THE SEVEN SLEEPERS

THE SEVEN SLEEPERS

FRANCIS BEEDING

INTRODUCTION

KARL WURF

John Leslie Palmer (1885–1944) and Hilary Aidan St George Saunders (1898–1951) were British writers who collaborated under the joint pseudonym "Francis Beeding." Palmer, born in Paddington, London, was an English author and theatre critic who spent nearly two decades in Geneva working for the League of Nations Secretariat. Saunders, born in Clifton near Bristol, was a decorated First World War officer who later wrote official wartime histories and served as Librarian of the House of Commons after the Second World War.

The two men first met while working in Geneva and soon began writing fiction together. Choosing to hide behind the shared name Francis Beeding, they created a body of work that spanned more than thirty novels between the 1920s and 1940s. Although they also used other pseudonyms, "Francis Beeding" became their most successful and recognizable identity, producing thrillers, espionage stories, and detective fiction.

Their spy novels often drew directly on their professional backgrounds and firsthand experiences of European politics. Many settings—Switzerland, Germany, France, Italy, and North Africa—reflect the international vantage point they had through their diplomatic and military service. The detail of these landscapes and the weight of contemporary political concerns gave their thrillers a distinctive realism uncommon in much of interwar popular fiction.

At the same time, they ventured into pure detective stories. Their most celebrated is *Death Walks in Eastrepps* (1931), a taut and innovative novel often cited as a pioneering example of the serial-killer narrative in Golden Age crime fiction. They also introduced recurring figures such as Colonel Granby, whose exploits provided continuity across a series of espionage adventures.

Their influence extended beyond the printed page. *The House of Dr. Edwardes* (1927), a psychological thriller set in a mental asylum, was adapted by Alfred Hitchcock into the film *Spellbound* (1945), starring Ingrid Bergman and Gregory Peck. This adaptation brought their work to an even wider audience and cemented their reputation as writers whose imagination could cross media boundaries.

Francis Beeding holds an important place in the history of mystery and spy fiction, standing between the traditions of the interwar British thriller and Golden Age detection. Their novels combined brisk pacing, international intrigue, and a willingness to experiment with form. For those wishing to explore further, recommended titles include the psychological thriller *The House of Dr. Edwardes* (1927), the inventive serial-murder tale *Death Walks in Eastrepps* (1931), and espionage adventures such as *The One Sane Man* (1934) and *The Four Armourers* (1935).

CHAPTER I

I LOSE MY LUGGAGE

It all started with the loss of my luggage.

I was returning home to England from a trip to the Tuscan towns by way of the Riviera, and I had registered my trunk to Genoa. On arriving at that city, however, I discovered, after much difficult enquiry, in the course of which I was assured that Italy, thanks to Signor Mussolini, was a great and glorious country which would shortly be undisputed mistress of the Mediterranean and the most efficient nation in Europe, that my effects had been despatched to Geneva. It was pointed out, for my consolation, that the difference between "Genova" and "Ginevra" was almost negligible.

Fortunately I was in no great need of consolation. I was, in fact, delighted with the discovery of my loss. It was an omen. All roads, it seemed, were leading me to Beatrice.

Beatrice Harvel, whom I had met in London during the War, was now on the staff of the League of Nations. She had been for two years in Geneva and I had not seen her during all that time. I had parted with her in the conviction that a penniless officer newly demobilised, as I then was, not yet broken to the paths of commerce, was in no position to lay his name and absence of fortune at her feet. During the last few days, however, my position and prospects had changed remarkably for the better. My Uncle James, calling me into his office some three weeks previously, had announced his immediate intention of making me a partner in his business, and had given me to understand that I might regard myself as his heir.

On the strength of these gratifying assurances, I was taking a short holiday, and confirming myself in the intention of going ultimately to Geneva in order to discover how I stood with the girl who had never ceased to be in my thoughts since I had waved her an affectedly cheerful farewell some two years ago at Victoria. It was stimulating to discover that my luggage had anticipated me and was calling me forward to the fatal moment. I decided then and there to go after it immediately, and within half an hour of this decision I had taken the express for Lausanne and was rolling towards the Swiss frontier.

But let there be no misunderstanding. The loss of my luggage was the pretext and not the cause of my sudden descent upon the city of Geneva. But for Beatrice, I might quite well have abandoned my trunk to whatever complicated doom was reserved for it under the appropriate regulations. To this day, in fact, I maintain that it was Beatrice who, in the last analysis, awoke the Seven Sleepers untimely. But I am anticipating.

I shall have little leisure, once this story is under way, to tell you anything about myself, so I had better take this opportunity, while I am still a mere member of the travelling public, to explain at any rate who I am, and how I am customarily employed.

I was born in 1894 in the village of Steynhurst, Sussex (where my mother still resides), and christened Thomas, Thomas Henry Preston. I was educated at Stowerbridge, where I took prizes for history, physical jerks, and running. I was also in the Rugger Fifteen and captain of the school boxing team. I was destined for Oxford, but before going up my people sent me for two years to the University of Bonn, where I learnt to speak German almost, if not quite, as well as a German himself. I think I must have inherited a gift for languages from my mother, who talks six or seven. I was about to go to Oxford when the War broke out, which upset my plans, for I entered the army instead, serving right through in the Royal Field Artillery, and emerging in the end with two wounds, the Military Cross and a captaincy.

For my personal appearance, it is shortest to quote from my passport:

> Height: 5 feet 11 inches.
> Colour of eyes: blue.
> Colour of hair: fair.
> Special peculiarities: none.

I should add that unkind friends have accused me of a certain resemblance to the sons of the Fatherland, owing, I suppose, to my fair hair and the rather crude blue of my eyes. I am apt, however, to become violent when this subject is mentioned, and it is not usually pressed.

Most of the men of my family are more remarkable for their physical prowess than for their business efficiency, and it was a lucky day for us all when my father's sister, Agatha Preston, married my Uncle James. Uncle James is widely known to commerce as Jebbutt, of Jebbutt and Jebbutt, Hardware Manufacturers, Birmingham. I have spent the last two years in learning the business; and, if you are interested, I can quote you a line in saucepans or sell you a thousand bedsteads without referring to the price list. I find it difficult to be enthusiastic in these activities, but at a time when the salt of the earth, who sacrificed four years of their youth to save the world, spends its abundant leisure for the most part in polishing the hard benches of labour exchange waiting-rooms, I can only thank the lucky stars that made me heir to a wholesale tinker.

I had caught my train at Genoa with only a minute to spare, and I had had no time to buy anything to read. There was one other occupant of the carriage. He was a Swiss, and, for the moment, he was absorbed in the morning papers. I had not seen them yet and wondered why he was so closely intrigued. He was not exactly excited—his race is seldom excited— but he showed a degree of mild interest in the foreign telegrams which was almost unprecedented in my acquaintance with his compatriots.

"*Vous permettez, Monsieur?*" I said, and I put my hand on the *Journal de Paris*.

He nodded and resumed his reading.

The news accorded well with my hopeful spirits, and the exhilaration of the December sunlight. There was, it appeared, a reasonable prospect at last of a European settlement. The long dispute between France and Germany seemed on the eve of conclusion. Germany had capitulated. She would pay any reparations that might be asked of her, down to the last farthing. There was to be some sort of inter-allied conference in Paris, and the German Government pledged itself in advance to accept its ruling. As a proof of her good faith, Germany was prepared at once to apply for admission to the League of Nations, to order an immediate resumption of work in the Ruhr, and to despatch to France large stocks of timber and coal that had been accumulated just outside the occupied territory. These announcements gave a finishing touch to the morning.

"Excellent news," I remarked to my Swiss companion.

Rather to my surprise, I found him frankly incredulous.

"Germany," he informed me, after some necessary preliminaries, "is still the most important country in Europe. She will never be found kneeling at the feet of her late enemies. Germany is a great nation."

I did not contradict him, and he proceeded to define his conception of national greatness in a final and comprehensive announcement.

"The German Government," he said, "has just purchased three hundred thousand aluminium saucepans."

"Three hundred thousand saucepans!" I exclaimed.

"*Aluminium* saucepans," insisted my new acquaintance. "No government could possibly require three hundred thousand saucepans, but it is conceivable that it might require large quantities of aluminium. It takes one back to the good old days."

"The good old days?" I echoed, in the tone of one who seeks an explanation.

"During the War," he explained, "we sold thousands of tons of aluminium to the German Government. I'm Albert Golay (Golay *fils*)"—he

9

bowed to me ceremoniously—"of Ufholtz and Golay of Neuhausen."

I knew the firm well by repute. Were they not my rivals in peace (now that I was a tinker) as they had been my enemies in war (when I was a soldier)? But for Ufholtz and Golay there would have been precious little aluminium for the friendly Zeppelins. I looked with interest at Golay *fils*. Here was the neutral trader incarnate. For him the War stood simply for the "good old days." And apparently, so far as he was concerned, they were coming back again.

"Three hundred thousand saucepans," I repeated softly.

"It was just two months ago," said Golay *fils*. "We are sending them via Basle to Hanover as fast as we can turn them out. Two thirds of the purchase price was paid in advance, and no haggling at the figures."

"And you suspect the German Government?"

"Private firms don't do business on that scale or in that manner. It's the government touch. Besides, I recognised the agent. He bought from us during the War. Funny fellow, tall and thin, bald as an egg. Stutters terribly. We met in Basle, by arrangement, to negotiate the deal, and as soon as it was concluded he slipped round right away to the bank and paid me in notes."

"I should like to meet that man," I said. "I'm by way of selling saucepans myself."

"*Aluminium* saucepans?"

"No, sir. I'm afraid I can't tell the precise nature of the material. It's a trade secret."

At this point we were interrupted by an attendant, who came along the corridor announcing that the first lunch was being served in the restaurant car.

We left our compartment and found that the restaurant was only half full. My Swiss companion, after a glance round the tables, saw someone he knew at the far end, whom we joined, on receiving from him a friendly sign. I was introduced as a brother bagman, and was soon listening to an interminable discussion of trade conditions in Europe.

Our new companion, it seemed, was a Swede, and the pair talked engagingly of supply and demand, of the exchange and of transport. Inevitably their conversation went round to the "good old days," more particularly as the Swede was a traveller for the Svenska Kullagar Fabriken. I had heard a good deal about this firm during the War from a friend of mine in the Ministry of Blockade. It was at that time the largest manufactory of ball bearings in the world, and the desperate need of our government for this essential commodity had virtually dictated our Swedish policy.

Then suddenly I pricked up my ears. Certainly it was a most extraordinary coincidence, though less extraordinary than it seemed perhaps. Europe is small and the routes into Switzerland are limited. That our Swiss friend, who was returning to Neuhausen, should encounter our Swedish friend, who was going to Basle, was not so very singular, nor indeed that they should both have done an excellent stroke of business with one and the same gentleman, who was conducting his operations in Switzerland. Anyhow, there it was. The Swede was also celebrating a partial return to the "good old days." He had met a tall, thin gentleman in Basle, and he was going to meet him again in Geneva—a gentleman who stuttered and was as bald as an egg. And he had received an order from this person for ball bearings that recalled the most prosperous days of blood and iron. Moreover, he had been offered two thirds of the purchase price in advance and a big premium for immediate delivery.

"This tall thin gentleman," I asked, "what does he call himself?" I spoke in German, this being a language common to the three of us.

"Herr Schreckermann," said the Swede.

"He was a government agent during the War," said Golay. "I assume he is still buying for the authorities at Berlin."

"I'm not so sure of that," said the Swede. "The German Government is bankrupt. It certainly hasn't hundreds of thousands of Swiss francs to squander abroad. It looks to me as though Schreckermann were acting for a big financial group. Stinnes himself would be hard put to it to find all that money at a moment's notice."

"Anyhow," said Golay, "the money's there," a fact which, so far as this neutral merchant was concerned, finally disposed of any international problem that might lurk behind these princely transactions.

I was getting tired of my neutral friends, and, bidding them a brief "Good day," I quitted the restaurant car, leaving them to their ball bearings and their aluminium saucepans.

Some hours later the tedious journey was drawing to its close. I had lost my travelling companions at the Swiss frontier, and the train was now running down the Rhone valley in the darkness. It would soon be at Lausanne, where I had to change for Geneva.

I remember that my mind, roused I suppose by the conversation over lunch, dwelt vaguely on the European situation. I am a very ordinary sort of fellow and have no special knowledge of what is styled foreign politics. I read the newspapers pretty regularly at my club, and occasionally chat for half an hour over a glass of sherry with old Thompson, whose special foible it is to carry about some new and sensational rumour of another crisis in Paris, Berlin or Moscow. I was, I must own, astonished at the utter and entire surrender of Germany, but there seemed to be no doubt whatever as to the facts. I glanced at the newspapers which were scattered about the carriage. All the news agencies agreed. Germany had capitulated and was advertising the fact broadcast.

By this time I had reached Lausanne, where I had an hour to wait. I bought a Swiss paper, and the news it contained confirmed and amplified the earlier reports. The paper gave the text of a proclamation issued by the German Government, which consisted in an exhortation to all German citizens to resume work immediately in the Ruhr. The War had been forced on the German people by a bad ruler, but that did not free them from responsibility. They must pay just reparations to the full. Only in that way could they hope to re-establish the prosperity of their country. Let every man put his shoulder to the wheel, and by united effort pay the former enemies of Germany, and thus ensure peaceful relations in the future.

I thought that I was to be alone in my carriage between Lausanne and Geneva, but, as the train was moving, another traveller scrambled up the steps, and, tripping over the top one, fell flat on his face in the corridor, where I happened to be standing, casting at my feet a small despatch case which burst open and scattered its contents over the floor.

With many apologies he picked himself up, and I saw that he was a short dark man between thirty and thirty-five. He was of the Southern French type, with the brownest eyes I have ever seen, eager and sanguine of expression, the obvious countryman of Tartarin and d'Artagnan.

I helped him to collect his belongings, which he packed roughly into the despatch case. He was profuse in his gratitude and explained that he had mistaken the time of the train.

As he was somewhat dusty about the knees as a result of his accident, I offered him the loan of a clothes brush from my own suit case, which he accepted and retired to make himself presentable, carrying his despatch case with him. When he had gone, I realised that the door of the coach was probably still open, and I went out to close it.

On returning to my compartment, I trod on something hard, which felt like a coin. I stooped down and picked up what proved instead to be a small, round disc, made of copper, with a hole in it for threading upon a chain or key ring. Stamped on one side of it were the letters "R.F.", and on the other side number "17."

I was still examining this when the traveller returned and handed me back my brush, with renewed thanks. As he did so, he noticed what I was holding in my hand.

"Pardon, Monsieur," he said, "but I think you have found something which belongs to me."

I assented and handed it to him. He looked at it sharply and then put it in his waistcoat pocket.

We talked together for the hour which the train took to reach Geneva.

I discovered him to be an extraordinarily pleasant and interesting companion. He was a French officer who had served right through the War and been wounded at Verdun, and, when he discovered that I too had seen some service on the Western Front, we soon found enough to talk about.

After exchanging various war reminiscences, I remembered the news in the paper and congratulated him on the triumph of the French policy.

For a moment his eyes lit with interest, and from a man of his type and origin one expected at once a stream of vivid comment and exclamation. To my surprise, however, he did not very readily respond. He was clearly about to do so, and then suddenly appeared to pull himself up, almost as though someone had tapped him on the shoulder and told him to be careful.

"It is a complete success," I ventured. "Germany is on her knees."

He looked at me queerly for a moment.

"*Vous croyez?*" he said.

There was a world of Gallic scepticism in that brief remark and in the tone in which it was uttered. I would have liked to discuss the position with him frankly and at large, but already the train was slowing down.

As I got up to collect my things, the Frenchman turned to me and said quickly:

"I must thank you particularly for having found my identification disc. It is an old war souvenir, which I should be very sorry to lose."

I said something polite to him in reply and hoped that we should encounter in Geneva. He answered me cordially enough, but said nothing of a further meeting, which, for a man of his obvious enthusiastic temper, seemed to me a little odd. I remembered then that he had not given me the slightest hint of his occupation, though I had been almost excessively communicative in regard to myself.

Had I had the least idea of the strange circumstances in which we were to meet again, I should have wondered less at his reserve.

CHAPTER II

I AM TWO DAYS LATE

I left the train and found myself on the platform of an ill-lighted station, in company with a large number of my fellow-passengers, who seemed to have entirely monopolised the few available porters. With some difficulty, I carried my two suit cases for a little distance, intending to leave them in a waiting-room while I went in search of the officials necessary to trace the missing trunk.

I pushed my way along the platform until I saw a notice "Chef de Gare" above a small, brightly lit office. There I was received by a magnificent functionary with a gold-braided cap, who told me that I must wait until the mails had been removed from the train.

"But not in here," he added, seeing that I was about to sit down on the only vacant chair; "this is the office of the stationmaster"—from which I inferred that, even in a democratic country, *lése majesté* may be committed unintentionally.

I accordingly betook myself to the platform again, where I presently found an enormous blue-smocked porter, to whom I explained my difficulties. I found it hard to convince him that anyone could have sent a trunk to Geneva instead of to Genoa. But at length we went together to the *douane*, only to discover it was locked. I enquired where the *douanier* might be, but was told that I could not see him that night.

"If you come tomorrow morning, perhaps you will be able to get it," said the porter hopefully.

Clearly the Swiss were a patient race.

I remembered the golden rule for travellers abroad, which is never to argue with anybody in a uniform, and I told the man to get me a taxi.

A thin, sharp rain, almost a mist, was falling as I left the station, and the air was very cold. I was wondering where to stay when I remembered that Beatrice, with whom I had kept up a regular correspondence, had put up for some time at the Pension de la Reine, on the Quai du Mont Blanc, where I had addressed letters to her. This seemed as good a place as any other, and would probably be not too expensive.

The drive there was short. We went down a broad street with cafés and shops on either side, turned off abruptly into a quiet square backed by tall, thin houses, and pulled up under an arch.

I took my room for a week. It was on the third floor, looking out over the square, in the middle of which was a dreary garden, the last leaves of the almost bare trees dripping with icy moisture, and a rusty fountain adding to the general dampness in the centre.

I had arrived too late for dinner, but they gave me some excellent *ramequins* and a rather tough steak, which I washed down with a bottle of thin Swiss wine. It was a meal that struck at once the prevailing note of the city —adequate but uninspired.

It was my first visit to the place, but I knew it well from hearsay—a city of spies and refugees and international organisations, where the more ancient traditions survived precariously in the *snobbisme* of its older families, entirely without distinction for the foreign visitor. I knew it best from the letters of my old friend Dick Braithwaite of the British Secret Service, who had been stationed there during the War, when Geneva had swarmed with agents of every nationality, who made of it a city of fantastic adventure.

Come to think of it, Geneva has always been a nest of unsavoury conspiracy. Here Elizabeth of Bohemia was murdered by a witless anarchist of twenty. Here Lenin lived for six years, hatching his great enterprise, and it was interesting to reflect that the town which had once resounded to Knox and Farel should have been the incubator of another and even more sinister revolution. Here too, it was said, Signor Mussolini had made his début as a Socialist, before he realised that the black shirt became him better than the red.

Tonight, it seemed, Geneva was *en fête*, and was even now completing the first of a three days' festival in honour of the annual carnival of the Escalade, held in commemoration of the attempt of the Duke of Savoy to capture the town in 1602. The Savoyards got into the town by night and were driven out after three days of desperate fighting by the gallant burghers in the bloodiest contest of the last three hundred years. The total casualties numbered fifty-four.

I was informed by my hotel proprietor that a number of *bals costumés* were in progress, and that some of the cafés would remain open all night.

Thinking it might be amusing to see how the Swiss enjoyed themselves, I went into the streets, being recommended by my host to go to the Moulin Rouge, where he said I should see dancing and other attractions. As I walked along, I met parties of disconsolate revellers, most of whom were masked, their hands, blue with cold, sticking out from soiled Pierrot costumes surmounted by bedraggled ruffs. Every now and then someone would blow a wheezy note on a tin horn, but for the most part the revellers

15

moved silently along with linked arms, seemingly conscious of their absurdity. Groups of young children would occasionally pass, wearing tall, conical paper hats, very moist and damp, walking hand in hand, singing a dull monotonous tune in shrill voices. At any other time I might have found all this depressing, but my spirits were proof against anything that auspicious evening.

I went down the street, the Rhone on my left side until, turning towards it, I crossed it by a footbridge in the middle of which was situated the dam controlling the water power for the electric light. Nearly all the sluices were up and the water roared through the confined space in a mass of foam and whirlpools. Turning again to the right and then to the left, I walked up a long broad street called the Corraterie, bounded on the left by the tall houses of the old town mounting to the cathedral. At the top I asked a gendarme the way, and was directed across the Place Neuve, with its opera house and conservatoire, until I reached a large open space called the Plain de Plainpalais, where a fair was in progress. Merry-go-rounds and swings were active, but the crowd was not large, and it seemed a dreary sort of business. Evidently the Genevese had exhausted their vitality on that famous night three centuries ago. Since then Calvin and the climate had been too much for them.

I crossed a corner of the plain and presently arrived at a side street in which was situated the Moulin Rouge.

On entering, I found the room very full, and with some difficulty secured a seat near the door, ordering a brandy and soda. A good proportion of the company were in some form of fancy dress. An orchestra arrayed in short black coats and white flannel trousers was in full blast at one end of the room, and when it paused for breath an electric organ crashed out behind me. The place was full of a mist of tobacco smoke, and the whole show seemed to me to be a tawdry imitation of Montmartre. Crudely painted women, alone, or in the company of what I presume were the local tradesmen, were seated against the walls, those on the dais which ran around the room sipping champagne, while the humbler, at tables on the dancing floor itself, contented themselves with glasses of a deep red liquid filled with an assortment of sliced bananas, oranges and apples.

Soon after I arrived, the lights were lowered and a tall, very thin girl in clumsily arranged draperies danced a classic dance barefoot among the tables, her expressionless face, framed in peroxide hair, bobbing up and down among the seated company in the room like a foggy lantern in the hands of a drunken man. There was a good deal of noise from several parties, and *serpentins* were being thrown about, so that the whole place was covered with dirty strips of coloured paper, which wound themselves over the tables, the chairs and the thick necks of the merrymakers.

So this was Geneva. It seemed at that moment a city in which most forms of excitement were at a discount, and at the end of half an hour I decided to go to bed in pleasant anticipation of my forthcoming meeting with Beatrice.

Then, quickly enough, it began. A man suddenly entered the room and, after a glance round the tables, came straight over and sat down in the vacant chair beside me.

He was a thin, undersized rat of a fellow, with black hair and a very prominent nose and teeth—obviously a Jew. He was breathing heavily, as though he had been running, and I noticed that his hands were trembling. I had scarcely had time to mark these details, however, when, to my utter astonishment, he suddenly put his hand on my arm.

"You're two days late," he said abruptly in German. "And what the devil do you mean by coming to this place? You'll hear of this from Ephesus."

I was staring at him incredulously when his expression changed. It was as though the words had been wiped from his lips, and he was looking with a fixed stare of terror across the room at a group of persons in fancy dress seated in the opposite corner.

Two of them rose and walked swiftly towards us. One was a tall, slim harlequin in black and silver, masked to the chin, who slipped easily between the revolving couples on the floor. The other was short and dressed as a clown in a single baggy garment and a tall conical hat. His face, which was painted in the conventional manner, seemed to me to be vaguely familiar. I could not quite place him at the moment, however, especially as I was much more interested in my companion, who, while these men were crossing the room, appeared to be stupefied with terror. He stared at them as though fascinated, and it was not until they were quite close to us that the spell was broken. They were only two tables away when he rose quickly, with a sort of gulp thrust something violently into my hand, and, turning, made for the door.

He reached it simultaneously with the harlequin and the clown, who bowed low, and, as it seemed, ironically, when he approached them. The harlequin tapped him lightly across the shoulder with his wand, while the clown grasped him by the arm.

To an ordinary onlooker, it appeared to be merely the unexpected encounter of three friends, but to me, who had seen the pitiable state of fright to which this little unknown Jew had been reduced, the gestures of the harlequin and the clown seemed charged with a sinister significance.

The clown immediately pushed open the door, and they all disappeared simultaneously.

I was too astonished to do anything for the moment, but, as the door swung to behind them, I came to my wits and got up, grasping the object which had been thrust into my hand, and which was apparently, from the feel of it, some form of pocket-book. I reached the door and entered the vestibule.

As I did so, the street door slammed. I fancied that I heard a scuffle going on outside and an instant later the *clas seur* who guarded the door reappeared in the vestibule from the street, breathing a little quickly.

I went up to him immediately and asked him if a small, black-haired man had just left the building with two companions.

"No, Monsieur," he replied, "no one has left. No one at all."

"But I'm sure of it," I said. "He left a moment ago. I saw him go out myself."

At this the *clas seur* brazenly changed his note. "For the good of the house," he said, "I beg Monsieur to say nothing. The man Monsieur mentions has just been arrested. Monsieur will realise we do not want any scandal."

"Oh, very well," I assented, "it isn't any business of mine."

I was still holding in my hand the pocket-book which had so mysteriously come into my possession, and I should then and there have handed it over to the *clas seur* if he had not already lied to me and given me every reason to doubt his honesty.

As it was, I called for my coat and returned to the Pension de la Reine, still in possession of the property of the little Jew.

18

CHAPTER III

I RECEIVE AN INVITATION FROM MY GRANDMOTHER

On reaching my room, I carefully examined the pocket-book.

It contained nothing but a sheet of stout note-paper, one side of which was half covered with figures arranged in groups. It was obviously some sort of cipher, but the document was signed by seven persons whose autographs were *en clair*. I did not, however, take the trouble to examine it any further that night, but soon turned in and slept soundly.

I was tired, and the peculiar events at the Moulin Rouge had not sufficed to do more than ruffle the surface of my good spirits. Anyhow, I could do nothing about it till the morning, and during the War I had acquired the habit, which remains with me still, of putting off till tomorrow the things which cannot be done today. I like to think that this is a habit which I share with all the more attractive people of the earth. My dear mother calls it laziness, and Uncle James of Jebbutt and Jebbutt frequently prophesies that it will land me and mine in the office of the official receiver.

I awoke rather late on the following morning, and I had not yet begun to think of the little Jew and his pocket-book when my coffee arrived, with hot water and a letter.

I opened the letter sleepily, without stopping to consider how odd it was for me to receive one when, as far as I was aware, no one knew my address. It was written in German, and was as follows:

> "Pension Ephesus,
> *December* 11th.

"My dearest Grandson,

"I am glad to know that you have arrived at last in Geneva. I am sorry, dearest boy, that circumstances, which you say in your telegram were inevitable, have caused you to be two days late. I trust, however, that you will lose no further time in coming to see me.

"I am accordingly expecting you to take tea with me this afternoon at 4 p.m. precisely, at No. 140, rue Etienne Dumont. Uncle Ulric and Uncle Fritz will be there, and we must have a nice little chat together. We have quite a number of things to say to you.

"I am anxiously awaiting the little present which you tell me you are bringing me. As it is small, I hope you will take the greatest care of it and that it will not be lost.

"I should add, dear boy, a word of warning, which I hope you will not misunderstand, since you know my great love and affection for you. You are of a high-spirited nature, and, as the city of Geneva is at the moment *en fête*, you may be tempted to indulge those high spirits of yours in the company of the other participants in the carnival. Now, the police here are lenient, but they do not permit undue brawling or noise in the streets. I therefore beg you most earnestly to be careful not to let your excitable nature run away with you, and thus bring you into unpleasant contact with the guardians of the law.

"Assuring you once more of my great affection, and of the warmth of the welcome which you may expect to receive,

"I am,
"Your loving,
"Grandmother."

To say that I was astonished by this letter is to put it mildly.

I read it through twice, and my first conclusion was that I must be the victim of a practical joke, but a moment's reflection showed me that there could be no one in Geneva who would wish to play such a trick on me. Lavelle, my French friend on the Secretariat of the League, was the last person from whom I should expect anything of the kind, and Beatrice Harvel had too excellent a sense of humour to prepare an elaborate hoax. Besides, neither of them yet knew that I was in Geneva.

My second thought was that the letter was directed to someone else, but, on turning to the envelope, I saw it was correctly addressed to "Herr Thomas Preston."

I read it once more, carefully, and noted that my estimable grandmother, whoever she might be, was evidently very anxious to receive the small present of which she spoke. The words of warning about not losing it, which one would not expect to find in an ordinary letter, were evidently meant to emphasise the importance of the gift. This seemed fairly clear, but the reference to the police and to the fact that I was two days late was beyond me.

"Two days late!" Where had I heard that phrase before? Then I remembered that the little Jew had opened upon me with precisely those words on the previous evening. "You're two days late," he had said, and he had added that I should hear of it from Ephesus.

20

Well, here was a letter addressed to me from the Pension Ephesus. Evidently there was a connection between this letter and the little Jew and the document he had thrust upon me in his panic.

But how on earth had he found me out, and who in heaven's name was my grandmother—not to mention Uncle Ulric and Uncle Fritz. I had apparently spent the night in acquiring a number of anxious relatives who were entirely strange to me.

I took the document out of the pocket-book and examined it. Of the cipher I could make nothing, but the signatures were more illuminating. Five of the names were unknown to me, but the sixth and seventh I seemed to identify. "Von Bühlen" I knew I had come across, though I could not remember where, and "Von Stahl" was even more familiar. Then, in a flash, I remembered where I had seen the latter.

We had had some dealings with German firms after the War, and I recalled a small order from Germany for hardware of some kind—I forget what—which had passed through my hands. The various documents in connection with it had been signed "Von Stahl." My uncle had told me at the time that he was perhaps the richest man in Germany, but that he was very little known and kept himself entirely out of politics. A dangerous man, my uncle had said, because he was so quiet and appeared to do nothing, although he was reputed to be very influential.

Now that I had placed Von Stahl, I remembered at once that Von Bühlen was the head of the big armaments firm which had constructed most of Germany's guns and munitions, and it was fairly certain that the enormous profits which the War had brought to the firm had been invested abroad and had not suffered from the collapse of the mark. Von Bühlen must still be fabulously rich.

This then appeared to be a document of some importance, and I soon came to the conclusion that the little present, to which my grandmother referred with such solicitude, was none other than the sheet of paper which had been so queerly thrust upon me at the Moulin Rouge. I had no idea what it meant, but clearly it was of value. Otherwise, the little Jew would not have been so eager to get rid of it before his arrest, and my "grandmother" would not have taken steps so promptly to retrieve it.

Here was a touch of mystery that set the wits pleasantly to work. I thought it over while I was shaving and decided to talk to Beatrice about it—a notion which gave to the problem an added attraction.

I dressed as rapidly as possible and rang her up at the Secretariat. It was pleasant to hear the cry of astonishment with which she recognised my voice, and still more pleasant to reflect that she recognised it at all—on the telephone, too—after so long an interval. I answered about thirty-five questions in as many seconds (or so it seemed) and then asked her to come to lunch with me. Luckily she was disengaged, and we arranged to meet at the grill-room of the Hôtel du Lac at one o'clock.

As I was leaving the telephone, I met the proprietor of the pension, who hoped that I had received the note which had been delivered for me that morning. The person who had left it had informed him that it was extremely urgent.

I took the envelope out of my pocket, and saw that what I had first thought was an ordinary letter did not bear a stamp.

I enquired who had brought it to the pension, and was told that it had been delivered by a lady who had come early that morning, before I was awake, about eight-thirty. She had given instructions that the note should be taken to me the moment I was called.

I asked what the unknown messenger had looked like. The proprietor said that he had not taken particular notice of her, but that she had been slight in appearance. He could remember no detail of what she wore except that, as she paused an instant in front of a mirror, to arrange her hat, he had remarked that it was trimmed with a pheasant's feather.

"You are sure she was young?" I queried

"One can never be sure," replied the proprietor. "Not more than twenty-five, I should say."

"She was not by any chance old enough to be my grandmother?" I suggested.

"Certainly not," said the proprietor.

I thanked him for his information and prepared to go for a stroll, before meeting Beatrice, to see the town and to think at leisure over possible ways and means of solving my mystery.

The rain of the previous day had ceased, though heavy clouds were still hanging over the city. I need not trouble you with a description of my walk, beyond saying that I set out vaguely in the direction of the university and eventually found myself in the Jardin des Bastions, marvelling at an incredibly ugly monument. Calvin, Beza, Knox and Farel, twice the size of life, looked out from the wall with a fixed uncomprehending stare, flanked by other figures and scenes in low relief. Among them I noticed the regicide Cromwell and his secretary, John Milton.

Suddenly a hand clapped me on the shoulder, and turning round, I found myself face to face with Jerry Cunningham.

Jerry had been the best of my battery subalterns, and I had not seen him since the day when he had been carried off, a blood-stained wreck of a man, from the remains of Number 3 gun, which had stopped a five nine on "the glorious 1st of July, 1916."

I was shocked at the change in his appearance. He had been something of a dandy, particularly about the cut of his tunic, and excessively proud of his field boots, which had been made by the most expensive bootmaker in London. Now I saw before me a medium-sized man, thin in the face, his forehead puckered with hard lines. He was slovenly dressed, although the clothes he wore were well cut, and he leaned heavily on a rubber-shod stick.

"Good lord, Jerry!" I exclaimed. "What on earth brings you to Geneva?"

"And what might you be doing?" he countered.

We walked across the gardens to a café where Jerry said the beer was from Munich, and, as he limped slowly by my side, he told me of his life since our last meeting. I found him as changed in spirit as in appearance. He had been the gayest and most delightful of companions. Now, every word was bitter and disconsolate. Nor was this to be wondered at.

After spending months in hospital, he had eventually been discharged with a pension of a hundred a year and a permanently game leg (poor old Jerry, the finest athlete of his year at Oxford). He had tried various jobs, but never for very long. Having a little money of his own, he had contrived to manage somehow. At the moment he was acting as tutor to two boys, sons of a rich French war-profiteer, who was anxious that they should learn English, and had made sufficient money out of the War—said Jerry with a savage sneer—to justify the employment of an ex-officer as a kind of superior servant. He had taken the job out of general boredom. He was in Geneva with his youthful charges, he explained, for a fortnight or three weeks, before taking them up to the mountains for the winter sports.

"Not much good to me, old boy," he said; and I remembered how he had won the golden skis at Villars in 1913.

As we were about to enter the café, Jerry turned to me and said jokingly, "Who's the lady?"

I looked at him in surprise.

"My dear chap," I protested, "I only arrived last night. Give me at least a morning to myself."

"You may not know it," said Jerry, "but all the time we've been walking along a girl has been following us at a distance of about fifty yards and she has a friendly eye for you.

"There she is," he continued, with a jerk of his head in the direction of a public building on the other side of the road.

I looked across and saw on the pavement opposite a small slim girl dressed in brown, and wearing a brown hat with a pheasant feather in it.

"Do you mean that girl over there in brown?" I asked.

Jerry nodded.

"I've never seen her in my life," said I. "Come into the café and I'll tell you about it."

We entered and sat down in front of two *chopes* of what proved to be excellent beer. I then told him all that had happened to me since my arrival in Geneva.

As I proceeded with my narrative, the look of boredom vanished from his face, and before I had finished he was eager to see the document.

"Here it is," I said, handing him the pocket-book beneath the table, "but don't display it too much. I'm beginning to feel that it has a way of exciting inconvenient interest in unexpected quarters."

"What are you going to do about it?" Jerry asked, after he had examined the document.

"It seems to me," I suggested, "that I ought at any rate to keep the appointment with my grandmother. The old lady arouses my curiosity."

Jerry again examined the document, but could make no more of it than I could, except that he identified another of the signatures as that of Herzler, who he said was a South African diamond magnate of German origin, and he thought of German nationality.

He was eager to accompany me to the tea-party, but I pointed out to him that my grandmother evidently desired to see me alone.

"Oh, all right," he said crossly. "After all, a lame fellow's not much good in a crisis."

"Confound you, Jerry!" I almost shouted. "Don't be a fool; you know very well that it isn't that."

We compromised by agreeing to dine together at the Plat d'Or whose *filet madère* Jerry assured me was one of the few good things in Geneva.

We sat on and discussed other matters till close on one o'clock. Then we left the café and, summoning a taxi, drove off to the grill-room of the Hôtel du Lac, arranging to drop Jerry at the Hôtel de France, where he was staying, on the way.

As we got into the taxi, I noticed that the woman with the pheasant feather was standing quite close to us, about five yards away, in fact, and just as we moved off she stepped forward with the evident intention of speaking to me. By this time, however, the taxi had gathered speed. Glancing back I saw her looking after me, and a moment later she waved her hand.

It has never been my habit to snub a friendly gesture, and I instinctively waved back at her.

"We'll stop if you like," said Jerry, with a touch of the old mischief.

"Not now," said I. "I have a presentiment that, whether I like it or not, I shall meet that lady again. She's evidently one of the family—Uncle Ulric's niece, or something of that kind."

We parted at the Hôtel de France, and a moment later I was shaking hands with Beatrice in the vestibule of the Hôtel du Lac.

Beatrice Harvel is one of the prettiest girls I have ever seen. Sitting up flat-backed opposite me, at a little corner table, in her trim coat and skirt, her dark hair neat and close beneath a small French hat, which set off her vivid eyes and colour, she presented a charming picture of an English girl who, while remaining essentially English, had none the less realised that in the art of dress the French have little to learn.

In mind, as in form and feature, she was compact and competent, her forearm drive at tennis having the same quality of precision and judgment as her observations on things and persons in general. In the first days of our acquaintance she had rather daunted me. She was so terribly adequate and assured. There was nothing about her in the least dependent or justifying a scorn of the weaker sex. I had felt the natural distrust of the gallant male for the girl who never pleads for a handicap. But I had soon found that with Beatrice there were moments that showed her unusually sensitive and intensely feminine.

I began by asking about her life at the Secretariat.

"They call me a bilingual stenographer," she explained, as a sole skilfully smothered in mushrooms made its appearance.

"That's a mouthful," I said.

"It means another fifty francs a month," she rejoined.

"I've heard all about you people in Geneva," said I. "You do hardly any work and you spend several guineas a week on silk stockings."

"You're going to correct that rumour, Tom. It annoys me. We live in a horrid little pension in a city which sees the sun one day in ten. The place is dull and drear and we work like Negroes. I should have left a year ago, only I was made private secretary to rather a nice Frenchman."

"Indeed," said I, suddenly wondering why I had postponed this meeting for nearly two years. "So you endure all these horrors for his sake."

"He's the best of the bunch," said Beatrice.

She always ignores sarcasm and never takes any occasion to be arch about her dealings with my interesting sex.

"Name, please," I demanded.

"Henri Lavelle. He's a member of the department that deals with political questions. Full of brains, and his work is most terribly interesting; among other things he's our cipher expert."

I breathed again. This was my old friend Lavelle of the French Army— the only man I knew in the Secretariat.

"A splendid fellow," I magnanimously testified. "I can just bear you to be his secretary. I'm coming to see him soon. In fact——"

I stopped. It occurred to me that here was a chance of light on my mystery.

"Do go on," said Beatrice. "You look as if you had something to say."

"Lots," I replied.

I told her then of all that had happened to me since I arrived in Geneva.

She took it much more gravely than I expected. In fact, it was the expression of her face when I had finished my story that first made me think that the affair might be really serious.

"I don't like it, Tom," she said. "All sorts of queer things are happening just now, and Geneva is always full of international agents of every kind."

"International agents!" I exclaimed. "But this is real life. I've got a British passport and I'm Thomas Preston of Jebbutt and Jebbutt."

"Don't make any mistake," said Beatrice. "My chief has told me a good deal about these things. He used to be in the French Intelligence Department."

"I don't see how on earth it can possibly concern me," I objected.

"You are going to this place in the rue Etienne Dumont?" she asked.

"Why not?"

"Be careful, Tom."

She laid her hand on my arm as she spoke, and I realised on meeting her eyes that she was really anxious. I think it was that instinctive anxiety for my safety and not the excellent Margaux, which suddenly made the world seem a better and brighter place.

"There's nothing to worry about," I assured her. "Geneva seems to have a sufficient number of gendarmes to the square *mètre* to keep everybody safe and sound. And they're all very splendidly dressed."

"You say the document is in cipher," said Beatrice, still serious.

"Yes. And I was about to suggest that Lavelle should have a look at it."

I put a hand into my pocket, but before I could take out the paper Beatrice suddenly nudged me under the table. I looked at her and saw she was gazing with an admirable affectation of no interest a little to my right.

I glanced casually round.

A couple of tables away were seated two men who were taking luncheon. The one nearer to me was tall and heavily built, with a closely-shaven head and light blue eyes. His face was criss-crossed with numerous scars, and I should have known him anywhere for a Prussian of the type which was caricatured in the Allied Press throughout the War. The scars were from the "Mensur" fights of his student days. Opposite him sat a man of middle age. He had a fine silky beard, neatly trimmed and of a bright gold, a broad forehead and well-set eyes, a straight nose, and a complexion almost feminine in its delicacy. At the first view he suggested an intelligent and sensitive philanthropist, reclusive in temperament. He had that air of distinction which surrounds the man who pursues some solitary purpose with little regard for the vulgar preoccupations of the worldly.

26

As I was secretly examining him he gave an order to the waiter, and I noted that the language he used was German. Then he became aware that I was gazing at him and turned his eyes in my direction. They were dark and the pupils were abnormally large. He favoured me with a short stare, penetrating but curiously soft and insinuating, and I caught myself staring back at him quite foolishly, seemingly without the power to withdraw my gaze. Then he dropped his eyes to his plate and I looked away, feeling as though I had been suddenly released.

The man affected me strangely. It may have been his eyes, or the abrupt warning conveyed by Beatrice as I had been on the point of producing the document, but somehow my disposition to make light of the adventure was shaken. I felt strangely called upon to behave like a conspirator; and, in the tone of a man discussing the *rognons brochette*, which the waiter had just placed on the table, I turned to Beatrice and enquired why she had assaulted me.

"They've been watching us for some time," she said in a low voice, "and I believe they're trying to listen to what we're saying."

"You may be right," I replied, "in which case I mustn't let them see me give you the document."

I beckoned to the waiter and asked him for the *carte dijon*. Tak ing it into my hand, I held it between me and the occupants of the other table and affected to be absorbed in its contents. With my right hand I extracted the pocket-book from the hip pocket, where I had concealed it, and pushed it up my sleeve, into which it fitted easily. A moment later I had slipped it into the card and handed the whole thing across to Beatrice, saying:

"You choose, my dear, but I recommend the *tarte de la maison*."

She picked up the card, and instantly bent down, apparently busy with her vanity bag. Then she agreed with my choice and we went on with our luncheon.

Over coffee we settled that I should ring her up later on in the afternoon, about six she said. I was to tell her of the result of my visit to the rue Etienne Dumont and to ask whether Lavelle had succeeded in solving the riddle of the cipher. It was further arranged that, before calling on my grandmother, I should go to the police and make enquiries about the little Jew, who had been arrested on the previous night.

I drove her back to the Secretariat and left her at the gate of a terrace garden, which gave upon a desolate quay and a mournful lake. But I had no eyes for the dismal prospect. The moment had come for Beatrice to depart into the vast building, all windows, in which the Secretariat was housed.

There was a disposition to prolong that departure. We stood for a moment on the pavement, Beatrice smiling at me in the old friendly way, and yet with a slight embarrassment which was new, but which I felt in an equal measure.

At last I said, most inadequately:

"Beatrice, it's terribly good to see you again."

Her smile deepened.

"Next time," she said, "you won't perhaps leave it for two years."

She left me at that, and I directed the taxi-man to drive me to the Bureau Central de Police, which was apparently in the Hôtel de Ville. We were soon proceeding slowly through the steep, narrow streets of the old town, where it is for a moment possible to recapture in a certain degree the charm of a vanished age.

After some difficulty, I arrived at a kind of municipal office, where I asked to see an inspector, and was shown into a small room with the usual official furniture. There I interviewed a typical policeman. Police officials are the same the whole world over, whatever their nationality. This man was enormous, with huge feet, and a black curling moustache. He seemed quite ready to answer my questions.

I explained that I had been in the Moulin Rouge on the previous evening, when, at about 11.30, a small dark man, who looked like a Jew, had been arrested by the police just at its entrance. As I had had some little conversation with him prior to the arrest, I was, I said, anxious to ascertain what was being done about his case.

He heard me to the end and pressed a bell, telling the clerk who entered to bring the police report of the previous day.

On receiving it, he studied it attentively for some moments and finally said:

"Three arrests took place last night outside the Moulin Rouge, Monsieur, but all were later on, between two and three o'clock in the morning —all women *faisant dıscan dale* in the street."

"Are you sure?" I asked. "I was certainly under the impression that the man I met had been arrested. The *chassen* told me so."

"The *chassen* was ly ing," said the official. "*C'était probablement ne blaga*. When the town is *en fête* many strange things happen, and there are always persons ready to play tricks on strangers."

I thanked him and took my leave. Outside I passed, uncertain what to do. I did not like this new development. The *chassen* had lied to me once when he had denied that the little Jew had left the dancing hall. Apparently he had lied again. The Jew had not been arrested. He had simply disappeared, and he had disappeared in the company of two men of whom he was obviously terrified.

As it still lacked half an hour or so of the time fixed for tea with my grandmother, I accordingly decided to find the *chassen*.

I walked straight down a steep street to the Place Neuve, crossed it and soon arrived at the Moulin Rouge.

I found the *chassen* in a dirty lit tle hole behind the vestibule, alleging as an excuse for my visit that I had lost an article of value and wished to see him about it.

He eventually appeared, in his shirt sleeves, heavy with sleep and inclined to be surly. I saw he was the sort of man that has to be bullied, as well as bribed.

"Why did you lie to me last night?" I began abruptly.

He started to protest, but I cut him short.

"The little dark man who left this building about 11.30 yesterday evening was not arrested. I know that perfectly well. What really happened to him?"

"I know nothing," said the man. "Monsieur is mistaken!"

"I'm sorry you know nothing," I replied. "I want to know what happened to that man, and I'm ready to pay for the information."

I produced a twenty-franc note.

"That's all very well," grumbled the man, "but in my position one must be discreet. I can speak when it is necessary and I can keep silent when it is necessary."

"Speak then," I said, and handed him the money.

"Well, Monsieur, you are right," he said. "The gentleman was not arrested; he came out in the company of two friends, the tall Monsieur in a harlequin dress and the clown. They were holding him between them, and they led him to a big automobile. They pushed him into it, and Monsieur l'Harlequin, turning to me, gave me ten francs to hold my tongue, saying that the gentleman whom they were taking away was a well-known person, who had been making a night of it and it would not do to have any scandal; so they were taking him home."

I saw the man was at last speaking the truth. I could even see the scene —the little Jew, hustled and trembling, carried off by those fantastic figures to some unknown destination.

I walked straight out through the vestibule and pushed open the outer door leading to the street.

I had not gone a yard when I found myself suddenly accosted by the girl in brown with the pheasant feather in her hat.

A taxi with its door open stood by the curb.

"*Kommen sie schnell, Karl,*" she said. "I am waiting to take you to your grandmother."

29

CHAPTER IV

I MEET MYSELF IN THE LOOKING-GLASS

I stared at the girl in astonishment and was about to protest when she put a finger to her lips, looking swiftly round, as though she feared to be watched.

"Be careful," she said. "We're probably under observation. We can talk in the taxi.

"Quick," she added, as I still hesitated on the pavement, "or your grandmother will be displeased."

I had already decided to see my grandmother, so why not take this way as well as another?

I entered the taxi, which, without waiting for instructions, at once moved off, turned the corner, crossed the big square and took the direction of the old town.

There was a moment's silence, during which I ventured a look at my companion. She was gazing at me in a kind of resentful expectation. Evidently I was not behaving as she had anticipated.

She was decidedly pretty on a nearer view—the prettiness of a china doll, eyes absurdly blue and all surface a fair complexion and flaxen hair. But she lacked depth—a creature who would, I thought, be easily moved by the small emotions, greedy, sentimental, easily spiteful and cruel as a thwarted monkey. You will perceive that I did not take to the pheasant feather.

The resentment grew in her eyes, and at last she said:

"Haven't you anything to say for yourself?"

"Nothing at all," I said, very frank and open.

Her eyes fluttered and fell coquettishly.

"Little heart," she cried (I spare you the German), "that means you want me to forgive you."

"Why not?" said I.

It is a phrase and a sentiment that has landed me in many scrapes. On this occasion it landed me in the arms of this blue-eyed damsel, her forgiveness taking the form of a sudden collapse on my chest, the flinging of two vigorous arms about my neck, and a succession of warm statements to the effect that I was an all-belovéd and a little treasure.

I forgot all about my grandmother and gave my undivided attention to feeling a perfect fool.

Then I took a firm hold of the arms about my neck.

"Fräulein," I protested, "there is some mistake."

"Oh, Karl," she murmured, "how can you be so cold?"

"Fräulein," I repeated.

She sat away from me abruptly.

"That is ungenerous," she said indignantly. "I forgive you and yet you continue the quarrel. It's hateful. You will break my heart. Why didn't you answer my letters?"

Some demon prompted me to proceed with the comedy. I always hate leaving things unfinished.

"You ought never to have written them," I said guardedly.

"I couldn't help it, Karl," she unexpectedly pleaded. "I know it was against the regulations, but I missed you so."

"I never received them," I declared emphatically.

I'm a plain, blunt man who loves to tell the truth upon a suitable occasion.

"I sent them to the Stahlhelm office in Leipzig," she said. "I suppose they were intercepted. I'm sorry, Karl."

The blue eyes fluttered and I became apprehensive of another demonstration.

"I thought you were being unkind just to pay me out for making love to that French spy in Munich. You oughtn't to be so jealous, my best-of-all-belovéds. You know quite well that I am obliged to do these things. Anyhow, you needn't trouble about that one any more. It went hard with him."

"Indeed?"

"Yes. He was dealt with by the Professor; you know what that means."

She shuddered.

"I could never get a word out of that mysterious Frenchman," she continued. "But the Professor did. They say it took him over three hours."

I suppose that, if I had been in a mood sufficiently prudent and collected, I should then and there have dismounted from the taxi and communicated with the police. But somehow, in proportion as the complications grew and as the adventure assumed a more threatening aspect, I became increasingly reluctant to forego that visit to my grandmother. Either the whole affair was a gigantic hoax, in which case I should look an utter fool if I took it to the authorities, or I had become seriously involved in some strange network of intrigue which it would be well to unravel even at the expense of a little time and risk. After all, I was a British subject and I still had tremendous faith in that honourable station. There could not possibly be any real need for alarm. I was merely visiting a private house in the middle of the afternoon, and I had a friend in Geneva who knew where I was going and expected to hear from me at six o'clock.

I believe, on subsequent reflection, that there was a deeper reason for my persistence. I am sure that men often do things from motives that are not altogether clear at the time, but which are fundamental. In this case I am convinced that a hostile curiosity was instinctively active in me from the first. I suspected mischief and divined that it was mischief beyond the resources and outside the experience of the local police. This, of course, may be wisdom after the event. All I can say for certain is that the determination which I had so lightly formed to visit my grandmother, far from being overthrown by the disquieting allusions of the girl in the taxi, was, on the contrary, confirmed and fortified.

My companion was again looking at me with an air of resentful expectation.

"Why don't you talk to me, Karl?"

"Fräulein——" I began.

She stopped me with a furious gesture.

"Fräulein, indeed!" she cried. "After all I have done for you—to speak to me as though I were a stranger. But you had better be careful, Karl; you will need every friend you've got. You're not very popular at headquarters just now. I can tell you that."

"It appears," said I, at a venture, "that I am two days late."

Her rage had already spent itself and she said anxiously:

"What have you been doing, Karl? They won't tell me anything about it, but I know it's something serious."

"I'm two days late, my dear lady. That is all I can tell you for the moment."

She put her hand on my wrist—a slender hand, very white, with an exquisite sapphire on the third finger.

"You're not in trouble?" she asked.

There was something rather appealing about her at that moment. She was evidently fond of Karl—the kind of fellow, I suspected, who systematically snubbed and ill-treated her, as the most likely way of securing her rather slavish affection.

"There's nothing wrong with me at present," I assured her.

She surveyed me earnestly.

"But you look so tired and thin. You don't seem at all like yourself," she continued.

She hesitated.

32

"Won't you make it up, Karl?" she pleaded. "We've only a moment now."

She put her hand on my shoulder, an act which filled me with immediate panic.

"Please," I protested. "Don't worry me now. I must have a moment to think things out."

"Very well," she answered sullenly. "But it isn't like you to be so terribly preoccupied."

She sighed.

"Do you remember that evening at the Indra? I told you then that the Professor wouldn't like it, but you said, 'Hang the Professor!' Now I suppose you've learnt to be afraid of him like everybody else."

By this time the taxi had reached the old town and was climbing a tall, narrow street, which ended in a small square with a fountain in the middle. Turning sharp to the right, it proceeded up a narrow and even steeper street, the name of which I caught sight of as we turned the corner.

It was the rue Etienne Dumont.

Our destination was close at hand. Should I even now explain to the girl who I was? I realised that if I did so my chances of seeing my grandmother would be small, and, more than ever, I wanted to make the old lady's acquaintance. I maintained an uneasy silence.

I was pondering who Karl might be, and why everybody was afraid of the Professor, when the taxi stopped with a jerk opposite a tall, narrow door.

My companion was first out, and had dismissed the driver before I had had time to do more than descend myself.

She went straight up to the door and tapped on it with the handle of her umbrella, one heavy rap and then a series of light ones, with two short, sharp knocks at the end. A small grille slid open in the door's face about the height of a man from the ground, and a pair of eyes surveyed us.

"Ephesus," said the girl.

"They are not dead, but sleep," replied the person on the other side.

Evidently it was some sort of password, for directly afterwards the door opened inwards, and my companion motioned me to follow her through.

I found myself in a dark, narrow passage, some thirty feet in length, running the whole depth of the house, which fronted the street. The man who had just opened the door closed it immediately behind us and turned to resume his seat in a little recess in the wall.

We went through the passage, which gave on a very small court or air-shaft, round which the house was built, and from which five or six stone steps gave access to another door.

My companion pushed it open. We entered a hall with several doors on either side. The girl opened the first on the left and we entered a room.

"Wait here a moment, Karl," she said. "I will tell them that you've arrived."

On that she went away, leaving me alone in the room.

I sat down in an armchair and lighted a cigarette to steady my thoughts.

The girl who had addressed me as Karl and who, to put it mildly, had shown herself of so friendly a disposition towards me, was one more factor in the mystery in which I had become involved since I had set foot in the grey city of Geneva. For the last time I wondered whether it was really wise for me to go on with the affair; but I found on reflection that my decision to do so successfully survived this eleventh hour. I can't accuse destiny of having hurried or entrapped me. I had received warnings enough to have sufficed for any sensible man. I wilfully disregarded everything that should have set me on my guard, and, on mature consideration, I must place this story to the account of my incorrigible curiosity and my impatience of routine. In brief, I had only myself to blame. I remember that almost my last feeling while waiting alone in that little room was a devout hope that my grandmother would prove less affectionate than the pheasant feather. You will judge from this the incurable levity of my disposition.

I presently rose from the armchair and began to examine the room in which I found myself. It was oblong in shape and very high for its length, obviously part of a much larger room, for one wall was merely a partition constructed some time previously in order to divide up into several pieces a single large room, a ballroom probably, or something of that kind. In its way, it was a beautiful room, white-panelled, and with a long, narrow window draped with heavy curtains, so hermetically sealed that there were cobwebs spun across the fastenings. I remembered that Beatrice had told me at lunch of the Swiss custom, observed by all classes in Geneva, to lock, bolt, and bar the windows on the first of October until the following first of May.

Opposite the window, in the partitioned wall, was a second door, presumably leading to another room. The room in which I was waiting was furnished partly as an office and partly as a sitting-room. Beside the window was a heavy oak desk on which several card board files were lying, in addition to the usual writing materials. A bookshelf stood in one corner, and I strolled over to examine the books. They were mostly on trade and economics, and amongst them I noticed Keynes' "Economic Consequences of the Peace Treaty," and Meneschkowsky's "Reign of Antichrist," that brilliant exposure of the theory of impersonality which is at the root of the Bolshevist system.

Then it struck me that I might learn something of the inmates of the house before meeting them in the flesh by examining the contents of the files lying on the desk. It will be seen that even at this early stage the instinct of the detective had already blunted the finer scruples.

I picked up a file and went rapidly through the contents, but it did not seem to contain anything of great interest. I took another, but that too only appeared to contain the records of various commercial transactions with different firms, most of them foreign, and related to the purchase of all kinds of goods, amongst which I noticed several large orders for Belfast linen, and six separate consignments of unfinished cotton goods from Manchester. There were also large orders to Dunlop and Goodrich, chiefly for tyres, and for consignments of rubber from the Dutch East Indies. The third file at which I looked seemed to be similar to the other two, but, glancing down the transactions chronicled, I came upon the words "Svenska Kullagar Fabriken."

I skimmed the relevant correspondence rapidly, and found several letters concerning the purchase of a large quantity of Swedish ball bearings. I was particularly struck by a letter requesting the Swedish firm to send a representative to Geneva to conclude the final arrangements, and I thought of my Swedish friend in the train.

The letters, being only carbon copies of the original, were simply initialled, so that I could not discover the name of the person who had made the purchase. This discovery set me wondering whether I could find any trace of the Swiss aluminium saucepans, and I searched through the rest of the file and through several others, until, finally, I came across a letter directed to Neuhausen, where, I remembered, the headquarters of the Swiss hardware firm were situated.

I was about to examine it, when I heard a movement outside the door in the hall, and, hastily abandoning the files, I moved across the room till I was opposite a large mirror, which was let into the wall above the mantelshelf and surrounded by delicate eighteenth-century moulding. There I made a pretence of adjusting my tie, and, as I was engaged upon this operation, I received the shock of my life.

While I was gazing into the mirror, replacing the gold pin which held my collar in place, my own face appeared in duplicate suddenly over my right shoulder.

I stared at it in astonishment. There it was, exact in every detail.

I thought at first that it must be some trick of reflection, and I grimaced into the mirror, to see whether the other face would register the contortion. But the face over my right shoulder remained solemn and unmoved, while I saw my own reflection by the side of it grimacing back at me with an expression of vacuous astonishment.

I whipped round and, standing behind me, I saw a man of my own height, wearing a light brown overcoat. The moment he caught sight of me, his face betrayed a similar astonishment to mine, and we both stood there for some seconds, dumb with amazement, so extraordinary was the likeness. Yet, even then, at the first encounter, I noticed differences between us. His hair was clipped very short over his head, in the German fashion, and his face was slightly rounder and had more colour in it than mine.

We must have stood gazing stonily at one another for an appreciable time, when the man's expression changed from mere astonishment to suspicion and from suspicion to blind rage.

Then, in a flash, without a word of warning or explanation, he sprang at me and seized me by the throat.

I was utterly unprepared for his attack and fell heavily backwards against the mantelshelf. Taken thus by surprise, I was at a serious disadvantage. I tore and struck at his hands and wrists, but his fingers would not loose their hold, and presently I felt my strength beginning to ebb. All the time we were swaying desperately up and down. We slithered along the edge of the mantelshelf till we came to the end, when a heavy kick on my shin felled me to the ground, and we rolled on the hearthrug.

Up to that moment I had been more amazed than frightened or angry, but, as I lay there on the floor, the breath being rapidly choked out of me, black rage took hold of me.

I stretched out a hand, with the object of trying to place a swinging blow at his head, and my knuckles came in contact with the hearth, in which I had deposited the butt of my cigarette, just before he had entered the room. Although I was fast losing consciousness, I was alive enough to act on the thought which came into my head as my knuckles touched the hearth, and, picking up the cigarette end, which was fortunately still alight, for my fingers touched the glowing end of it, I applied it to the nape of his neck.

It was a good fat stump, the remains of one of those big Virginian cigarettes, the "Greys," I think they call them, and it must have burnt him properly, for, with a yell, he loosed one hand and clapped it to the back of his neck. The same instant I knocked his other hand away and staggered to my feet, gasping, everything swimming before me in a mist of red.

He was up a moment later, and, as he rose to his feet, I hit him with all the force I could muster on the point of the jaw—I hadn't delivered such a punch as that since the day when I had knocked out the Ashingford middleweight, when I was fighting as captain of my school boxing team—and he fell with a thud. I had knocked all the consciousness out of him.

I stood leaning on the mantelshelf breathing heavily, and feeling slightly sick. My rage had departed, and I was trembling a little at the knees. My first coherent thought was, "I wonder whether anyone heard us fighting?"; my next, "Why did he attack me?"

I listened, but could hear nothing but my own breathing. The hearthrug, which was a good thick one, had deadened the sound of our fall.

I had now sufficiently recovered to examine my late opponent. There was no doubt about it. I had knocked him clean out, and the blow which he had received in falling against the corner of the hearth had completed his discomfiture. I thought rapidly what I should do.

The gentleman on the hearthrug was evidently Karl, who was clearly some kind of agent of the gang into whose house I had so wilfully penetrated. The little Jew. in handing me the pocket-book, had mistaken me for Karl, and so had the lady with the pheasant feather. The consequences of that mistake were so undoubtedly serious that Karl had attacked me at sight.

I looked down at the fellow. He was an ugly brute (though I say it who shouldn't) and I hoped that, in spite of the resemblance of feature between us, the likeness was not really fundamental. He was certainly not the kind of man for whom anyone would substitute himself without considerable misgiving.

Meanwhile, grandmother was presumably preparing to receive me, and I realised that she was likely to be annoyed if she found me there in studied contemplation of the inert figure of her dearest grandson. I remembered also that Uncle Fritz and Uncle Ulric were likely to be there, and I had no reason to believe that they would be less sudden or less resourceful than Karl on realising the mistake which had been made.

My blood was up and my throat hurt me abominably, so that I doubt whether I should have left the house even if I had been given the chance to do so. Anyhow, it was impossible. Already I heard steps and voices in the room adjoining.

I bent down hastily, seized my late opponent by the ankles and dragged him between the desk and the window, where his head and feet were covered by the falling curtains.

No sooner had I done this than the second door, which I had remarked when examining the room, opened, and the girl in brown appeared.

"This way, Karl," she said. "They're waiting for you." I passed my handkerchief once or twice across my forehead, gave a rapid glance into the mirror, which showed that I was less dishevelled from my late encounter than I had feared, and passed through the open door.

I entered a larger room than the previous one, and my eye instinctively noted that it was decorated in the same way, that is to say, its walls were covered with white painted panelling, and there were two tall windows. I had no time, however, to note further details, for my attention became immediately engaged with the person, or rather persons, who were awaiting me.

They were three in number and were seated behind a table covered with a red cloth.

Two of them I instantly recognised. The man in the centre was the dark-eyed man with the silky beard, who had favoured me with such a penetrating glance at luncheon in the grill-room of the Hôtel du Lac. The man on the left was his companion, the bullet-headed Prussian type, with the Mensur scars on his face. The man on the right was tall and thin, bald as an egg and wearing an eyeglass. I remembered at once my neutral friends in the train. This was evidently Herr Schreckermann, who had bought the aluminium saucepans and the ball bearings.

I walked up to the table and came to a standstill opposite the man in the centre. Meanwhile the girl in brown had slipped out behind them and vanished through another door, giving me an encouraging smile as she did so.

It was the man in the centre with the silky beard who spoke. I had already made up my mind that he was the most important member of the tribunal. He looked at me a moment with that same disconcerting stare which had so strangely affected me at the restaurant. I find it difficult to describe its precise quality. It was as though he were cautiously groping in the recesses of my mind, cutting painlessly at secret tissues of the brain with a velvet knife.

His voice when he spoke had the same quality, musical, but with a latent rasp. Every syllable of his utterance fell distinct and yet no note of it was forced. It reminded me of the taste of olives—oily, with a tang.

He fell upon me, softly as a cat.

"Why did you find it necessary to kill the chauffeur?" he demanded.

The three men all had their eyes fixed upon me inexorably—the man of the Mensur marks with the glassy stare of a commanding officer, the bald-headed man with the awe which deeds of violence inevitably inspire in the sedentary, and the man in the centre with that gradual, soft regard which I had already begun so greatly to dislike.

"Let me explain," I began.

"You will do no such thing," said the man with the silky beard. "We haven't any time for explanations. My question was intended to inform you that we already know precisely what has happened."

"If you will allow me——" I began again.

The man with the beard held up his hand in a gentle movement of arrest.

"Your action was careless and unnecessary," he continued; "you will do well in future to be less impulsive. You appear to be, I regret to say, much too liable to be moved by the primitive instincts. You were right in assuming that the man was a spy, but he was not really dangerous, and you had received strict orders to report to us here on the ninth of the month and not to allow yourself to be delayed by any circumstances whatever. Your behaviour in that affair was altogether contrary to the spirit of your instructions. To aggravate the offence, you left behind you a sufficient number of clues to convict you ten times over——"

"There's been a mistake," I protested. "If you'd only allow me to explain——"

"You are not here to explain," he said with an air of tranquil authority. "You're here to receive orders. You are already two days late, and, what is worse, it will take the whole of our organisation to get you safely away from Geneva. It is solely due to our vigilance that the complete description of your personal appearance and the warrant for your arrest, which have been forwarded to Geneva by the Zürich police, have not yet reached their destination."

He paused for the fraction of a second.

"One moment," I interrupted; "may I be permitted to know who is addressing me?"

"Our names do not immediately concern you," replied the man with the beard. "For the moment I have the honour to be your grandmother, and this gentleman," he continued, indicating the man with the Mensur scars, "is your Uncle Fritz, while on my right sits your Uncle Ulric.

"You have received a certain document," he resumed, before I could utter a word. "You will now deliver it to a person whose name for the present we are instructed to withhold. I should prefer to send it by a safer messenger. Unfortunately, however, the person to whom you are going is suspicious of strangers. He has been told to expect Karl von Emmerich, whom he trusts, and he is not likely to welcome a substitute. Luckily, some of our best men are at present in Geneva, and it should not be very difficult to baffle the local police."

He paused, but, before I could take advantage of the fact, the man with the Mensur marks abruptly intervened.

"Most deplorable," he said, in a voice that had evidently done excellent service on parade. "Like a lot of nursemaids. Finest organisation in Europe wasted in looking after a young blockhead who goes and commits a murder under the very eyes of the police."

"It's true," stuttered the bald-headed man, "that Karl, is a b-blockhead, but they trust him in Hanover, and he has g-gifts. When you s-send Karl, you may be sure he'll g-get there."

"Better give the young fool his instructions and get rid of him," growled the man with the Mensur marks. "I don't want him on our hands for another twenty-four hours. I've got picked men on every bridge in Geneva and on most of the main roads. But I can't keep up this sort of thing indefinitely."

"Evidently not," said the man with the silky beard. There was a world of unpleasant insinuation in his voice, and his military friend, plethoric by constitution, flushed a dull red, the slack veins swelling visibly on his temples.

"You demand impossibilities, Herr Professor," he said. "The whole organisation has been strained to the utmost, and this murder on the top of everything else was the last straw. I admit that the arrangements broke down yesterday evening—but only for a moment."

He regarded with his glassy stare the man whom he had addressed as Herr Professor (presumably the professor to whom the pheasant feather had alluded), but his eyes fell almost immediately before the mild scrutiny which they encountered.

"My estimable Fritz," the Professor kindly expostulated, "it is not a function of organisations to break down—even for a moment. During that moment our friend Adolf contrived to disappear completely. Perhaps Karl can tell us something about that most unfortunate occurrence."

"I know nothing whatever about it," I said shortly. "And I don't suppose you'd let me tell you if I did. Several times already I've tried to explain to you——"

"A bad habit, Karl," sighed the Professor. "If you do not know the whereabouts of Adolf, there is nothing you can usefully say. Adolf in any case is a side issue. He carried out his instructions in handing a certain document to you, and the fact will be noted to his credit. You will now please endeavour to emulate his example. To begin with, your Uncle Fritz, as chief of staff, will give you some good advice."

The man with the Mensur marks cleared his throat in a manner that reminded me painfully of certain disagreeable interviews in the orderly room, which, in common with most young men of my generation, I had not altogether succeeded in avoiding.

"No more monkey tricks, young feller. You've done quite enough harm as it is. You come late. You cause us endless trouble. You disobey instructions. You put up at the wrong hotel under an unknown alias, you talk to unknown men and lunch with unknown women; you interview the police; in fact, you're a—er—confounded nuisance. Now listen to me."

He took up a sheet of paper which was lying in front of him on the table, and looked it over.

"These are your instructions. I'll read them to you, and you'll obey them to the letter."

"The person to whom the document is to be delivered left Basle last night and has gone back to Hanover. We couldn't persuade him to stop.

40

Well, you'll have to go after him, and it'll be difficult, very difficult. You'll travel to Munich by air, starting at nine o'clock tomorrow. Until then you'll remain here. The Professor," and he looked at the man with the silky beard, "will give you fresh papers and see that you're properly disguised.

"Meanwhile," he concluded, "as a simple matter of form, you will please show me the document you had last night from Adolf, and sign a receipt to the effect that it has been formally entrusted to you by Section Q."

There was a slight pause as he ended, and the three men looked at me expectantly. The moment had at last arrived when I was to be allowed to speak.

I seized the occasion the more readily as I thought I now saw a way of escape.

"I cannot show you the document," I said.

The man called Fritz glared at me angrily.

"Insolent puppy!" he exclaimed. "My authority isn't good enough for you, I suppose. Only Karl von Emmerich, with friends in Hanover, may be allowed to see such writings."

"I cannot show you the document because I don't happen to possess it— not at this moment," I responded coolly.

"What?"

Fritz, the man with the Mensur marks, bounded in his seat. Schreckermann, the bald-headed man, had a stricken look.

The Professor leaned gently forward.

"Do I understand," he asked, "that you have seen fit to come here this afternoon *without* the document?"

"That is so."

"Is not that rather extraordinary?"

"It is all rather extraordinary," I answered wearily. "And since you don't appear to need any explanation from me, I suggest that, if Uncle Fritz really wishes to see the document I received last night, you would do well to let me go and fetch it. I shall be with you again in twenty minutes.

"With all the largest policemen I can find"—I added silently, for my own information.

The Professor was looking at me intently; so I stared defiantly at Fritz, whose glassy eye was much more easily met.

"This begins to be interesting," the Professor meditated aloud. "Do you know, Karl, I am almost beginning to have a doubt as to your good faith— nothing much, only the merest small suspicion.

"What do you say, Major Adler?" he concluded, turning to the man with the Mensur scars.

"He hasn't t-told us yet where he has p-put the d-document," observed Schreckermann.

"He's coming to that," said the Professor. "I feel sure that sooner or later he will tell us everything we wish to know."

"It's perfectly simple," I assured him. "The document is now at my hotel. I can fetch it for you in less than a quarter of an hour."

Fritz thumped the table.

"Then be off with you at once," he shouted. "And next time perhaps you'll attend to your instructions. I don't like your behaviour, sir. It's damned irregular."

I turned to go—perhaps a little too eagerly.

"One moment!" It was the silken voice of the Professor, but it conveyed infinitely more authority in its casual and quiet tones than the blustering of Adler.

I turned and found myself looking straight in his eyes.

"You left the document at your hotel?"

"Yes."

"For greater safety?"

"Yes."

"Is it, I wonder, possible to be so foolish?"

He said this in the manner of one carefully weighing an unlikely hypothesis.

"I was a marked man," I pointed out. "At any moment I might be arrested and searched. What more natural than to hide the paper in my rooms before venturing into the streets?"

"I wonder," murmured the Professor.

He continued to look at me, and I collected all my powers to withstand his penetration. In less than ten seconds I could feel the perspiration starting on my forehead as the result of the mental strain of meeting those persuasive eyes. I knew he was asking himself whether I, Karl von Emmerich, was blundering but honest and whether I might be trusted to go and fetch a certain document. I did my best to keep my eyes utterly candid and fearless, and tried to look the biggest fool in the universe.

Apparently I succeeded, for the Professor turned suddenly to Fritz.

"Very well," he said. "Send him off at once to the hotel, but have him closely watched."

I did not repeat my former mistake of seeming to be in too great a hurry. I stood motionless for an appreciable moment, and then said:

"Well, gentlemen, am I dismissed?"

Fritz nodded, and I turned without undue haste. In another moment I should be free, with the knowledge that I had stumbled by an extraordinary chance on what appeared to be a formidable but mysterious conspiracy.

I had almost reached the door when the Professor held up a slim forefinger.

"One moment," he said.

Again I stopped, though every nerve in my body tingled to put a closed door between me and those three men at the red-covered table.

There was dead silence, and I became aware of a sound in the adjoining room, a shuffling sound as of a heavy body dragging itself across the floor in the way of a caterpillar. This was followed by stertorous breathing and a faint scratching on the lower panels of the door.

Fritz leaped to his feet, and in three strides was across the room. He seized the handle, tore open the door, and there, on all fours, vainly trying to rise to his feet, his face uplifted, bulked the veritable Karl.

CHAPTER V

I HANG MYSELF

I have an instinct for danger when it is sufficiently obvious and immediate, and I lost no time meditating this new development. I made straight for the door, and was on the point of assaulting Fritz with Nature's weapons, which unfortunately were the only ones at my disposal, when I found myself looking plumb into the muzzle of an automatic pistol.

"Hands up," he commanded.

For an instant I thought to close with him, pistol or no pistol, but a click behind my back warned me that I was covered by more than one of these effective and disagreeable weapons.

Shrugging my shoulders, I walked back to the table, noting as I turned that it was Schreckermann who had me covered from the rear. The Professor had not moved from the table. He still sat in his chair. He had the air of one speculating on the intrusion of a new and interesting factor in a problem of purely academic concern.

"G-Gott in Himmel!" cried Schreckermann. "They're like as two p-peas."

"It certainly is not very easy to tell which of them is which," mused the Professor, "particularly as our four-footed friend in the doorway has for the moment lost the full use of his faculties."

Karl, who was trying to stand up, pulled himself heavily to his feet and stood swaying dizzily, holding fast to the jamb of the door. He glared vaguely into the room till his eye lighted on me, when he suddenly recovered his powers of perception and speech.

"Take care," he gasped. "That's a damned impostor."

He pointed an unsteady finger in my direction. His wits had not yet recovered from the terrific blow he had received, and his primitive instincts were still uppermost.

"I'll cut your blasted throat," he muttered thickly.

The Professor smiled from the table.

"I think this must be Karl," he said, surveying the swaying figure with benevolent interest. "I seem to recognise his psychology. However, we will

44

soon clear up this little difficulty."

He pressed an electric bell standing on the table.

It was answered by two sleek, dark-looking men, wearing the uniform of continental menservants.

"Search these men," said the Professor.

At the same time Fritz levelled his pistol at my head in the manner of one who would use the weapon if necessary. Schreckermann, I noticed, performed the like office for my twin.

"Hands up, both of you," ordered Fritz.

There was nothing for it and I raised my hands helplessly in the air. The two servants rapidly ran their hands over us. Nothing is more ignominious than being pushed and prodded by another man—though I must admit that my searcher was not unnecessarily violent or offensive—and it was with the utmost difficulty that I could restrain myself from knocking the fellow down. I had no doubt whatever at that moment that if I had made the least movement to do so, Fritz would have emptied his pistol into me without any hesitation.

The searchers coolly and methodically emptied our pockets, and laid the contents on the red-covered table.

The Professor examined the articles as they appeared; and, when he picked up my British passport, I realised that the game was up. And so it proved.

The Professor looked up from my passport.

"An Englishman," he said pleasantly—to my surprise he addressed me, for this speech only, in my mother-tongue, with no trace of accent. "And I perceive that your handsome gold watch was purchased in Bond Street—a pleasant thoroughfare."

"It's quite true," I said, "that I'm a British subject. It's a fact which you will do well to keep in mind. The British Foreign Office will certainly not lose sight of it."

"The British Foreign Office is in Whitehall if I remember rightly," said the Professor, "and Whitehall is in London. We are now in the rue Etienne Dumont, and the rue Etienne Dumont is in Geneva."

"There are friends of mine in Geneva——" I began, but suddenly stopped short.

The only person in Geneva who knew where I was at that moment was Beatrice Harvel. These men were desperate and unscrupulous. They had resources which I had not yet been able to measure. They apparently were engaged in a scheme of great importance, but of the nature of which I was unable to form any clear idea. This was a dangerous labyrinth, and it was out of the question to allow Beatrice to become involved.

"Yes?" prompted the Professor. "You were saying something about friends in Geneva."

"I'm only suggesting that if I do not return to my hotel enquiries will be made."

"We will deal with the enquiries when they arise," said the Professor. "There are rather more pressing matters which demand our immediate attention. You have confessed to knowledge of a certain document, and you have informed us incidentally that it is at present secreted in your hotel. Do you confirm that story now that we have come to know you better?"

I decided at once that I must stick to my original tale to the effect that I had hidden the document in my hotel. If I confessed that Lavelle was even at that moment attempting to decipher it, I was pretty sure that the whole gang would in a moment be at his heels, possibly with serious consequences not only for him but for Beatrice, who had acted as my messenger. The whole body of them would be put upon the track of my supposed accomplices, who would be without warning and without defence.

My object must be to get away to my hotel—if possible with not more than one member of the gang. Once in the open street, I had an infinitely better chance of escaping.

I endeavoured to meet the Professor in his own vein, smooth, reasonable, and unflurried.

"I don't think I have given you any good reason to doubt my word," I protested amiably. "I have never attempted to deceive you. I tried to explain who I was the moment I arrived; but you didn't give me a chance. It appears that I have been mistaken for this gentleman" (I indicated Karl, who was, I observed recovering slightly the use of his wits). "No one regrets it more than I do. The merest accident has placed a certain document in my possession, to which it appears you all attach considerable importance. I ask nothing better than your permission to restore it as soon as possible. If one of you will accompany me to my hotel, I'll hand him the paper that was thrust upon me yesterday evening, and count myself well quit of the whole affair."

"Then you assure us quite explicitly that the document is at your hotel," said the Professor.

"Do not be in too great a hurry to answer," he added kindly. "Should the statement prove to be incorrect, our faith in you would be rather badly shaken."

"I have made my statement," I said, with the air of an honest man justly aggrieved. "I can't think why you should doubt it."

"Instinct," said the Professor. "I never really took to that story of the hotel. However, we will give it a chance. What do you say, Fritz?"

"Perhaps Karl has something to say about it," suggested Fritz. "Can't he throw some light on this confounded business?"

Karl, who stood supporting himself at the table, put a hand to his head.

"I found the fellow waiting in the room outside," he said huskily.

"How did he get here?" demanded Fritz.

"I don't know anything about it," said Karl.

"Elsa brought him to the house," said Schreckermann. "She must have made the same mistake as Adolf."

"It's all the fault of this blundering idiot," said Fritz wrathfully, indicating the unhappy Karl. "Why are you two days late?" he harshly demanded.

"I couldn't help it," muttered Karl. "I'll explain as soon as I can, but my head's swimming so badly that I can't think. Give me a drink," he ended feebly, and collapsed, half-fainting, into a chair.

Schreckermann nodded to one of the servants, who left the room and returned with some brandy for my late opponent.

"Well, gentlemen," I intervened, "you don't seem particularly anxious to recover that document. I've informed you that it is at my hotel, and I have offered to fetch it. I have even invited one of you to accompany me as a proof of my good faith."

"B-better send F-Fritz," suggested Schreckermann.

"Yes," said the Professor, "we will send Fritz, and Mr. Thomas Preston shall remain with us till Fritz returns."

My face must have fallen visibly, for the Professor continued pleasantly.

"I am sorry to disappoint you, but, if your story is correct, you will be released in another half-hour at the latest. I am afraid it will be necessary for us to borrow your keys for a moment."

He picked them out from among the articles on the table, and, assuming the bored indifference of a man to whom the whole affair was simply an infernal nuisance, I pointed out the key of my despatch case on my key ring.

"I suppose I may trust you to take nothing but the document," I said resignedly.

Fritz glared at me for an answer.

"Certainly," said the Professor with dignity. "You will find that we are perfectly honest folk, and that we shall deal with you as is right and proper. I much regret the apparent lack of courtesy with which we have been compelled to treat you.

"Josef," he added, turning to one of the servants, "hand the gentleman his things, and conduct him to Room Number 4."

One of the servants approached me with my small change, my pocketbook, and my passport upon a salver, a which he held out to me for all the world as though he were handing coffee or liqueurs.

I picked them up and put them in my pockets.

"This way, sir," said the man respectfully, and motioned me across the room.

I followed the servant, and his colleague, as we passed him, stepped into the rear behind me, and we all three marched from the room.

We walked a short way down the corridor, and a door was flung open. The servants stood aside for me to enter and closed the door gently behind me. An instant later I heard the key turn softly in the lock.

I examined the room into which I had been conducted. It seemed to be a servant's bedroom. There was no window, but only a skylight high up in the roof, too small to admit a man. The room was very tall and narrow, so that its height greatly exceeded its breadth. It was barely furnished—a small wooden bed, a chair, and a table were all it contained. Round the four walls, at a short distance from the ceiling, was a shelf supported on iron brackets on which stood various pots and jars.

I sat down on the bed and thought things over. If Fritz took a taxi, he could, in about twenty minutes or half an hour, reach the Pension de la Reine, enter my room, discover that the document was not there, and return. Then, apparently, I should have the pleasure of a further interview with the Professor, and I had more than a suspicion that he and his confederates would stick at nothing to obtain from me the information they desired.

At this point my eye fell upon a small quarto volume bound in vellum, lying incongruously on the deal table of the attic. I picked it up and found it to be an exquisite bibelot containing some really beautiful reproductions of some of the more famous pictures, which depict the death by torture of the early saints, together with what appeared to be a complete history of the art of torture as practised, not only in Europe during the Middle Ages but in China and Persia and among the savages of Polynesia.

The various methods were described with great erudition and in amazing detail, apparently by an author who loved his subject, and the book was illustrated with zest and particularity. Some of the tortures I recognised as having been taken from mediæval pictures, such as the tortures of the rope and the brazier and the *peine forte et dure*, dear to the ancient judicial system of France. Others were more esoteric, such as the Chinese torture of the seven gates or the careful impaling practised by certain tribes of Eastern Mongolia. The artist had been especially skilful in conveying the great agony of the sufferers, whose limbs and faces, hideously twisted, registered forcibly the screaming protest of mutilated flesh and exposed nerves.

I was still examining the book when the door opened and the Professor entered. He was alone, and, for all I could see, unarmed. My first instinct was to grapple with him, but he met me with a smile which seemed at the

48

same time to divine my impulse and to rebuke its folly. He sat down companionably in the vacant chair.

"A man in your position, my English friend," he said, "should only employ violence as the last expedient. Particularly," he sarcastically added, "as you are at present merely awaiting your release. Fritz will find a certain document at your hotel and you will give me a solemn promise to say nothing that might cause your poor dear grandmother to regret her hospitality. Then we shall just shake hands and part company."

"That's all very well," I grumbled. "But how can I be sure that you will be as good as your word. I'm pretty sure that some of you—Karl von Emmerich for instance—would much prefer to cut my throat and have done with it."

"Karl would certainly prefer it," said the Professor. "Your Uncle Fritz would probably favour it too, and even Schreckermann would appreciate the very distinct advantages of such a course. But I am a sentimentalist, Mr. Preston, like all my countrymen, and in my youth I formed an attachment for your admirable country which recent historical blunders have failed to destroy. I should hate to be needlessly harsh towards an Englishman, a countryman of Kelvin. I was at Cambridge, Mr. Preston, with your wonderful J. J.—quite the greatest man of science I shall ever meet. Such memories are not easily ignored. It was a sad day for me, Mr. Preston, when England so foolishly decided to send her armies to the Continent. I foresaw the whole terrible tragedy—my own country and yours, exhausted with untold hardships and suffering, left at last to make their final reckoning with France, the ancient incorrigible militarist of Europe, determined never to forgive either the country which attacked her or the country which sprang to her assistance.

"You will realise," he concluded, "that I am moved by no national animosity towards England, and I hope you will believe that I feel no personal animosity towards yourself. On the contrary, Mr. Preston, I have taken rather a fancy to you."

I listened to this strange discourse with amazement, wondering to what on earth it was leading.

I was not left long in doubt. The Professor leaned gently forward.

"Now, Mr. Preston," he said, "will you not tell me, please, where you have put the document?"

"I have told you time and again," I stubbornly rejoined. "The document is at my hotel."

The Professor sighed.

"I am sorry," he said. "I had hoped that a little friendly persuasion would have induced you to take me into your confidence."

"At my hotel," I repeated firmly.

The Professor rose.

"Well, I hope you are right," he said. "Should Fritz fail to find a certain document at the Pension de la Reine, we shall be obliged to take other steps. I have, as I have said, taken a fancy to you, Mr. Preston, but I never allow my personal likes and dislikes to interfere with my duties as a public servant. I shall, in fact, be obliged to inflict upon you a certain amount of physical inconvenience. I find that the human will is subject to much the same laws as material substances. Individual specimens vary according to kind and quality; but just as every oil has its flash point, so every individual will has a limit beyond which it is powerless to resist the application of tests which are purely physical. At this particular moment you are rather a fine fellow, Mr. Preston; but in half an hour we can reduce you to a knot of purely reflexive nervous impulses, among which the impulse to confess will gradually begin to predominate. I see that you have already examined the admirable quarto which is kept in this room for the amusement and instruction of visitors. Study it well; for, if Fritz should return to us empty-handed, I assure you that within the next hour it will possess for you more than an academic interest."

He was now at the door, and, as I looked at him there, smiling and courteous, I knew he was speaking the truth and not merely trying to frighten me. These brutes were desperately determined to get the document, and I was convinced that the Professor would think no more of dissecting me alive than he would of vivisecting a laboratory rabbit.

Again he read my thoughts, for he added:

"I perceive, Mr. Preston, that you are a reader of men; so I need not assure you that I am not wasting your time with idle fancies. You are also sufficiently observant to have noticed that this is not a room from which it is possible to escape in a quarter of an hour. There was a man who escaped from us here on one occasion, but the way he took was as disagreeable as it was ingenious."

"Indeed?"

"Yes, Mr. Preston. He opened his veins with the blade of a safety razor."

He left me at that as quietly as he had come, shutting the door and turning the key in the lock.

It would be quite useless to pretend that I was not thoroughly intimidated, though I told myself that this was precisely the object which the Professor had hoped to achieve. I was horribly afraid, not only of the torture but of the condition to which it was possible for torture to reduce even the most stubborn of men. It was well enough for me, as I sat there more or less master of myself, to resolve that these blackguards should never wring from me the whereabouts of that accursed paper, but, with those confounded pictures fresh in my memory, it was impossible to be sure that the

50

secret would not issue from me as naturally and inevitably as the yelp of a mangled cur. I again opened the book and turned sick with horror at a vision of bare flesh blistering under heated steel.

I rose, feeling a little faint, and looked again for a way of escape.

I examined the bed, which was covered with two coarse sheets and two blankets; there was also a pillow in a case. I racked my brains for a device, but got no further than planning to stand near the door with a blanket up ready to throw over the first man that entered, after which I would try to fight my way out. The chances of getting free that way would, however, be pitiably slight.

Then, as I strode feverishly up and down the room, my eye suddenly lighted on the high shelf which ran round the top of it. It was, as I have already said, supported on iron brackets of an ordinary pattern, that is to say, a right angle of cast iron, one side of which was screwed into the wall, with the ends joined by a rod to give it greater solidity. There was a space within the triangle formed by the two sides of the bracket and the iron rod, through which it would be possible to pass a cord or rope.

My thoughts went instantly back to the Professor's parting words concerning the man who had escaped by taking his life. That gave me my idea.

I stripped the bed, and with some difficulty tilted the wooden frame against the wall. Next I laid the table flat on the floor and wedged it between the narrow space which separated the edge of the bed and the side of the room. This was to prevent the bed from slipping. I mounted upon it and discovered that, when standing on its topmost edge, my outstretched hand was only about a foot below one of the iron staples.

Climbing down again, I seized the sheets and tore them into strips with the aid of my pocket knife; and from these I rapidly constructed a rough rope of sufficient length for my purpose. Last of all I slipped the case from the pillow, and then my arrangements were completed.

I took a pencil from my pocket and, on the back of an old envelope, I wrote in German:

"My dear Professor,
    "Thanks for your friendly warning. Hanging is an easy death.
                                        "Thomas Preston."

I placed the note in a prominent position on the chair, which I had planted in the middle of the room, where the last rays of the sun passing through the skylight caught it and threw my message into high relief.

Throwing my sheet rope and the pillow-case over vain attempts, succeeded in threading one end of the my arm, I climbed on to the bed and, after one or two rope through the aperture in the staple. I pulled the other towards me and made a noose, into which I slipped my head, drawing it fairly but not too tight.

The most difficult part of my task was yet to come. It was necessary for me to pass the rope two or three times through the staple to prevent the noose from tightening about my neck. Fortunately, I am fairly athletic, and I succeeded in jumping for the staple and grasping the rod connecting the ends. I passed the rope through the staple, at the same time doing what is called an arm's bend, so that the length of rope between my throat and the staple was considerably shortened.

Already I could hear steps in the passage outside, and I remember inwardly thanking God that at least it would soon be over, and that I was to be spared the terrible anxiety of waiting for the moment of my desperate experiment.

Seizing the slack end of the rope with one hand, I pulled the pillow-case over my head with the other and swung off from the bed. The pillow-case would, I knew, be a handicap when the moment for action arrived, but I realised that it was imperative to hide my face if I were to deceive my enemies. I knew how a man was expected to look when hanged—especially the eyes.

As I swung from the bed I slithered along the side of the wall, all the while gripping the slack end of the rope desperately, for if it slipped I knew I should be strangled. The perspiration broke out on my forehead with the physical effort of maintaining myself in that position.

I forgot to explain that the staple to which I had tied my sheet rope was not directly above the bed, but somewhat to the right, so that, as I hung from it, I was clear of the uppermost edge of the bed.

Not more than ten or fifteen seconds could have passed before I heard the door swing violently open. There was a noise of entering feet, a momentary silence, instantly followed by a chorus of exclamation.

CHAPTER VI

I RIDE IN A HEARSE AND AM TRANSFORMED

I like to remember that in that moment I remained astonishingly calm and clear-headed. Though I could see nothing of what was passing under my feet, my head being completely enveloped in the pillow-case, I vividly imagined the scene which confronted the invaders. It was now late in the afternoon and the light was beginning to fail. They would see first the disorder of the room, then the chair full in the last ray of the sun, and finally a dim, swaying figure, hanging just clear of their heads in the far corner. I prayed for two things: that they would not turn on the light and that they had not closed the door.

It was now or never. I drew my legs up as quietly as possible, placed the soles of my feet against the wall behind me, slipped off the pillow-case and the noose, pushed myself off from the wall and jumped towards the centre of the room.

I saw them all in a flash, collected in a group near the chair. The Professor, with Schreckermann, was reading the note, and Fritz was advancing in my direction. I had timed my jump perfectly, for in another moment he could have caught me as I went over his head. As it was I sprang clear of them all and landed, stumbling forward, in the open door.

In an instant I was up and running for dear life. Behind me rose a medley of angry voices.

I ran down the passage, through the door at the end of it, down the steps and across the little yard to the outer entrance.

I remembered the man who sat by the door into the street and wondered whether he would be in his place, and if I should be able to deal with him before they caught me. Sure enough he was there, seated in his alcove.

"Quick, open the door. Ephesus!" I cried.

He got down and unlocked the door, but, as he opened it, my pursuers appeared at the other end of the yard and shouted that he was to stop me. He paused for a second, bewildered by the noise. I did not wait to argue the matter but, before he had recovered himself, I dealt him a heavy blow on the side of the head, which knocked him flat on the stone floor of the passage.

The next moment I was through the door and safe in the open street. I ran swiftly, turned a couple of corners and was immediately in the steep, narrow, and winding streets of the old town.

I had explored this portion of Geneva sufficiently well to realise that it was almost hopeless for a stranger to find his way to the more open parts of the town. This ancient quarter was a perfect maze of courts and alleys, many of them blind, and the danger of running at hazard in this labyrinth was brought home to me by the fact that I had already been obliged to turn two right angles and had thus been running for that short distance in a circle. I saw no one to whom I could appeal. The narrow streets were empty; the old houses apparently deserted. I knew that I could not be more than a few hundred yards from the headquarters of the Genevese police, and yet I verily believe that my pursuers could have knocked me on the head with complete impunity.

I could never have been more than fifty yards ahead of my enemies, and at any moment, if I continued to run aimlessly about, I might find myself driven into a trap.

I looked hastily around for a refuge. I wanted a moment to collect my wits and think the matter out.

I soon perceived a likely shelter. In the basement of one of the houses I saw a black hole yawning almost on a level with the pavement.

I dived into it and found it to be the entrance to a small cellar, nearly filled with potatoes and other market produce.

I attained this welcome refuge not a moment too soon, for quick steps were already sounding at the far end of the street. I shrank into a dark corner, panting for breath; and a second later I could hear my pursuers as they trooped past my hiding-place, their feet clattering on the uneven cobbles as they ran.

It was the first interval I had yet had for reflection since my desperate jump for freedom, and I took a decision which may seem odd to those of a more methodical turn of mind. I suppose the wisest course would have been to run at the first opportunity as directly as possible to the police. It was true that my double was wanted for murder and that I should be involved in endless difficulties explaining who I was. But at any rate, my personal safety would have been assured, and my final release a matter at most of several hours.

Meanwhile, however, the gang would almost certainly be on the track of Beatrice with whom I had been seen lunching just before the visit to my grandmother, and I had already a strong feeling that anyone with whom I could be connected even remotely was in serious and immediate danger.

My instinct was to get at all costs to the Secretariat of the League in order to warn Beatrice, put Lavelle on his guard, and recover the document, which was clearly of the highest international importance. It was true that I had not the slightest interest, so far as I knew, in upsetting the unknown plans of the conspirators into whose affairs I had so strangely stumbled, but when a man has been assaulted at sight, detained at the end of a pistol, threatened with torture and pursued with evident intent to kill, he is disposed to regard himself as in a state of enmity with his pursuers. I already felt that it was my duty not only to protect my friends from being molested by these mysterious people, but to prevent them if possible from recovering a certain document which, for some obscure reason, was necessary to their doubtless malevolent enterprise.

My immediate object, therefore, was to reach the Secretariat of the League, but the Secretariat of the League, it must be remembered, was on the far side of the lake, and my only way of reaching it lay across the Pont du Mont Blanc or one of the other bridges across the Rhone. Fritz had said that all the bridges were watched by men who were on the alert for Karl, and would soon be warned to be on the alert for me, if the organisation directed by Fritz were as efficient and as numerous as he had boasted.

Moreover, I had yet to reach the bridges. At present I was lost in the old town, without a clue to the labyrinth and with my enemies drawing the covert and likely to put me up at any moment. I was almost certain to be captured within the next five minutes, if I remained in my present place of refuge; and it was just such a place where I would least like to encounter the Professor and his friends. I must make a move at once.

I crept towards the entrance of the hole and looked up and down the street. Sure enough there were no less than four men walking towards each other from opposite ends of the thoroughfare and carefully examining the houses as they passed.

I drew back from the entrance and groped about in the darkness to find another way out. There was a door at the far end, but on examination it proved to be locked. It looked as though I had stayed too long in that wretched cellar and that I was to be caught like a rat in a trap.

Just at that moment, however, I heard a sound of wheels outside and I made my way back to the opening and looked out. A large hay-cart was coming down the street. It passed the two men who were methodically searching their way along and was soon abreast of the cellar. Almost simultaneously another vehicle, which had been approaching from the opposite end, came to a standstill almost on a level with the hay-cart, whose driver at once entered upon a heated argument with the new arrival.

Looking between the wheels of the hay-cart, I saw that its passage was obstructed by an empty hearse drawn by two black horses, which was trying to proceed in the opposite direction, presumably on its way back to the mews. The two vehicles between them completely filled the narrow thoroughfare.

I crawled out of the cellar on all fours and crept underneath the hay-cart, where for the moment I was hidden from view.

From there I was able to examine the hearse in detail. It was an ornate affair with a silver gilt roof, its woodwork covered with the ornamental scrolls dear to undertakers. The black cloths which had covered the coffin were lying in tumbled confusion on the floor.

Both vehicles were stationary at the moment, but, with much shouting, creaking of harness and grinding of wheels, the hearse began to move slowly past the rear wheel of the hay-cart. I gripped its edge with both hands and succeeded in pulling myself inside, at the risk of being jammed between the two vehicles. The driver of the hearse, a man in rusty black whose professional solemnity had been somewhat ruffled by his recent encounter with the hay-cart, was fortunately too closely preoccupied with his horses to notice my singular behaviour.

Once in the hearse I crawled beneath the cerecloths and arranged them about me as artistically as possible. They were of some heavy material and very voluminous, so that I could reasonably hope to escape notice under their ample folds. I lay there motionless while the hearse moved slowly down the street. The excitement under which I laboured may be judged from the fact that I did not spare a thought for the grisly nature of the conveyance which had so providentially come to my rescue, though I still remember small details such as the faint smell of camphor given off by my sombre wrappings.

As the hearse turned the corner of the narrow street, I could not resist looking out from under the black cloth. Sure enough, at the corner, stood Fritz and Schreckermann, waiting for the vehicle to pass before resuming their search. As I drew back into the hearse and it rumbled slowly past them, I noticed with grim amusement that my pursuers mistook it for a genuine and complete funeral cortège, and that they removed their hats with the mechanical reverence of the well-bred Continental.

The hearse proceeded through the old town at a pace truly funereal and from time to time I looked out to see where we were going and whether I was being pursued.

I noted with satisfaction that we were going steadily downhill and apparently making towards the lake. It was not long, in fact, before we turned into the rues basses, at the foot of the hill on which the old town was constructed.

The streets were already thronged with pierrots and other persons in fancy dress beginning their revels in celebration of the second day of the

Escalade. I was surprised at the sudden gaiety of the streets. Evidently on the preceding evening I had seen only the conclusion of the ceremonies. The Genevese took their pleasures early and the streets were now packed with citizens celebrating the ancient prowess of their forefathers. The hearse picked its way incongruously through the noisy crowd, cumbrously rebuking the levity of the masquerade.

I often remember that strange progress, vividly recalling details of which at the time I was only mechanically aware. I particularly remember how a Columbine, having thrown a *serpentin* which twined itself about the neck of my lugubrious driver, suddenly realised the nature of the vehicle he was conducting. She stepped back with a startled look and instinctively crossed herself, a gesture of which the syndics of the city would have deeply disapproved.

The condition of the streets at the foot of the old town gave me an idea, and, as we rounded a corner, I looked about for an opportunity to leave the hearse. It happened just at that moment to be passing one of the *chariots* (a kind of large flat tray mounted on wheels) which Genevese tradesmen use for delivering goods to the houses of their customers. I slipped from beneath the cerecloths, jumped on to the *chariot* and thence on to the ground.

The streets were so crowded that I doubt whether my dramatic rising from the dead was even noticed. In any case, I did not give the public any time for comment, but walked quietly across the road into a little shop that stood conveniently near at hand.

The shop contained cheap masks and dominoes for the revellers, and on reaching the interior I rapidly looked through a variety of costumes. Eventually I chose an elaborate cardboard face painted to represent a red Indian, with the appropriate head-dress and a scarlet domino to match, and, having donned my disguise, I asked the old woman in charge of the shop if there was a back entrance thereto, alleging that I wanted to play a joke on some friends who were waiting for me outside.

"*Bien*, Monsieur," she said, "if you will come this way."

She led me to the back of the shop and out through a side door, directing me under an arch to the rue de la Confédération.

I thanked her and walked through the arch and along the street, determined to make for the first bridge I saw and walk boldly across it, trusting to my fancy dress to avoid recognition.

I was within a few hundred yards of the Pont du Mont Blanc when I attracted the attention of three or four merrymakers, dressed in soiled finery. They intercepted me, commented vivaciously on my appearance, and, after dancing round me in a noisy ring, they insisted on linking arms with me, and we proceeded on our way, my companions chanting uncouth Swiss rhymes and I untunefully bellowing the "Madelon" which, with the exception of the Marseillaise, was the only French song I knew. I was not sorry to have met this merry band, since, being in their company, my chances of slipping across the bridge unrecognised were greatly increased.

I found that the crowd mostly confined itself to the streets through which I had already passed, and that it thinned rapidly as we came within view of the lake.

On approaching the bridge I looked eagerly for any sign of a watcher, but at first saw nothing to give me any cause for alarm.

I was soon to realise, however, that the resources of Fritz and his intelligence service were by no means to be despised. Half-way across the bridge stood a ragged member of the unemployed selling bunches of those small pink carnations which seem to be perpetually in season in this part of Europe. As we came near him a powerful green touring car drew up with a grinding of brakes, out of which stepped a man, apparently with the object of buying a posy. He picked up and rejected several bunches of flowers, talking rapidly to the flower-seller all the time he was doing so. Eventually he chose one, paid for it and turned back towards the car. He glanced in my direction a moment, and I recognised him immediately. It was none other than Fritz himself. He climbed back into the car, which continued on its way across the bridge.

We were now abreast of the flower-seller, whom I now knew to be primed and posted for my arrest, when it came into the head of one of my unknown companions, who had evidently chosen to honour the occasion with copious libations, to break into a dance. He executed a few ungainly steps in front of us, insisting that we should pause to admire, while he illustrated what he described as "*Le vrai pas d'apache.*" Then, all at once, filled with some freakish spirit of mischief, he ran up to us, seized the hat of one of my companions, which he threw into the lake, while with his other hand he tore off my mask, just as the flower-seller thrust a faded bunch of carnations under my nose, asking me to buy.

It would be difficult to say which of us was the more disconcerted. So suddenly had I been unmasked that the flower-seller was for an instant entirely at a loss. He recognised me at once, but he obviously did not know what to do. I turned abruptly, hoping to get away before he had recovered the use of his wits, and, abandoning my companions, I walked on, intent only on crossing the bridge and reaching the Secretariat before he should have time to give the alarm and raise my pursuers. I had not gone fifty yards before I heard a sharp whistle behind me, and looking back saw that it came from the flower-seller, who was walking rapidly in pursuit.

I ignored his signal and hastened across the bridge past the Pension de la Reine, and then to the left into the Place des Alpes.

There were no taxis in sight, but as I ran across the square, shedding my now useless disguise as I went, I suddenly saw a tram inscribed "Palais des Nations," which is local hyperbole for the Secretariat of the League. It was already moving off towards the rue des Paquis and I jumped into it. Nothing could well be safer than the interior of a municipal tram, and I regarded it as sent from heaven. It took me the whole way to the Secretariat, and I alighted opposite the main entrance, which is situated on the side remote from the lake. It is approached by a small courtyard bounded by an iron railing. At each corner of the railed court there are two gates, one for the entrance and the other for the exit of vehicles, and in the centre is the gate for persons on foot, through which I passed.

Just as I started to walk across the court (the door is about ten yards from the gate) I saw a large green car heading from the right entrance to the court, presumably with the intention of stopping opposite the door by which I was seeking to enter. Its great headlights were full on and I was clearly defined in their glare.

The next instant I heard a guttural exclamation, and the car, instead of slowing down on approaching the door, gathered speed and made straight for the opposite or left entrance to the court, a manœuvre which, as I was crossing the court full in its path, entailed my immediate and sure destruction.

I gave a wild leap forward and fell head foremost through the door, which was opening to admit an elderly gentleman, whom I have since ascertained to be a delegate of the Kingdom of the Serbs, Croats, and Slovenes, knocking him headlong with myself on top of him, in a confusion of silk hats, attaché cases and blasphemy.

CHAPTER VII

I BECOME AN INTERNATIONAL PROBLEM

We sorted ourselves out on the mat, and by that time the car had crossed the court and disappeared into the street. Two *huissiers* came forward and the ruffled old gentleman with whom I had collided was pacified with a clothes-brush, while I knelt on the floor in search of his papers. Presently, still grumbling, and grasping his despatch case tightly under the arm, he went up the steps, approached the *concierge* and thereafter disappeared from view, leaving his accompanying secretaries to dust themselves and recover their equanimity at leisure.

Meanwhile, two chauffeurs had appeared mysteriously from some hidden office in the basement, and were offering professional comments on the car which had so narrowly failed to run me down. One considered the driver's conduct "*un peu trop fort*," while the other went so far as to style him "*un imbécile au point de vue de la circulation.*"

I asked them whether they had noted the number of the car, but they replied in the negative. They had seen that there were two men in the driver's seat, one in livery and the other tall, big and in plain clothes.

I mounted the steps and walked up to the desk of the *concierge*, reflecting that my friends of the rue Etienne Dumont were not leaving much to chance. If they were prepared to assassinate me in front of a large building and in full view of several people, they were evidently men who would stick at nothing.

I gave my name to the *concierge*, an Englishman, stout, broad, typically British, with our national readiness to be respectfully, but unaffectedly, amused by the spectacle of a number of foreign gentlemen brushing themselves in a condition of high excitement.

I asked to see M. Lavelle of the Political Section. He sent my name up by the lift boy and requested me to wait until he had ascertained whether M. Lavelle was disengaged.

I spent a few moments in the hall, examining the place with interest. It was large, with two corridors running into it backed by a long glass screen shutting off a huge committee room. There was a lift, and I noticed that the shaft was in two portions, accommodating a passenger lift, in which the boy bearing my card had ascended, and, immediately behind it, what I took to be a service lift.

The lift boy returned, after a lapse of some minutes, and informed the *concierge* that M. Lavelle would see me immediately.

As I turned towards the lift, I heard the *concierge* dealing with a party of tourists, who, with a laudable desire to obtain as much information as possible in the shortest space of time, had enquired whether the League was still in session.

I noted with satisfaction that my countryman behind the desk was entirely equal to the occasion.

"No, gentlemen," he said. "But I can show you a room in which two wars were stopped."

Lavelle's office was at the end of a long corridor on the second floor. I knocked on the door and an instant later was vigorously welcomed by my old friend. He was just as I had remembered him, except that he was now out of uniform, bright, alert, with a mobile, responsive French face, dark eyes and hair greying a little above his ears.

"Come in, my dear Preston. So it's really you. I'm more than delighted."

He gripped me by the arms, smiling and taking a long look at me. It was pleasant to receive so cordial a reception after my experiences of the afternoon, and I breathed happily again, like a man released.

"Not half so delighted as I am," I replied. "In fact, I'm sadly in need of a few friendly words."

I suppose the strain of the last two hours had told on me unperceived, for I suddenly felt a little faint, and Lavelle was now gazing at me in some concern.

"Why, my dear chap, you look done to the world."

Lavelle, who spoke perfect English, prided himself on his idiom.

"Here," he continued, "sit down at once."

He pulled up a chair, into which I thankfully subsided, and went to a cupboard by the window. I smiled as he produced a bottle of cognac and a glass.

"Yes," he said, as he poured me out a stiff double. "I've not quite forgotten the old habits—though heaven knows how quickly one degenerates. Besides, dear friend, I need such aids to reflection, being in the habit of working here late at night. Drink this, and tell me afterwards what on earth you've been doing with yourself."

"I'm afraid it's rather a long story," I said, taking the cognac.

He watched me approvingly as I dealt adequately with the grateful draught.

"Has it anything to do with the paper which was brought to me by Miss Harvel this afternoon?" he asked.

"I suppose Miss Harvel has told you how that paper came into my possession," I said.

"She told me a terribly quaint story about a little Jew and a letter from your grandmother," Lavelle answered. "I suppose you have come straight from the tea-party?"

"As straight as was possible in the circumstances. Have you looked at the document yet?"

"It's a cipher document," he replied, "signed by the seven richest financiers in Germany; but I haven't had time to examine it properly.

"You'd better tell me your story," he continued. "It may help to throw light on the subject.

"And I'm sure Miss Harvel would like to hear it, too," he concluded.

He pressed a bell and Beatrice entered from the adjoining room. She smiled at me, but her face changed to an expression of concern as she noted my appearance. It was curious that I hadn't realised, till now, that I was hardly a fit figure for an official interview. In the course of the afternoon I had wrestled savagely with a man who had tried to choke me, I had hanged myself, dived into a cellar, lain in a hearse, scrambled into the costume of a red Indian and out of it again, and finally measured my length in the vestibule of the Secretariat. I began to feel that in all probability my tie was no longer straight.

"What *have* you been doing with yourself?" she exclaimed.

"I'm getting tired of that question," I said. "The fact is," I continued, "I appear to be two days late, which seems to account for the fact that at the present moment I probably look like a man who has been badly hustled."

I finished my cognac, rose, walked to the mirror over the mantelpiece, and was there confronted by a pale face, hectic eyes, a collar hopelessly crumpled, a neck which faithfully recorded the finger-prints of Karl von Emmerich, hair disordered, a tie that had almost ceased to exist, and shoulders badly in need of the brush.

"The truth of the matter is," I said, as I tried to repair the worst of the damage, "that for the last two hours I haven't been devoting any very serious attention to my personal appearance."

"But your neck!" exclaimed Beatrice. "What a horrible bruise."

She drew in her breath sharply between her teeth. I noted with pleasure that she did not like me to be hurt.

"That was my grandmother," I explained. "First she tried to strangle me, and I was finally obliged to hang myself in order to escape from her affectionate embraces."

And then and there I told them the whole story.

They listened attentively, and, as I told them what had happened to me in the rue Etienne Dumont, I must confess that I was myself considerably impressed. It appeared stranger in retrospect than it had seemed in the heat of the moment.

"Obviously," I concluded, "the document which came into my possession in so curious a manner is of supreme importance to someone, but I do not know at all who it can be, though my uncles ordered me to take it to Hanover, where there is apparently a personage anxiously waiting to receive it. What do you make of it, Lavelle?"

He shook his head.

"I don't know what to think. It looks like the kind of conspiracy which a short while ago was pretty general throughout Germany, but that sort of thing has been completely discredited since the celebrated Kapp Putsch. We hoped it was a thing of the past. The German Government, as you know, has capitulated, and applied for admission to the League. The Secretariat here is humming with this new development and the optimists among us are already rejoicing over the prospect of a general European settlement. Personally I can't quite believe it, though I must confess I have no real evidence to go upon. Things are quiet everywhere and we have lately ceased to hear anything of the German secret societies."

"Tell me about them," I begged.

"I thought most of it was common knowledge," said Lavelle.

"You forget, my dear old boy," I protested, "I've no time or use for common knowledge these days. I'm merely a wholesale tinker."

"In a drawer here," said Lavelle, "I have a list of fifty-nine German secret societies, which will show you to what extent Germany is honeycombed with these organisations. Some of them masquerade as gymnastic societies, sporting clubs, associations of comrades of the War, or of civil servants. Hardly a month passes that one or other of them is not dissolved by the Government. But they are invariably reconstituted under another name. I suppose you've never heard of the Consul Murder Club, or the Oberland Free Company, led by the notorious ex-Captain Ehrhardt, with whom the German Government has never been able to cope? No one knows the full extent of their numbers. Their adherents are mostly young; they are all well-disciplined, and they have only one object in view, which is to tear up the treaty of Versailles and wipe out the German republic."

We talked for some little time of the German secret societies, and I became very interested in the picture drawn by Lavelle. He made me realise as never before that there were vast forces in Germany, burning with resentment at their country's humiliating defeat in the War and eager for revenge. These forces were under capable subordinate control, but they had hitherto lacked a leader of adequate ability and prestige and had failed to secure any sound financial backing.

It seemed not unlikely that the document which had come into my hands concerned one of these societies, and, if this were the case, I had become unwittingly involved in preparations for another Putsch, whether monarchist or communist I did not know.

"Moreover," I pointed out, "they seem to have the money for this particular show." In proof of which I told him of the astonishing purchases of aluminium and ball bearings which had recently been made by Schreckermann, not to mention the evidence I had seen in the files kept at the rue Etienne Dumont of other extensive and costly transactions.

"That's the really striking element in the problem," said Lavelle. "Your document, as I have said, is signed by the seven richest men in Germany. That alone gives it an unusual significance."

He unlocked a drawer, produced the document, and spread it on his desk in front of us.

All the time he was speaking, in spite of my keen interest in what he was saying, I was acutely aware of Beatrice. I was like a man suddenly enchanted; and, as the three of us bent over the desk to look at the sheet of paper spread before us, I realised that I was far more aware of her, near to me and, as I felt, conscious of a growing intimacy, than of the mystery and peril in which I had so strangely become involved.

I was recalled to earth by Lavelle saying:

"It seems an ordinary enough cipher, but I must submit it to various tests before I can read it. Most modern ciphers, or rather most number ciphers, depend on a code word. Did you by any chance hear anything in the rue Etienne Dumont which might serve the purpose?"

"I don't think so," I replied hesitatingly, trying to concentrate my thoughts.

"Try Ephesus," suggested Beatrice. "It was your grandmother's password and it was the word used by the little Jew."

"Well, let's try it," said Lavelle.

He took a sheet of paper and drew a square on it, which he subdivided into a series of small squares, putting each letter of the word Ephesus into one square. He then made a series of calculations, and soon the sheet became covered with little groups of figures similar to those on the document. He worked rapidly, whistling under his breath as he did so, which was a trick I remembered him to have had in the old days, while Beatrice and I watched him in silence.

"*Sapristi!*" exclaimed Lavelle at last, in an excited tone of voice. "You're right, Miss Harvel. Ephesus is the code word. Look!"

He took the document and copied the first three groups of figures into the large square which he had previously drawn on the paper. Then he wrote down the letters of the alphabet beside the figures in a certain order, and they automatically formed the words, *"Wir, die Siebenschläfer"* (We, the Seven Sleepers).

I leaned forward eagerly, and Lavelle bent down to resume his work. At that moment, however, the telephone bell rang.

"Zut," he said. "Answer it, will you, Miss Harvel?"

Beatrice went to the telephone and took up the receiver.

"Yes," she said, "M. Lavelle's secretary speaking. Certainly."

She handed the receiver to Lavelle, saying as she did so, "The Secretary-General."

Lavelle put the receiver to his ear.

"Yes, it's Lavelle here. Yes. Immediately? Very good. I'll come down at once."

He replaced the receiver.

"Sorry, old man," he said ruefully, "the Secretary-General wants to see me at once. I must go down, but I don't suppose I shall be long. You'd better wait for me here, and I'm sure," he added, with a smile, "that Miss Harvel will be able to entertain you."

The assumption of Lavelle that Beatrice and I enjoyed some kind of special understanding put a sensible constraint between us. At least I know that for a moment I was clearly out of countenance myself, though I suspect Beatrice was more amused at my momentary awkwardness than conscious of her own. Anyhow, it was she who came to our rescue.

"Well, Tom," she said, "safe at last."

"I don't *feel* particularly safe," I replied. "I'm pretty sure that Uncle Fritz is waiting for me round the corner, and that there will be precious little peace for any of us while we continue to have that wretched document in our possession. That's why I was so keen to get here this afternoon. I felt it was essential to put you on your guard."

Beatrice looked dubiously at the sheet of paper, spread on the table as Lavelle had left it a moment ago.

"I wish we were well rid of it, Tom," she said.

"If," I replied, "we are right in suspecting that it has to do with a German conspiracy, I'm inclined to think that the best place for it is at the Quai d'Orsay. In fact, I'm inclined to offer my services as *courrier*. Isn't there a fast train to Paris this evening?"

"At ten o'clock."

"Could I get a sleeper?"

"Easily. There's always a spare compartment at this time of the year. But"—she hesitated a moment—"isn't it rather a risk, Tom?"

"I should have thought with a false beard and a revolver and a *wagon-lit* locked on the inside, and the French frontier within forty minutes run of Geneva it was a fairly safe proposition."

"And I should have thought that the forecourt of the Secretariat of the League of Nations in a neutral city was a fairly safe proposition. But they tried to kill you on the doorstep all the same. Thank heaven that, for the moment, at any rate, you're out of reach. We're extra-territorial, you know."

"What on earth does that mean?" I asked.

"We have diplomatic privileges."

"Beatrice dear, don't be so terribly technical."

"In plain terms, you ignoramus, the offices of the League are like an Embassy or a Legation. Nobody can touch you here—not even the Genevese police."

"I see," I said. "I've taken sanctuary, as they said in the good old days. I'm holding on to the horns of the altar."

She nodded.

"It was a stroke of genius to make for the Secretariat," she said.

"It was an inspiration," I exclaimed, with an ardour that surprised even myself.

I was seeing Beatrice at that moment in a light that made me oblivious to any advantages or disadvantages that might lie in being extra-territorial or whatever the term might be; my exclamation, in fact, had an unavoidably personal significance that was by no means lost on my companion. She looked at me a moment and then, her eyes dropping suddenly, she suggested a clothes-brush, and disappeared, before I could protest, in search of it.

She came back in a moment and started to brush me down. I submitted in silence, and her performance of this small office gave to our relationship at that moment of respite from fantastic adventure a sense of the familiar, I had almost said of the domestic, which remained with me all through the nightmare incidents of the succeeding days.

She finished the brushing and, as one who cannot endure to leave her work incomplete, she readjusted my tie, and smoothed out, as well as she could, my crumpled collar. I can shut my eyes to this day and recall the light movements of her hands as she tried to make me presentable.

"Heavens, what a bruise!" she cried, as she saw more closely the marks left upon me by Karl von Emmerich. "It was not one of your lucky days when you lost your luggage and came to Geneva."

I took quickly the hands that had just fallen from my collar.

"It was the luckiest day of my life," I said.

She drew back a little, but her fingers, after the first instinctive movement of recoil, remained quietly in mine.

"Touch wood, Tom. The story isn't finished yet."

"It was a lucky day, whatever happens. It was today I came to my senses and realised that I hadn't seen you for ages."

"So that's why you arrived in Geneva, Tom—two days late."

"Two years late," I corrected.

I drew her towards me, but she held away.

"Beatrice," I pleaded. "It's the real thing. I bless the day that I came and found you again."

"Not now, Tom," she whispered.

The door opened and Lavelle came quickly into the room.

I saw at once that he brought bad news. He looked unusually serious and did not stop to rally me, as even the best of Frenchmen must certainly have done at any other time, on the subject of Beatrice, whose hands I still held fast in my own.

"Preston," he said, "I'm afraid you'll have to run for it."

"But, my dear chap," I protested, "I've just this minute been told that I've taken sanctuary and can't be touched."

"That's what the Secretary-General wanted to see me about. The Geneva police have called with a warrant for your arrest. They want you for that murder in Zürich. Either you must run or be laid by the heels while the authorities discover that you're not merely an alias for Von Emmerich."

"Nonsense," I said. "I've got my passport."

I put my hand to my breastpocket.

"No use," said Lavelle.

"But *you*, at any rate, can swear to me," I said in bewilderment. "You've only to assure the Secretary-General that I'm your old friend, Thomas Preston, and he'll send the police about their business."

"It won't do, I'm afraid. They've already told the Secretary-General that, if questioned, you will claim to be Mr. Thomas Preston and that you carry a British passport, but that this is merely a masquerade, which you are quite likely to support with the most incredible and fantastic tales. In fact, they were obviously ready to deal with any objection at once, and were quite clearly aiming at you rather than at Von Emmerich. I couldn't quite make it out."

"But didn't you tell the Secretary-General——" I began.

Lavelle interrupted me.

"My dear chap," he said in great distress, "we haven't time for this. The Secretary-General personally took the view that, if you were really my old friend, Mr. Thomas Preston, it was only necessary for you to go round to police headquarters and establish the fact. Officially, he considered that if the warrant were in order, it would be highly improper for him to resist the police in the performance of their duties, seeing that you were not yourself a member of the Secretariat. So he decided to waive the privilege which attaches to this building, and to surrender you if the warrant were found to be genuine. I thought it best, in the circumstances, to accept the decision without any more ado. After all, it doesn't make matters very much worse. I'll keep the document safe and decipher it this evening. Meanwhile, you can either go to the police station, where you will at any rate be safe, or show a clear pair of heels before they arrive."

I thought hard for about five seconds.

"Lavelle," I said, "what was the policeman like?"

"There were two. One of them was tall, with cuts on his face, the other ____"

"Never mind the other. The tall one is Fritz."

"Incredible!"

"On the contrary. It couldn't possibly be anybody else. The Genevese police know nothing of Thomas Preston. The gang have followed me here with a false warrant. Were they in uniform?"

"No."

"Did you see their papers?"

"Their papers are at this moment being examined by the Legal Section."

"And if they are in order?"

"If they're in order, I shall be instructed to receive the police in this room and formally invite them to perform their duty."

"Then you must go back to the Secretary-General at once and challenge their identity."

"That will be merely one of your incredible tales."

"But he can ring up the police and corroborate your statement."

Lavelle seized the telephone.

"I'll do that at once. If the police deny that any of their officers have come to the Secretariat, it will be proof positive that Fritz is impersonating."

I breathed again as Lavelle took up the telephone.

The telephone service in Geneva is the most efficient in the world, and in less than a quarter of a minute Lavelle was speaking to police headquarters.

He asked whether anyone had been sent to the Secretariat to effect the arrest of Karl von Emmerich, alias Thomas Preston, for murder. His expression changed to one of the completest amazement as he listened to the answer.

He hung up the receiver.

"*Mon Dieu!*" he cried. "*Ces Messieurs sont épatants.*"

68

"The police?"

"No, your friends of the rue Etienne Dumont. They leave nothing to chance. The superintendent of police tells me that they were warned twenty minutes ago by telephone of the presence at the Secretariat of Karl von Emmerich, wanted in Zürich for murder and now passing under the name of Thomas Preston, a British subject. Two genuine policemen were at once despatched to effect the arrest."

"Very well," I said coolly. "We've only to delay the proceedings a little, and the real police will arrive just in time to unmask my ingenious uncles."

Lavelle shook his head.

"I wouldn't risk it if I were you," he said, with a shrug.

"What do you mean?"

"My dear fellow, a gang which is sufficiently ingenious to warn the police at the very moment when two of its members are actually impersonating two of their officers isn't likely to be defeated by their arrival at an inconvenient moment."

"You mean?"

"I mean that the real policemen are probably at this moment being firmly, but let us hope gently, detained by some of these gentlemen who guard bridges and drive powerful motorcars at express speed through the forecourt of the Secretariat. Why, my dear chap, they would have been here at least ten minutes ago if they had not been intercepted. I doubt if Fritz would even have started till he had them safely detained."

"But can't you explain all this to the Secretary-General?"

"It would be hopeless. Fritz will at once suggest telephoning to the police to ask whether they have sent to make the arrest. The Secretary-General will be informed immediately that two men have been dispatched. Am I to suggest that the real policemen have been detained by the friends of the false policemen? The Secretary-General would infer either that I was stark mad or that I was pulling his leg. A man in his official position couldn't possibly risk accepting such a story for five minutes, in the presence of officers who are *prima facie* genuine government officials."

Lavelle had not for nothing served for three years in the French Intelligence Service. I admired his quick diagnosis of the position and his decided view as to what was likely to happen. I had little doubt as he finished that, if I stayed in the Secretariat, I should very probably leave it under duress in the company of Fritz, and that the green car would shortly be taking me for the last excursion of my life.

The telephone bell rang as Lavelle concluded, and he had already taken the receiver.

"Yes," he said. "Lavelle speaking—Very well—Yes, I'll receive them here."

He hung up the receiver.

"Not a moment to lose," he said. "The Legal Director informs me that the warrant is in order and that the police are coming up at once to arrest you. My instructions are to introduce you to the officers, and not to obstruct them in the discharge of their duty."

He turned to Beatrice, who had followed our conversation with anxious concern.

"Take him through your room and show him the service staircase. These fellows are either coming up by the front staircase or in the lift. You can leave by the garden gate. I'll receive them and take care of the document."

"We must have a *rendezvous*," I said.

"I shall be here tonight from nine o'clock," Lavelle replied. "Ring me up or come if you can. By then I shall have deciphered the document, and we shall know what these blackguards are trying to do."

I seized my hat and coat and left the room hurriedly with Beatrice, who took me down the corridor towards the lift. We soon reached a glass door, through which I could see some uncarpeted stone stairs. Beatrice tried the handle, but found it locked. That way out was barred.

Her presence of mind was admirable, for she took me without hesitation to a recess where, just as we reached it, the service lift drew up with a jerk, and the lift-man came out, carrying a great pile of documents.

"Going down?" Beatrice asked.

"Yes," he replied.

I stepped in. On the threshold I paused for a fraction of a second. I hated to leave Beatrice in this hurried way without a work or look of farewell. But she pushed me urgently forward, and the last I saw of her was the upward rush of her slim figure as the lift swept me down and out of sight.

Halfway down we passed the other lift—which, as you may remember, was in the same shaft—going up, and I caught a glimpse of a party of visitors ascending. Evidently Uncle Fritz was losing no time.

Arrived at the ground floor, I slipped out of the lift and found myself in the hall. The back of the *concierge* was fortunately turned, and he did not see me.

I did not go out by the front door, however, for I thought it extremely probable that the big green car was in waiting outside.

I went instead into the big glass committee room, behind the desk of the *concierge*, which proved to be empty. It had long French windows giving on to a verandah, and I opened one of them without much difficulty. A flight of steps led from the verandah to the garden. I descended them rapidly and made for the little gate, where I had said good-bye to Beatrice after lunch. It was unlocked, and I was through it in a moment, finding myself alone on the Quai du Mont Blanc with the leaden lake in front of me and a few stars showing faintly through a cloudy sky.

I paused on the pavement, uncertain what to do next. I had a couple of hours at least during which I must hide myself before it would be safe for me to communicate with Lavelle. How he would contrive to throw off my pursuers I did not know, but I was content to leave it to him.

I soon came to the conclusion that it would be unwise to make for the town, so, turning to the left, I started up the Quai, which ended at this point in a public park, intending to strike the high road to Lausanne, and stop at the first likely refuge.

I had only gone two or three hundred yards when an open touring car driven by a chauffeur in livery and containing two men came level with me and drew up alongside, with a grinding of brakes. One of the men jumped out and approached me.

"Quick," he said, "you've no time to lose."

He spoke in French with an accent that could only have been the gift of Nature.

I looked at him, hesitating for an instant.

"We're your friends," he said.

The other man leaned suddenly from the car.

"Don't you remember me, Monsieur Preston—yesterday evening in the train from Lausanne? Jump in, quickly. Or do you perhaps prefer the green automobile?"

Bewildered, I climbed into the car, and a moment later we were speeding down the main road into the night.

CHAPTER VIII

I ENTER THE SERVICE OF THE FRENCH REPUBLIC

I was now seated in the back of a large open touring car between the two men, the one on my left a complete stranger and the one on my right the little Frenchman with the brown eyes, whom I had met in the train from Lausanne on the previous evening, and whose despatch case had fallen open at my feet. I had recognised him at once. Those brown eyes of his were unmistakable. At the present moment they twinkled merrily, and his whole appearance was one of suppressed high spirits and delight at what he evidently regarded—which indeed it was—as a wholly unexpected encounter.

His companion was tall and dark. He had a thin kindly face with an indiscriminate sandy moustache cut close and almost level with the ends of his mouth.

Uncle James of Jebbutt and Jebbutt is always impressing upon me the necessity of summing up men at a glance if I am ever to succeed in business, and I have consequently formed the habit of trying to tell the character of anyone with whom I come into contact. The tall Frenchman had the eyes and habit of a student, and I put him down with little hesitation as a man of exceptional gifts. He had the downcast, stooping manner of the overtrained official, and, from my wide acquaintance among French officers during the War, I judged him to be a brilliant product of the Continental system of education, which forces the intellect at the expense of the more ardent and engaging qualities of youth. Nor, on further acquaintance with him, did my first estimate prove to be incorrect. He was a very finished product of the *école normale*, and typical of the hundreds of able functionaries whom France seems to possess in inexhaustible numbers for her administrative needs. By this I mean no disparagement. They are men trained to devotion, at all times ready to subordinate their personal feelings in obedience to official instructions. Etienne Réhmy has ever been my true and staunch friend; and it was his training, and not his character, which seemed prematurely to have thinned his blood and kept his more ardent

72

emotions under control. The real man was to emerge later in a fashion that has endeared him to me for as long as I can tell one man from another.

His friend on my other side, Gaston de Blanchegarde, I have already partly described; and for the moment I have nothing to add, except to note the striking contrast between him and his companion. I was shortly to realise that Réhmy was as clearly the cool, competent brain of that curious partnership, as de Blanchegarde was its impulsive and occasionally rash executive.

This, however, is by the way, and when I first met Réhmy and de Blanchegarde I only had time to gather a first general impression created upon me by two persons whose courage and fortitude neither Beatrice nor I shall ever be able to forget.

"Well, gentlemen," I said, as the car sped through the darkness in the direction of Lausanne, "to whom am I indebted, and may I enquire where we are going?"

I was answered by a merry laugh and a hand laid lightly on my shoulder.

"Ha, ha, my Capitaine!" replied the little brown-eyed Frenchman. "It was a trifle sudden, *hein?*—and a lucky chance we caught you. Allow us to introduce ourselves. On your left you have M. Etienne Réhmy, of the French Secret Intelligence, Permanent Staff, and on your right you have M. Gaston de Blanchegarde, of the French Flying Corps, temporarily attached."

"I have met you before, at any rate," I said, turning to M. de Blanchegarde. "We travelled together from Lausanne yesterday evening. Otherwise I should have been less ready to accept the hospitality of your extremely well-appointed automobile."

M. de Blanchegarde laughed again.

"In that case, my English friend, we should have found means to persuade you."

I had a sudden recollection.

"We met again yesterday evening," I said. "But you were dressed somewhat differently."

"So you recognised me, did you?" he rejoined. "Yes, I was the clown—at the Moulin Rouge—and Etienne there made a splendid harlequin, don't you think?"

"You both looked very well indeed," I replied.

"Come now, Gaston," remonstrated M. Réhmy mildly. "I'm sure Captain Preston is much more anxious to know how it is we were fortunate enough to capture him just now than to discuss the merits of our masquerade. I'll explain if you'll allow me to do so."

"But certainly, my friend, I detest explaining," said his companion.

Réhmy turned to me in a business-like way, and during the next five minutes I was subjected to a very close and searching interrogatory, at the end of which he appeared to be satisfied that I was a person to be trusted. "Captain Preston," he concluded, "we are anxious to obtain possession of a certain document. We have reason to believe it was handed to you in the Moulin Rouge last night at about 11.30 by a little German Jew. Is this correct?"

I hesitated.

"Well, gentlemen," I said, "although I do not for a moment doubt your identity, before I answer that question I should like to take a look at your credentials."

"Naturally," assented Réhmy, and, taking something from his waistcoat pocket, he handed it to me.

It was a small disc with the letters "R.F." stamped on one side and on the other the number "31."

"This is my badge as an accredited agent of the French Republic," he said. "You picked up a similar badge, belonging to Gaston, in the train yesterday."

"I did," I acknowledged. "But he told me it was an identification disc, which he was cherishing as an old war souvenir."

"He didn't know you then, Captain Preston. We have to be very discreet with strangers."

"But you don't know me now," I objected.

"Oh, yes, we do," said de Blanchegarde. "We are extremely well-informed."

"As I was saying," continued Réhmy, "we believe that a certain document came into your possession yesterday evening."

"Well?" I queried.

"We only discovered that the little Jew had succeeded in passing this document to you when we came to search him in this very car."

"So you kidnapped him, did you?" I said.

Réhmy nodded.

"We have great need of the document," he said, as though apologising for a misdemeanour.

"You must have been very disappointed when you failed to find it," I remarked.

"We were, exceedingly disappointed," returned Réhmy. "Failing to find it on the person of the little Jew, I went back again in a taxi to the Moulin Rouge."

"Not, I hope, with the object of kidnapping *me*," I expostulated.

"But, yes, most certainly, if it had been necessary," said Réhmy gravely. "Unfortunately, when I got there you were nowhere to be seen. I enquired of the *chasseur*, who informed me that you had left the building almost immediately after us. So I got back into my taxi and drove off, and, by the merest chance, passed you as you were walking down the Corraterie. I accordingly abandoned my taxi and followed you as far as the Pension de la Reine."

He told his story in the manner of one reporting progress to a committee.

"The rest was easy," he continued. "I called next morning at the hotel and asked the proprietor if a friend of mine, whose name I invented, was staying there. By this means I was able to look at the hotel register. The only male guest who had arrived on the previous day was yourself, and I accordingly enquired for you, saying that you would probably be able to give me news of my friend. The proprietor informed me that you had gone out about half an hour previously."

He paused a moment and resumed.

"We have since taken turns in watching your hotel continuously, but you never returned to it, and we decided at last to interview again your Jewish friend. Then, only a moment ago, suddenly, to our great content, we saw you leave the Secretariat of the League of Nations—and here we are."

"Thank you," I said, "but in one point you're mistaken. The little Jew is not a friend of mine. I saw him yesterday evening for the first time in my life, not five seconds before you yourselves laid hands on him."

"As I thought," said de Blanchegarde. "I felt sure, Etienne, that a man with Captain Preston's record wasn't the man to consort with German agents."

"What do you know of my record?" I enquired.

"Oh," said de Blanchegarde, "that was easy enough. You told me in the train that you were a British officer. You even mentioned your regiment, and, though you may not know it, our department carefully preserves the army lists of all who were our allies during the late War. We just rang up Paris and had you identified."

"I see," I said. "So now you know all about me."

"We do," assented de Blanchegarde, with a friendly smile. "And I've an idea that you won't be at all sorry to part with that unlucky document. It's not exactly an insurance policy."

"I've discovered that—to my cost," I replied. "Unfortunately, however, I can't oblige you at the moment. The document is not at present in my possession."

"You've been robbed of it already!" cried de Blanchegarde, in dismay.

I hesitated. Was this perhaps an inspired manœuvre of the resourceful Fritz? A glance at the eager little Frenchman reassured me immediately. I found it impossible to doubt his good faith.

"I'll tell you the whole story," I said.

The car, which had turned off the main road, had entered a carriage drive, and it stopped a moment later in front of a capacious wooden *chalet*, which was vaguely outlined in the darkness. De Blanchegarde jumped out, went up to the door and rang the bell. A moment later the door was opened by a short, grizzled manservant, addressed by de Blanchegarde as "Jules."

"How is our guest?" de Blanchegarde enquired.

"Tolerably quiet, M. Gaston," replied Jules, "but inclined to be nervous. He prays that we shall refrain from cutting his throat."

"Good," said de Blanchegarde.

We all descended from the car and a few minutes later we were seated in a warm and pleasantly furnished sitting-room.

"And now, please," said Réhmy, "we'll have that story you promised to tell us."

"Certainly," I said, "but for the love of heaven give me a drink!"

I sank into an armchair, and de Blanchegarde was immediately all concern.

"*Mon pauvre ami!*" he exclaimed. "Etienne, you're a perfect savage. Can't you see that Captain Preston is tired out?" and in a few moments he was shaking me up what proved to be an excellent and very welcome cocktail.

After that we settled down, and I began the history of my adventures.

They heard me to the end, and as I proceeded with my tale, I found myself adopting more and more of an official manner, as though I were making a report, as I used to do in the army.

"I think that's everything, gentlemen," I concluded.

I could see that my new friends were, each in his individual way, tremendously impressed. De Blanchegarde could with difficulty restrain his excitement. Now and then he would bound in his chair and his eyes light with the joy of battle as the more striking episodes were recounted. Réhmy looked more and more concerned, and at the end he had the worried look of a man faced with a problem unexpectedly difficult. It was amusing to note how, when my tale was finished, de Blanchegarde, though it was clearly difficult for him to restrain his exuberance, waited becomingly for his more collected official superior to take the lead.

Réhmy allowed himself a moment for reflection before breaking the silence which had fallen between us. He then spoke with a grave courtesy that accorded well with his somewhat ascetic face and tired eyes.

"As we have already informed you, Captain Preston," he began, "we are accredited agents of the French Republic. Owing to an entirely unforeseen and extraordinary series of coincidences, you have become involved in our operations. You will, I am sure, as a man who has served his country, understand only too readily how difficult it is for us to take you completely into our confidence, since, although you possess information of inestimable value, we cannot expect you to accept the risks and hazards which we ourselves are necessarily called upon to face as incidental to the performance of our official duties."

"It seems to me," I replied, "that I have had my share of them already."

"That's no reason why they should continue," said Réhmy; "and we wouldn't for an instant involve you in unnecessary danger."

These words put me on my mettle. I am not a brave man, nor a particularly rash one, but I had too much national pride, and, it must be confessed, too much personal curiosity, to abandon an adventure which by now deeply intrigued me, merely because a French officer informed me that it was dangerous. Besides there was Lavelle to consider, and even Beatrice was implicated. I must at least go through with the affair till they had been successfully and finally extricated.

All this I explained in a confused way, and my new friends nodded sympathetically, helping me out with those little turns and phrases of the French language which are quite inevitable, but which express so much better than any other form of human speech our stumbling emotions.

"Anyhow," said Réhmy, "your immediate help is essential to us. You say you left the document with M. Lavelle, in the offices of the Secretariat of the League of Nations?"

"Yes," I replied. "He promised to take care of it, and I was to ring him up after dinner if I could. Oh, and that reminds me," I added, thinking of Jerry, "I was also to dine with a friend of mine at the Plat d'Or, but I'm afraid that will be impossible."

"Quite impossible," agreed de Blanchegarde. "Social engagements are at a discount just now. You'd better send him a message or ring him up."

"This document," Réhmy began; "you say that your friend at the Secretariat had begun to decipher it. How much of it did he make out?"

"Three words," I answered.

"Which were . . . ?" queried Réhmy.

"*Wir, die Siebenschläfer*," I replied.

The two Frenchmen looked at one another, and de Blanchegarde emitted a low whistle.

"*Nom de Dieu!*" he muttered. "The gang that murdered poor Raoul Duplessy!"

"You know all about them then?" I asked.

"I wish to heaven we did," said Réhmy. "We know enough about them to realise that this whole affair is probably ten times more serious than either you or your friend, M. Lavelle, can possibly realise."

77

There and then he told me a tale which, had it been recounted to me twenty-four hours earlier I should have judged to be impossibly fantastic. It seemed that the French Intelligence Service had received information some months previously of an effort on the part of several of the more important German secret societies and murder clubs to amalgamate. There had been a good deal of negotiation between the heads of these societies, and three big financiers, Von Bühlen, Kaufmann and Von Stahl, were known to be involved. It was at this point that a French agent, one Raoul Duplessy, had succeeded in getting on the track of a mysterious unit or organisation referred to as "*Die Siebenschläfer*." But he had never been able to divulge whatever information he might have obtained, for he had been found murdered and hideously mutilated in the streets of Munich a few weeks previously. His last message to headquarters had been to the effect that he had come into contact with a little Jew of the name of Adolf Baumer, and my two friends had been sent to find Baumer, and to endeavour to extract information from him.

They had come upon his traces in Munich, but at the last moment he had slipped through their fingers, and they had then pursued him to Geneva. They were all the more eager to capture him as, while in Munich, they had discovered him to be in possession of an important document, which was to be transmitted to a certain Captain Z. This, of course, was the document which had been thrust into my hands at the Moulin Rouge.

My description of the gang in the rue Etienne Dumont confirmed them in the belief that they were on the track of operations of international importance. Schreckermann was known to them as a prominent buyer for the German Government during the War, and the Professor, whose name was Anselm Kreutzemark, was, it seemed a figure notorious in the archives of every intelligence service in Europe. De Blanchegarde could scarcely contain his fury when the man was mentioned.

"It was he that tortured Raoul," he said, "I'm sure of it. Among other things, he is one of the finest chemists in Germany and responsible for a dozen foul inventions. He it was who discovered Yellow Cross gas, though, like many of the really important men in Germany, his identity was kept secret."

"Well," I said, "one thing seems pretty clear. You'll want all the help you can get, and you must let me go in with you. I somehow feel that at this stage I can't decently withdraw, and I'm certainly not prepared to allow our friends of the rue Etienne Dumont to take a hand in the settlement of Europe. I dislike their methods."

De Blanchegarde looked for a moment at Réhmy, who nodded; and then jumped enthusiastically to his feet.

"On behalf of France, we accept your offer," he cried; and, to my great embarrassment, he kissed me tempestuously on both cheeks.

The die was cast; and from that moment I never once thought of withdrawing from the enterprise, but regarded myself as equally pledged with Réhmy and de Blanchegarde to fight this affair to a finish.

We fell to discussing details, and, on my recommendation, we decided to let Jerry Cunningham partially into the secret. The great difficulty with which de Blanchegarde and Réhmy had been faced was that they needed someone at Geneva, whereas they might suddenly find it necessary to go in search of the headquarters of Captain Z, which we now knew to be at Hanover. Jerry might usefully hold a watching brief in the city of Calvin if at any moment we found it necessary to go elsewhere.

Réhmy had hired the small chalet in which we were sitting. It was situated in the outskirts of Versoix—a large village on the lake some eight or ten kilometres distant from Geneva—and his establishment consisted solely of the grizzled manservant, whom I had already seen, an old retainer of de Blanchegarde, and a chauffeur, an ex-noncommissioned officer attached to Réhmy.

I scribbled Jerry a note saying that I was unavoidably prevented from dining with him; that strange developments had arisen in connection with the visit to my grandmother; and that I would explain everything on the morrow. Meanwhile, I asked him either to remain in his hotel or to keep the proprietor informed of his whereabouts. The note was taken into Geneva at once by the chauffeur and delivered at the Plat d'Or, where Jerry was awaiting me in vain.

By this time it was close on eight o'clock, and there was nothing further to be done until it was time to ring up Lavelle at the Secretariat. We accordingly dined—a ceremony to which de Blanchegarde was able to impart a surprising atmosphere of good cheer, thanks to his extraordinary high spirits and the convivial effects of a bottle of excellent dry Perrier Jouet.

CHAPTER IX

I RING UP A DEAD MAN

I rang up the Secretariat about nine o'clock and asked for Lavelle.

The *concierge* informed me that I could not be put straight through to him, because there was no night service on the internal exchange, but he volunteered to go and fetch him while I held the line.

After an interval of some minutes, the *concierge* returned to the telephone and told me that M. Lavelle had not yet arrived at the Secretariat.

I asked whether he was absolutely sure of this, to which he replied that he had come on duty about eight thirty; that no one had passed either in or out since that hour; but that M. Lavelle might quite possibly have come in before, as his room was locked, though he had received no reply to his knocking.

I rang off and reported the news to my friends.

"Probably he hasn't yet arrived," said de Blanchegarde.

We decided to give him another half-hour, and we waited restlessly, talking and smoking but finding it very difficult to be patient. De Blanchegarde could scarcely contain his excitement. He fidgeted about, turning over the leaves of books which he did not read, looking at pictures which he did not see, and lighting innumerable cigarettes which he did not smoke.

Réhmy observed him with the sympathy of an old campaigner for a young recruit.

"This waiting is the most difficult part of our job," he said. "I'm afraid Gaston will never be very good at it. He wastes half his energy in trying to advance the clock."

I must confess that my sympathies were with Gaston on this occasion. I tried in vain to imitate the professional calm of Etienne Réhmy, but it was with the greatest difficulty that I could keep my hands from the receiver.

Punctually at a quarter to ten I telephoned again, but with the same result as before. Lavelle's door was still locked.

"Did you knock on it?" I asked of the *concierge*.

"Yes, Monsieur," he replied. "I knocked and shouted, but there was no reply."

I hung up the receiver.

"That settles it," I said. "We must drive round to the Secretariat and look into this matter on the spot."

Réhmy and de Blanchegarde instantly agreed, and we all three found hats and coats and packed ourselves into the car.

A quarter of an hour later we arrived at the Secretariat.

As we walked up the steps towards the *concierge's* desk, we saw a group of cleaners and the *concierge* examining something which was lying on the ground. They were in a state of considerable excitement and I knew at once that something untoward had happened.

I pushed my way into the circle and saw that a large wolf hound—*a chien de garde*—was stretched on the floor, apparently *in extremis*. Close beside him lay a great St. Bernard.

I went up to the *concierge* and asked for M. Lavelle. It was not my English friend of the afternoon but a Swiss official of the night shift.

"I haven't yet seen him, Monsieur," he replied.

"What has happened?" I asked, looking at the men who were bending over the sick hound.

"Why," he answered wrathfully. "The dogs have been poisoned."

I looked quickly towards my French colleagues and saw at once that my apprehensions were shared.

"Indeed," I said. "When was it done?"

"Not very long ago," he replied. "When I came on duty they seemed perfectly all right. But when I came down to the hall after I had been up to look for M. Lavelle the first time, Baril, the St. Bernard there, was in great pain, and Apollon was ailing. Baril died in a very few moments, and I'm afraid that Apollon won't last long."

He looked again at the dog, which was lying with its mouth wide open. Its tongue was hanging out and great tremors and shivers were passing over its body.

"Poor beasts!" I said. "Who can have done it?"

"I don't like this," broke in de Blanchegarde suddenly. "Let's go up and look for your friend."

We prevailed upon the *concierge* to accompany us and climbed the stairs to the second floor.

I had continued to think of the Secretariat as I had seen it in the afternoon, blazing with light, clicking with typewriters, messengers on every floor, stenographers passing to and fro, and officials promenading the corridors. I was ill prepared for this vast and shadowy building, silent as the grave, where our voices lost themselves in the remoter spaces and our eyes were drawn into dark recesses. I thought of Lavelle working alone in this obscure labyrinth, and my sense of foreboding increased. Mentally I cursed the idle hours we had spent in the chalet. I remember that I almost ran up the stairs in my impatience to be reassured that nothing serious had happened.

We arrived at Lavelle's room. It was approached by a tiny vestibule and the *concierge* switched on a light that hung above the door. He knocked and shouted, but there was no response.

We stood for a moment, uncertain what to do. Réhmy suggested that we should go to his private address, which the *concierge* said he could obtain for us from the office register. As we were on the point of retiring, however, the *concierge* switched off the light in the vestibule and in the darkness I could see that there was a light in Lavelle's room, which showed plainly in the crack between the door and the ground.

I grasped Réhmy by the arm.

"Look," I said, pointing to the light.

The *concierge* turned at this.

"Zut," he said. "M. Lavelle has gone away, locking the door and leaving the light on. I'm afraid I shall have to report this to the Establishment Officer. It's against the regulations."

He moved away, apparently proposing to leave the light burning all night rather than effect a forcible or unauthorised entrance to the room. It was a characteristic official decision. A regulation had been broken, he had duly noted the fact, and suitable action would be taken on the morrow.

Apart from my irritation with the *concierge* for his senseless servility to the routine of his office, nothing would have induced me to leave that locked and lighted room uninvestigated. I was about to suggest forcing the lock or breaking down the door and preparing to encounter a horrified protest from the *concierge*, when I remembered that in the afternoon I had noticed a balcony running past the window in Lavelle's room and communicating with the rooms on either side. Despite the remonstrances of the *concierge*, who seemed to think the proceeding a highly doubtful one, we decided to make use of this balcony to look into Lavelle's room and see whether it was possible to enter by the window.

We all four went into the room next door.

Once in the balcony, two steps took me to Lavelle's window, and I looked into the room.

Lavelle was seated at his desk, his head bowed over a pile of documents. He looked as though he had fallen asleep over his work. I tapped on the window, but he did not move. A sense of uneasiness came over me. I tapped again louder. Still there was no movement. Uneasiness deepened to fear.

Snatching at Réhmy's stick, I drove it with all my force against the window. The panes shattered, with a crash, but the figure at the desk remained motionless.

I put my hand through the hole in the glass, lifted the catch and a second later was in the room. I went straight to my friend and laid a hand on his shoulder. He slipped sideways, inert, like a dummy figure. The wooden handle of a knife was sticking out of his ribs.

"Good God!" I said faintly. "He's been murdered."

With the assistance of the *concierge* I laid him gently on the floor. He was quite dead, stabbed to the heart, the body still warm.

"The fiends," I muttered; "the fiends."

De Blanchegarde was instantly beside me.

"He was your friend?" he said, his eyes shining with sympathy.

"One of the best men I ever met," I replied.

"That makes two," said de Blanchegarde, clenching his fists. "The first was Raoul Duplessy. Two gallant gentlemen foully murdered by these ruffians."

There was a rustling of papers beside us, and, turning, I saw that Réhmy was already searching through the litter on the desk.

Everything was in utter confusion. Lavelle's papers were helter-skelter on the floor and on the desk itself. The drawers had been forced open and their contents scattered about the room, but there was no sign of the document anywhere.

"One thing seems pretty clear," I pointed out. "Lavelle can't have been working on the document when he was killed. Otherwise they would have found it at once."

All this while the *concierge* was standing wide-eyed and trembling.

"I must telephone for the police," he said at last.

"Would you gentlemen please stay here while I do so?"

I nodded, and he left the room.

De Blanchegarde stooped over the body of my friend, folded his arms over his breast and closed the eyes.

"He died for France," he said simply.

Réhmy was still looking through the litter on the desk and in the drawers.

"Lavelle could not, as you say, have been working on the document when he was surprised. Perhaps he had finished deciphering it before dinner and concealed it pending our arrival. Probably it has been found and taken by the men who murdered him. On the other hand, he may have hidden it too well. Perhaps his secretary can tell us something about it."

"There's just a chance," I replied. "But it's unlikely."

"Perhaps you could ring her up and enquire," suggested Réhmy.

I went to the telephone, only to remember that I should have to go into the hall to get into communication with the town.

I went down through the deserted and silent building, still numb with the shock of our discovery.

As I went up to his desk, the *concierge* was just hanging up the receiver after informing the police.

With some difficulty I got through to the *pension* where Beatrice was staying and enquired for Mademoiselle Harvel. I was informed to my amazement that Mademoiselle Harvel was ill.

"Ill?" I exclaimed, taken with a sudden deadly fear. "Are you sure of that?"

"No one has seen her," said the proprietress, "but a hospital nurse and a doctor have just called and are even now in the hall, asking to be taken to her room. You may speak to Mademoiselle Harvel yourself, if you like."

And before I could say another word she had put me through to Beatrice's sitting-room, which Beatrice shared in common with two other girl friends, and which possessed a telephone.

A moment later I heard her voice.

"It's Tom speaking," I began hurriedly. "Are you all right, Beatrice?"

"Quite all right, Tom. So you got safely away?"

"I'll tell you about that later. The proprietress of your *pension* has just told me you are ill."

"Nonsense. I was never better."

"Well, she says there's a hospital nurse and a doctor enquiring for you downstairs."

"Impossible, Tom."

"Are you alone?"

"Yes."

"Listen, Beatrice," I said earnestly. "Don't on any account let anybody come into your room. Do you understand? Nobody at all, on any pretext whatever—at least, not until I have seen you myself. I shall probably come round or send you a message within the next half-hour. Meanwhile can you tell me anything about the document I left with Lavelle?"

"He worked upon it before dinner."

"Do you know what he did with it afterwards?"

"Yes. He put it safely away."

I hesitated a moment, but decided almost at once not to tell Beatrice yet about the murder.

"Then you know where the document is concealed?"

"Yes, Tom. Is it safe, do you think, to tell you on the telephone?"

"We must risk it. I must get hold of that paper at once."

"Well, it's rather amusing. We wondered what would be the safest place and we hit on one at last that was absolutely sure. Even if you knew where it was, it would take at least a month to find it."

"Is it somewhere in the Secretariat?"

"Yes."

"Does anybody, except Lavelle, know where it is?"

I waited anxiously for her reply.

"Nobody in the world," she answered, "except of course your humble servant."

"Beatrice," I said, "I must get the document immediately, and Lavelle cannot for the moment be found. I want you to tell me at once where it is concealed."

"Certainly, Tom," she replied. "You will find the document——"

And then I heard the fall of a telephone receiver to the floor, a sort of gulp and a thin strangled cry, followed by utter silence.

CHAPTER X

I CONSENT TO MY ARREST

I cannot clearly remember what I did at that moment. I seem to see myself, a man of stone, with the receiver to my ear, listening vainly for some further sound, all my faculties strained towards that unknown room where Beatrice had suddenly ceased to speak. So intense was the effort that it left me weak and trembling. The first concrete thing to break in upon that awful moment was the voice of the *concierge*.

"What is it, Monsieur?" he asked in astonishment. "Are you ill?"

I pushed past him and dashed up the stairs, repeating mechanically, "Beatrice! My God, Beatrice!"

Half-way up, I encountered de Blanchegarde and Réhmy descending. I must have been looking quite ghastly, for, before I could speak, Gaston cried,

"My poor friend! What has happened?"

"They've got Beatrice," I said.

"Beatrice?" he repeated.

He was for a moment at a loss, not remembering her part in the story.

"The lady who took the document to Lavelle," said Réhmy, who never forgot details.

Gaston, with his quick instinct for romance, at once knew that Beatrice was more to me than a casual friend. He pressed my hand impulsively.

At the same time, Réhmy laid a firm grasp on my shoulder.

"You must calm yourself, Captain Preston. We can do no good by losing control."

I leant back against the banisters. The first shock was passing and my brain was at work again. I explained as coherently as I could what had happened on the telephone.

"She knows where Lavelle hid the document," I ended. "My God! They may have killed her too."

"Steady, man," said Réhmy quietly. "They wouldn't do that. They're not so foolish. They're far more likely to have put her safely away."

His calmness restored my nerve.

"We must act at once," I said. "She may still be at her *pension*. We may yet be in time to catch them."

De Blanchegarde, with his usual impetuosity, ran down the broad stairs ahead of us, so that when we reached the entrance to the Secretariat the engine of the car was already running; and a moment later we were speeding to the Boulevard des Tranchées, where Beatrice lived.

Throughout the short journey I deliberately refused to think, for I verily believe I should have lost my reason if I had faced the terrible possibilities that suggested themselves. I looked unseeing at the buildings dripping with moisture (the town was again enveloped in its usual mist). Once we were compelled to slow down almost to a standstill at a crossing of two streets, to allow the passage of what I took to be the local fire brigade, which leisurely crossed our path in single file on bicycles. They wore large brass helmets and blue uniforms, and carried hatchets, but they did not appear to be in any great hurry, and their presence was only forced on my notice by the sudden slowing down of the car.

It could not have been, I suppose, much more than ten minutes or a quarter of an hour since I had heard the receiver fall from the hand of Beatrice when we found ourselves on the pavement, ringing the front door bell of a grey flat building, in the upper stories of which lights were to be seen. It was a dreary looking place and Beatrice's remarks at luncheon about horrid little *pensions* recurred vividly to my mind as the door was opened by a tousled Swiss in shirt sleeves and a green baize apron, with a large smear of dirt on one cheek.

Réhmy, as leader of our party, requested immediate speech with the proprietor.

The man admitted us into a small hall, which smelled of mackintoshes and vegetables recently cooked, and, after some delay, on the ground that the *patron* was probably in bed, went off to find him, while we waited, myself in an agony of impatience.

After some minutes, a comfortable woman in black came down the stairs to meet us and enquired our business. Her husband, she said, had gone to bed and she did not like to disturb him.

"We wish to see Miss Harvel immediately," said Réhmy.

The lady shook her head.

"That is impossible. Messieurs," she said. "Poor Mademoiselle Harvel has suddenly been taken ill and——"

"But I spoke to her myself," I protested, when a gesture from Réhmy silenced me, and I realised that it would be unwise to awaken the curiosity or suspicion of the proprietress.

"This illness," said Réhmy, "is sudden."

"Yes," continued the proprietress. "She was here to dinner as usual and appeared to be in good spirits. But shortly after ten o'clock a hospital nurse and a doctor arrived in an ambulance. They said that they had received a telephone message from the friends of Miss Harvel, who had very suddenly been taken seriously ill. A maid at once conducted them to Miss Harvel's room, and five minutes later the poor lamb was carried down unconscious. She looked very ill indeed. They have only just gone," she added—"barely ten minutes ago."

"Did they leave the address of the place to which they were taking Miss Harvel?" asked Réhmy.

"No, Monsieur."

"Did you know the doctor?" said de Blanchegarde eagerly. "Was he a local man?"

"I couldn't say, Monsieur. I've never seen him before."

"What was he like?"

"I didn't notice him particularly, Monsieur. But he had a golden beard."

We all three looked at each other. I knew of only one man with a golden beard, and dread settled slowly down upon me like a black cloud obliterating every ray of hope.

"The Professor," whispered de Blanchegarde.

We turned to leave the *pension*, Réhmy explaining to the proprietress, with the quick address of the trained secret service agent, that we were members of the staff of the League of Nations who desired to see Miss Harvel on urgent official business.

"There is a last chance," I said, as the street door closed behind us.

"The rue Etienne Dumont!" cried de Blanchegarde. "And please God we find someone there. Etienne, *man ami*, there will be no holding me tonight. I shall shoot at sight."

As we got into the car, Réhmy turned to me.

"Are you armed?" he said.

"No," I replied, "I'm not."

That question, which Réhmy put to me in such a matter-of-fact manner, brought home to me more forcibly than anything else the utter nightmare in which I had become involved since my arrival in Geneva. The average traveller nowadays no more thinks of carrying arms than he would of travelling without a railway ticket. But if ever a man needed weapons I needed them now.

Réhmy leaned forward and pulled an automatic from a pocket in the car's upholstery. He handed it to me.

"Do you know this make?" he enquired.

It was a French army automatic of small pattern with two extra magazines of cartridges. I slipped it into my pocket, as we speeded towards our destination.

We swung sharp round a corner and pulled up with a jerk in a narrow street, which I found was the top end of the rue Etienne Dumont.

Our further progress was rendered impossible by a large and ever-increasing crowd which completely blocked the narrow street.

"What is it now?" said de Blanchegarde, as he jumped from the car.

We followed him, and soon the three of us were elbowing our way through excited Genevese citizens, some of whom I noted were arrayed in portions of their night attire. Anxious as we all were, the irrepressible de Blanchegarde could not refrain from pointing to the ludicrous spectacle of an elderly citizen, stuck half-way through a window, a large nightcap on his head, looking not unlike a continental Mr. Pickwick.

We were informed that there was a fire farther down the street on the right. It had apparently broken out very suddenly. As we fought our way through the crowd, I saw ahead of us a dull glow of flames obscured by dense volumes of smoke. A strong smell of burning pervaded the air. By hard pushing we eventually won our way to the forefront of the crowd.

"As I thought," Réhmy observed suddenly in my ear.

The dread tightened about my heart as I realised the significance of his exclamation.

The burning house was some fifty yards ahead of us, for a police cordon prevented any unauthorised person from approaching nearer to the scene of the disaster. Some dozen men, in the blue uniform and brass hats of the fire brigade, were running aimlessly about dragging lengths of hose along the pavement. I remembered the file of cyclists, similarly attired, whom I had seen a short time previously.

Réhmy approached a gendarme and enquired whether we might be permitted to go farther down the street.

"No," replied the gendarme firmly. "In no circumstances whatever, Monsieur."

"But we have urgent business with some gentlemen in Number 140," expostulated Réhmy.

"In that case," replied the gendarme, "you are a little late, Monsieur. Number 140 is in flames."

We looked at each other, our dawning apprehension confirmed.

"The *sapeus pom piers*," the gendarme volunteered, "were called out about half an hour ago. But there is no cause for alarm on behalf of your friends," he continued, "for the house was empty."

"Empty?" I echoed.

"Yes, Monsieur. The heroic fire brigade succeeded in penetrating to every room before the flames became too much for them. There was no one at all in the house. The gentlemen whom you wish to see have evidently escaped."

"Well," said Réhmy briefly, turning as he spoke, "it's no use standing here. Back to the car."

We pushed our way slowly through the crowd back to the spot where we had left the Peugeot standing. As we went, de Blanchegarde laid a hand on my arm.

"*Mon Capitaine*," he said, "I've known worse moments than this," and he gently squeezed the muscles of my forearm with a friendly gesture. It was kindly meant, and I tried to respond, but without much success.

Arrived at the car, we paused to take counsel. It appeared to be quite checkmate. The document, the conspirators, and Beatrice were lost, and there appeared to be no possible clue to their recovery.

Even at that bitter moment, I could not help noticing, as we talked, the difference in my two companions. Réhmy, I could see, was primarily concerned about the document. He took from force of habit the professional view; the official work must at all costs go forward. De Blanchegarde—or Gaston, as I soon learnt to call him—was chiefly preoccupied by the personal aspects of the adventure, the escape of the Professor, the murder of Lavelle, and the abduction of Beatrice. As for me, international problems, conspiracies, and even the brutal murder of my friend Lavelle all dwindled before the supreme and terrible fact that the girl whom I loved was in the hands of a man whom I dreaded above all other men in the world, while I was ignorant alike of her fate and of her whereabouts.

"He is clever, that Professor," remarked Réhmy, as we climbed at last into the car. "He has covered his tracks completely."

The burning of Number 140, Etienne Dumont, was certainly a masterstroke, for it left us without any means of tracing the gang, besides effectively destroying all incriminating evidence against them.

We remained silent while once more we took the road for Versoix. I was gradually recovering from the first shock of these disasters and setting my brain to work, groping for some plan which might give us a chance of rescuing Beatrice. Ponder as I could, however, I could hit on no solution. To go to the police at this stage would be fatal. It would, at best, result in a process which could only be lengthy and tedious, since the quarters of the gang were unknown. At the worst I might find myself indefinitely laid by the heels. Fritz had denounced me as a murderer, and it might take several days for me to convince the authorities of my identity and to prove an effective alibi (especially now that poor Lavelle, who might have been able to help me, had been murdered). Meanwhile, time was all on the side of the conspirators.

Then, suddenly, Réhmy, who had been very thoughtful since we got into the car, exclaimed:

"But of course there's Adolf!"

"By Jove, yes!" I said. "I'd quite forgotten Adolf."

"He may know another headquarters," continued Réhmy. "It's not unlikely that they've more than one place of meeting in Geneva."

"It's scarcely probable," I said doubtfully. "They are much more likely to be on the way to Germany by now."

"You forget the document," replied Réhmy, in the tone, eager but calm, which I afterwards came to know for a sign that he was on the track of a possible way out. "They will never leave Geneva without the document, and they don't even know where it is to be found. That's why they've taken Mademoiselle Harvel."

He ceased abruptly, for I suppose my face must have shown the direction of my thoughts.

"Courage, my friend," he said, and added with a grave conviction, "It will be our turn presently."

"If they touch a hair of her head," I began, and stopped, realising the uselessness of empty threats.

My French friends looked at me with quick sympathy, and Réhmy said at once:

"Our next step is obvious. We must question Adolf."

"If he refuses to speak," said Gaston savagely, "we'll see what a riding whip will accomplish."

An idea flashed across my brain.

"I know a better way than that," I said. "Adolf mistook me for Von Emmerich at the Moulin Rouge, and he has been in your hands ever since. He will mistake me again. Shut me up with him. I will pass for Von Emmerich and say that you have captured me too. Once we are imprisoned together, it will be strange if I can't get some information out of him."

"Excellent," Réhmy agreed, and during the rest of the journey we discussed the details of my behaviour.

It was settled that as soon as we reached the *chalet* I should be locked up in the cellar with Adolf. During the night I would suggest to him that we should try to escape, and thus entrap him into revealing the nearest refuge of the conspirators. I would plan with Adolf to attack Jules when he brought us food in the morning, and pretend to overpower him. Adolf and I would then make our escape, Adolf being immediately recaptured by Réhmy and de Blanchegarde. This little comedy would lend verisimilitude to my impersonation and still leave Adolf ignorant of my real identity.

"I must get my hair cut," I concluded, as the car stopped opposite the door of the *chalet*. "Karl shaves his skull in the most approved Prussian style."

Gaston laughed.

"My poor friend," he said. "It's a sacrifice, but it will undoubtedly help you to win the confidence of little Adolf. Jules is an excellent valet, and will doubtless be equal to the task."

Jules opened the door to us as Gaston finished speaking.

Shortly afterwards I was seated in a chair, Jules cropping my hair in a most professional manner, while Gaston and Réhmy, looking on, explained to him the part he had to play in the approaching drama.

It was extraordinary, now that there was a prospect of action, how my spirits rose.

Beatrice must at all costs be rescued, and this was the first step.

CHAPTER XI

I CONNIVE AT MY ESCAPE

As soon as my hair was cut, Jules, under the direction of Réhmy, carried down a mattress and blankets to the cellar.

"I'm afraid we can't make you more comfortable than Adolf," said Réhmy, "and the hard-hearted Gaston is treating him to a somewhat limited hospitality."

"I'm not exactly hoping for a bed of roses," I rejoined.

"You look pretty tired, my friend," said Gaston, "and you've certainly every reason to be. Wait a moment, and we'll make you a cup of coffee."

"Hadn't I better go down at once?" said I. "Adolf may have heard us arrive, and he'll think it strange if I'm not locked up immediately."

"I don't think you need worry about that," Gaston replied. "If Adolf has heard anything, he will merely suppose that we are asking you some necessary questions."

The excellent fellow was soon boiling coffee in one of those glass machines, remarking as he did so that it should be "hot as hell, black as night, and sweet as sin," while Réhmy and I discussed what we should do if I succeeded in obtaining the necessary information from our prisoner.

We decided that if I discovered the new quarters of the gang, we should all three go to their hiding-place and trust to our wits to find Beatrice and set her free.

I swallowed the coffee and immediately afterwards was conducted down some narrow stone stairs leading out of the small hall, preceded by Jules and followed by Gaston. Gaston brandished a pistol, with a broad grin on his face, which changed to an expression of grim ferocity as Jules opened the cellar door and stood aside to let me pass.

"You can cool your heels for a time in there," said Gaston in German, "with your little friend, and if you are still obstinate tomorrow, we shall try other, and less pleasant, means to make you talk."

The door closed and I heard him lock it.

It was very gloomy in the cellar, the only light coming from the hall through a square of thick glass let into the wall at the level of the ceiling. In one corner a heap of blankets indicated my companion's bed. It was very cold, there was a sort of damp frost, very unpleasant, and a faint smell of spilt beer.

I did not, however, immediately take in these details, for my attention was at once attracted by the little Jew, who had sprung to his feet on my entrance, exclaiming:

"Who's that?"

"Von Emmerich," I replied. "Who the devil are you?"

And I moved into the darkest part of the cellar, so that it would be difficult for him to examine me closely, though I had little fear that he would discover my impersonation.

"I'm Baumer," he said. "Have they caught you too?"

"Looks like it," I rejoined surlily. "How long have you been here?"

"Since yesterday evening."

"And how much have you told them?" I asked in a bullying tone.

I had decided that it was best to take a high and mighty line with him. From what I had seen of the real Von Emmerich he would obviously have adopted this attitude.

"Nothing," he said. His teeth chattered, whether with cold, or terror, I could not immediately determine. He came close up to me and laid a hand on my arm.

"Those Frenchmen are devils," he said, in a low voice. "The little one has been threatening me, and I can't bear it much longer."

I saw that the man's nerve was already almost broken. His hand trembled on my arm, and he made no pretence of keeping up appearances. He seemed a poor-spirited fellow to be engaged with others on a desperate enterprise, but I reflected that he evidently had his uses, and that he was probably not fully acquainted with the details of the conspiracy.

"When did they catch you?" he continued.

"Not an hour ago," I said. "It was all the fault of that blundering fool Fritz."

I pitched him a story to the effect that I had received a telephone message from Fritz ordering me to return to the house in the rue Etienne Dumont, and that on arriving there I had found it in flames.

"I was standing in the crowd," I said, "when someone touched me on the arm and told me that the Professor was waiting for me. I made my way out of the crowd and turned down a side street after the fellow, who was some distance ahead of me, and there I was set upon. They must have used some sort of anæsthetic, I think, for my head is still thick and muddled, and I don't remember in the least how I got here."

I sank down, as I finished, upon the mattress which Jules had provided.

"But why did Major Adler ring you up?" asked Adolf, sitting down beside me, and drawing a blanket round his shoulders.

"I don't know," I said savagely. "It's not the first of his blunders."

"I don't believe it was he who rang you up at all," said Adolf. "It was one of those Frenchmen upstairs."

"What?" I exclaimed, pretending to the astonishment of a stupid man.

"Yes," said Adolf. "That was how they outwitted me."

"What do you mean?"

"They telephoned to me in your name last night, saying that you, Von Emmerich, would meet me at the Moulin Rouge. I went there, though I knew it was dangerous, and I couldn't imagine why you had appointed that place of rendezvous."

"Humph!" I said. "That's their little ruse, is it? Well," I continued, in the tone of a surly man grudgingly according credit to a superior intelligence, "I suppose you're right. Anyhow, here we are, both in the same boat—or rather cellar. We must get out of it somehow. I'm not going to stay here, and, as for you," I turned and gripped his shoulder roughly, so that he winced, "you're not going to stay here either. You'd soon begin to give the game away. What do they propose to do to you?"

"Nothing definite," stammered Adolf. "They talked about other means, and I-I'm not strong," he ended weakly.

His voice broke, and I knew by the heaving of his shoulders that he was sobbing.

I hate to see anyone break down, especially one of my own sex, and there was something almost indecent in the little Jew's collapse. I began to dislike the scene excessively.

Presently he took his hands from his face and poured forth a piteous tale. His was a dog's life, he whimpered, all kicks and never a reward. He was bullied by everyone with whom he came in contact. Schreckermann had threatened him. Fritz had apparently used violence on more than one occasion; and before the Professor he cringed with a terror that was positively abject.

"I can't bear to think of him," he said in the manner of a man whose inward eye is obsessed with the object of which he is speaking. "His eyes are not those of a mortal man."

And now, to crown his misfortunes, he had blundered into the hands of these Frenchmen. It was the last straw, and he was on the point of a complete nervous collapse.

I realised that my chances of getting any coherent information from him were small unless I could to some extent restore his faculties.

"You must pull yourself together," I said firmly. "We've got to get away from here somehow. If we escape, I'll square it with the Professor as far as you're concerned. Remember, I have friends in Hanover. They can none of them dispense with me."

My change of tone had the desired effect, for Adolf rapidly grew calmer, and a submissiveness never too absent came into his voice. Evidently a man who was able to face the Professor was, in Adolf's opinion, a man to be treated with respect. It was a point of view with which I was destined to sympathise increasingly as time went on.

The moment had now come to bring Adolf to the point. I assumed an air that obviously meant business.

"The first thing," I said, "is to escape, and we must settle at once where we are going as soon as we get away."

"One moment," interposed Adolf. "Have the Frenchmen taken the document which I handed to you last night?"

"No. You don't suppose I'd allow myself to be caught with a paper like that," I replied, assuming again the truculence of Von Emmerich.

"No, no, of course not," he hastily assured me. "But where have you hidden it?"

"That's my affair," I said curtly. "It's safe. You needn't worry."

He breathed a sigh of relief.

"Come now," I went on. "We haven't any time to lose. We must make our plans. Take a cigarette. They've had the decency to leave me my case."

Adolf took the cigarette eagerly.

"So the Professor has burnt Number 140," he said musingly.

"I don't know," I replied. "At any rate, it was on fire when I saw it last."

"That was part of a prearranged plan," said Adolf. "If ever we had to leave quickly, it was to be destroyed. There are lots of things in Number 140 which the Professor wouldn't like to expose. I expect they have gone to the Villa Mortmain."

"And where's that?" I asked.

He seemed surprised. He even looked at me suspiciously.

"Surely you know that?" he said. "It was Schreckermann's private house before he moved to Geneva."

"You appear to forget," I said, "that my instructions were to go to the rue Etienne Dumont. I know no other place."

"The Villa Mortmain is at Bellerive, on the other side of the lake," said Adolf. "It's not very easy to reach from here."

"Time enough to see about that when we get away," I rejoined.

We discussed various plans of escape, and eventually he agreed to my suggestion that I should endeavour to overpower Jules when he came to bring us food in the morning.

"If he does come," said Adolf.

"Of course he'll come," I declared, in the manner that, with Adolf, brooked no further question. "There's no reason why these people should starve us."

We settled to take it in turns to sleep, so that one of us would always be on the alert when Jules arrived.

I took the first watch myself, and, as I sat huddling into my blankets, cold and very tired, I revolved all the incredible happenings of the day. It was not till I sat in that dark and damp cellar, with nothing to occupy my mind, that I realised the full horror of all that had happened. Up to my arrival at the Secretariat in the early evening, there had been the exhilaration of action and novelty; and, looking back, I found that I had almost enjoyed my fantastic progress through the streets of Geneva. But swift on the heels of these events had come the foul and dastardly murder of my friend. And now, added to this, was the capture of Beatrice. It required all my self-control to prevent my mind from dwelling on the possible actions of the Professor in her regard, and I look back to the time I spent in that cellar as possibly the most miserable hours of my life.

Adolf, waking after some two hours or so, suggested that I should try to sleep for a while.

I lay down on the mattress and presently fell into an uneasy doze, visited by nightmares of past happenings in the War, mercifully totally absent from my conscious mind. I dreamed I was once again in St. Pierre Vaast Wood among the rotting corpses, pursued by a nameless thing with silken, yellow hair and piercing eyes, and that as I fled I stumbled and fell repeatedly over the French and German dead and the black stumps of shell-torn trees.

I wakened with a start to find Adolf's hand on my shoulder.

"Someone's coming," he whispered.

It was pitch dark, for the light in the hall had been put out, and there was no window in the cellar. The illuminated dial of my wrist watch, however, showed that it was eight a.m.

I listened and heard footsteps approaching. Here was Jules with the food.

Now that the moment for action had arrived, I was astonished to find that Adolf seemed to have regained his nerve. He was cool and even voluble.

"You stand over there on the left and jump on him as he comes into the cellar," he said. "The door opens inwards. I'll get hold of his keys. I've put a mattress under the door to deaden the noise of his fall."

"Good," I said, and, rising to my feet, I took up the position he had indicated.

A moment later the door was opened and Jules stood revealed, a lantern with a single candle in it in one hand, and a tray with some bread and coffee on it in the other. He came forward and stooped to deposit the tray.

At that moment, I jumped on his back, whispering in his ear.

"Fall down and put the light out."

He did as he was bidden, falling heavily forward on to the mattress, and as he did so he gave a deep groan.

"Lock the door after you," said Adolf, and he bounded up the stairs.

I followed, but omitted to do as he had suggested.

The house was still quite dark, for the sun had not yet topped the mountains which surround the lake of Geneva. We stood a moment in the hall.

"Through the windows in the sitting-room," I whispered.

"Yes," nodded Adolf.

We crossed the hall and entered the sitting-room. The windows were fastened, but Adolf, with a skill evidently the result of practice, noiselessly opened one of them and the shutter outside. As he did so, he whispered to me.

"It's all right. I've settled that Frenchman, I think. I kicked him in the belly as we passed."

Little Adolf, it seemed, had a great spirit in him when he was roused.

By this time both windows were open, and we stepped cautiously through. We had arranged to slip through the garden, go down to the lake side, and endeavour to hire or steal a boat and row across the lake to Bellerive, which was about a couple of miles away on the other side. I had arranged with Réhmy and de Blanchegarde that they should lie in wait at the bottom of the garden, ready to take Adolf as he passed.

To my great annoyance, however, Adolf, once outside, turned to the right instead of to the left, and began to make his way uphill and away from the lake.

"Where are you going?" I protested. "That isn't the way to the lake."

"I know," he replied, "but sometimes the longest way round is the shortest. Perhaps they have heard us, in which case they're sure to come straight into the garden. This will throw them off the scent."

He broke into a run as he spoke, and I followed him, wondering what I should do. If I assaulted him, I could scarcely continue to impersonate Karl von Emmerich, should it be necessary to do so on some future occasion. On the other hand, we certainly did not want Adolf to go free.

At this point, I heard a shout, and, looking round, I saw de Blanchegarde and Réhmy emerging from a small plantation of firs at the bottom of the garden and running in our direction.

"Quick," said Adolf.

He increased his pace, turning sharply to the right, so as to head for the lake, which was distant some four hundred yards.

I ran after him. But, glancing over my shoulder, I noticed that Gaston, who was evidently something of a sprinter, had jumped the garden wall and was running to cut us off, while Réhmy laboured in his rear.

We had reached the main road, which was very close to the lake, some fifty yards ahead of our pursuers, when, to my astonishment, instead of making for the water, where I could see some boats drawn up on a pebbly foreshore, Adolf stopped. At the same moment, I became aware that an errand boy was passing along the road on a bicycle, in the direction of Lausanne.

Adolf, without a second's hesitation, sprang in the way of the bicycle. To avoid a collision, the boy swerved to the left, and, skidding, fell off into the ditch. Adolf immediately picked up the bicycle.

"We must separate," he shouted.

"Not so fast," I said.

I was now determined to capture him at all costs, and I made ready to close. Unfortunately, however, I was quite unprepared for what happened next.

I had intended to knock him down, but, in a flash, he divined my intention, assuming probably that I wanted the bicycle for myself. Being unversed in Continental methods of fighting, I got the worst of it, for, as I approached him, Adolf suddenly lifted his right foot and planted a heavy blow in the pit of my stomach, laying me gasping and momentarily windless on the side of the road, just as de Blanchegarde arrived, with Réhmy close on his heels.

I could only point speechlessly at Adolf, who was already on the bicycle, pedalling as fast as he could in the direction of Lausanne.

The errand boy had picked himself up from the ditch and was running down the road after him, shouting furiously.

Gaston, without pausing, ran after Adolf, but Réhmy stopped beside me.

By this time I had to some extent regained my breath.

"Quick," I gasped. "He mustn't get away, or he'll give the alarm."

Réhmy turned.

"I'll go for the car," he said, and sped quickly away to the villa.

I lay for a moment in the ditch getting back my wind. The blow had caught me shrewdly, and if it had been slightly lower would have got me in the groin, in which case it might have injured me seriously. As it was, I soon recovered and, getting to my feet, mechanically brushed myself down, as Réhmy glided up in the Peugeot.

"Don't wait for me," I shouted, as he slowed down. "I'm all right now. I'll go back and wait for you at the villa."

He nodded assent, gathered speed again and was soon lost to view round a bend in the road.

I walked back slowly to the chalet, where I found Jules suffering from a similar injury to mine, and in a state of furious indignation. We condoled with one another and comforted ourselves with hot coffee, to which Jules added a liberal dose of Kirsch.

Half an hour passed, and there was still no sign of Réhmy and de Blanchegarde. I began to get uneasy.

"They must have caught him by now," I said.

"He'll be leading them a fine chase, Monsieur," said Jules. "He's a keen little customer when it comes to saving his skin."

Another half-hour went slowly by, and still the Frenchmen had failed to return. At last I could bear it no longer.

It might be hours before they came back, and meanwhile there was no knowing what might be happening to Beatrice. I feared the worst. Had circumstances been different, I should have hesitated to set out on so dangerous a venture alone, but thinking of Beatrice, perhaps no farther off than the other shore of the lake, which I could see plainly from the windows of the chalet, I could not remain inactive.

I told Jules that I could not wait any longer; that I was going to the Villa Mortmain at Bellerive, and that when de Blanchegarde and Réhmy returned they should follow me immediately.

I put on a hat and coat and walked into the little town of Versoix. There I found a garage, from which I succeeded in hiring a car to take me to Bellerive.

The journey took about half an hour. We drove back to the end of the lake at Geneva, crossing the Pont du Mont Blanc, of famous memory, and then skirted the lake on the other side until we arrived at a small village on its edge, containing a few houses and a restaurant with a terrace commanding the lake.

Here I dismissed my car and, enquiring from a small boy the whereabouts of the Villa Mortmain, was directed a few hundred yards down an old, disused road, which ended in a modern villa of fair proportions, but badly in need of paint. The name "Mortmain" was written on the gateposts.

I took cover in the wooded garden and carefully reconnoitred the new headquarters of the gang. It was the ordinary type of Swiss villa, of indifferent architecture, with a verandah shading long windows running right round the ground floor. I could see no sign of activity in the house and, after remaining for some ten minutes or so in the garden, I decided to effect an entry, in order to discover what was happening inside and, if possible, to take a hand in the proceedings, pending the arrival of my French friends.

I slipped from cover and crossed the garden at a run, reaching the shelter of the verandah, where I was secure from the observation of anyone unless he happened to be at the window which commanded that particular section.

After a further cautious examination of the house, I approached a long French window with a curtain on either side of it, which, by the greatest good fortune, proved to be half-latched and gave upon an empty room. With the blade of my pocket-knife, I pushed up the fastening on the inside. The window swung open and I stepped into the room.

It was an ordinary Swiss sitting-room. On the farther side, opposite the windows, was a pair of folding doors, which I cautiously approached, my pistol cocked. With infinite care, I pushed them and, fortunately being well oiled, they slid apart almost without a sound.

I entered a second room and found myself in what was evidently a laboratory. There were shelves, with retorts and test tubes and chemicals in bottles, lining the walls, and in the middle there were two square deal tables and several Bunsen burners with other apparatus. At the farther end of the room was a pair of heavy curtains covering what I took to be a kind of alcove. I listened intently, but could hear nothing. I accordingly tip-toed across the room and, reaching the curtains, I peered between them. They covered, as I had thought, an alcove containing a couch and several chairs.

It was then that I saw Beatrice. She was lying on the couch full length, asleep, unconscious or dead, I could not tell which, and seated on either side of her, in close attendance, were the Professor and Schreckermann.

"I think we are now ready to begin," the Professor was saying.

I do not know what it was in my mind to do in that frightful moment, but I feel pretty sure that I should have been unable to restrain myself from some kind of immediate intervention. I only know that I had already, with a gesture almost mechanical, raised my pistol in order to cover the Professor, when a raucous, screaming voice shrieked out suddenly above my head, "I spy strangers! I spy strangers!" And then it gave a piercing whistle.

I looked up, startled out of control by that eerie voice which stabbed at me from the air, to see, perched on the curtain rail above my head, a red parrot of malevolent appearance. It was gazing at me with its beady eyes, its cunning head cocked on one side.

Then, before I could recover my wits, I felt my arms gripped roughly from the rear, and, at the same instant, a blow behind the knees stretched me helplessly on my back.

CHAPTER XII

I WITNESS AN EXPERIMENT

Prone on the floor, I saw that I was in familiar company.

The man who fell heavily on my chest was Fritz Adler. It was Karl von Emmerich who had knocked the pistol from my hand, while Schreckermann passed a noose round my ankles, drew it tight, and thus prevented me from kicking. I tried to hit Karl with my free hand, but, as he was behind me, twisting the arm he had collared into the small of my back, I failed to reach him properly, and my fist only grazed the side of his head.

"Not this time!" he shouted, remembering the knock-out blow he had received at Number 140, rue Etienne Dumont. "Quick, Major Adler!"

My other arm was seized, a rope passed round my wrists, and an instant later I was as helpless as a lobster on a fishmonger's slab.

All this time Beatrice had remained motionless on the couch, while the Professor stood waiting with an air of patient boredom until I was secured.

"So," he said quietly, when Fritz and Karl had finished their job. "It is Mr. Thomas Preston again, and it is to Ahasuerus that we owe the pleasure of renewing your acquaintance. His bad manners on perceiving for the first time persons whom he does not know are occasionally of advantage."

And, stretching up his hand to the curtain pole, he stroked the parrot and ruffled its feathers, while it chuckled and gurgled with a malicious satisfaction.

"I am sorry," he continued, "that we should have been compelled to receive you with so little ceremony, but you must lay that to the account of your reputation. You are of a violent temperament, Mr. Preston, and any indulgence of it at the moment would be particularly unfortunate, especially for the charming young lady who at present enjoys our hospitality."

"If you lay a finger——" I began, but was interrupted by Karl, who said viciously:

"Hold your mouth, you dirty spy, or I'll cut your pig's throat for you."

The Professor turned his eyes towards Karl.

"I admire your simple disposition, Herr von Emmerich, but I think we shall dispose of Captain Preston when the time comes in a manner more in keeping with the dignity of science. In these modern days," he continued, turning to me with a pleasant smile, "it should be a point of honour to refine upon the cruder practices of our ancestors. I hope to convince you shortly and without much difficulty that the new ways are better than the old. At the moment, however, we are about to begin a small experiment upon a lady who is not unknown to you, with the object of ascertaining the whereabouts of a certain document."

"You devil!" I said, and struggled desperately, but in vain, to free myself.

The Professor drew back, and his face assumed a pained expression.

"These men of action," he sighed; "their vocabulary is at times deplorable. In this case, moreover, the epithet is quite unwarranted. I assure you that the young lady will suffer no pain or injury of any kind. It is essential, however, that the experiment should be conducted in complete silence."

He pressed a bell-push standing on a little table at the foot of the couch, and I heard a bell ring sharply twice somewhere in the house. As he did so, he favoured us all in turn with that mild penetrating stare which was at once so disarming and so disconcerting. We submitted to it in different ways, Karl like a naughty schoolboy who has been caught writing "Mr. Bloggs is a fool" on the blackboard, Fritz flushing beneath his scars and looking for all the world like a London policeman submitting to a spiteful cross-examination, while Schreckermann, who had remained silent since my arrival, shuffled his feet uneasily and dropped his eyes. As for myself, though I was raging with an impotent desire to spring at the Professor's throat, I could not, even in that moment, for the life of me meet his gaze.

I at once divined what was coming. I was to be forcibly gagged in order to keep the silence that was necessary for whatever devil's work was toward. From the moment I had seen Beatrice lying there motionless on the couch, I had been conscious of her still, helpless figure within the alcove.

"Beatrice!" I called desperately, anxious that she should at least know that I was there.

The Professor held up his hand.

"Silence," he said sternly, "unless you wish to do her an irreparable injury."

Somehow I knew that he was speaking the truth. I was convinced at that moment that it would be fatal to call again to that motionless figure, which lay as under some accursed spell, beyond any help that I could see or summon.

The bell was answered by one of the menservants who had conducted me to my prison in the rue Etienne Dumont.

"A white silk handkerchief, please, Josef," said the Professor.

The man bowed and left the room.

The Professor, with a motion of the hand, directed Karl and Fritz to bring me to the alcove. This they did, half dragging, half carrying me, for the cord round my legs was too tight for me to move. They bound me securely to one of the iron hinges of a shuttered window situated only a few feet behind the couch. As they were tying me up, the servant returned with a salver, bearing an old-fashioned white silk neckerchief, of the kind used by elderly gentlemen to wrap round their necks beneath an overcoat. He handed this to Fritz, who twisted its ample folds securely about my mouth, effectively preventing any attempt to speak again.

"Now," said the Professor, and, taking up from the little table at the foot of the couch a hypodermic needle and some cotton wool, he approached Beatrice, who throughout had not moved, but who, I had noted with thankfulness, was breathing naturally and regularly, as though asleep.

She was wearing, I saw, her nightgown and a silk dressing-gown. I remembered then that she had been taken from her room by the hospital nurse and the doctor. She must already have gone to bed when I telephoned to her from the Secretariat. Her hair was lying in two long plaits on each side of her cheeks, and her feet and the lower part of her body were covered with a quilt.

But what kind of sleep was this which had held her fast through the noise and violence of my struggle with her captors? She lay as in a trance, immobile and curiously aloof from the group that surrounded her. It seemed as though she were not actually there in presence; that she was sleeping remote from the figures which moved about her; that for the moment she was as far beyond their malice as she had been beyond the urgent call which I had addressed to her. This impression lent an added horror to the deliberate approach of the Professor towards the couch. It seemed as though he were about to summon her from the distant tranquillity in which she lay in order to impose upon her his own evil and alien purpose. I was aware, in my impression of the scene, of something that transcended the horror of a mere physical approach. I felt as though he were about to touch the mind and being of the girl I loved, and I felt it as more than a merely physical indignity.

I watched him, helpless and fascinated, every fibre crying out against this infamy, as he bent over the couch, drew back the sleeve on her left arm and, inserting the hypodermic needle a few inches above the elbow, pressed home the plunger. He stepped back, watching her quietly. After a few moments she opened her eyes and stretched herself quite naturally, as though she were just waking from an ordinary sleep. Her eyes wandered round the room for a moment, and her face assumed a puzzled expression.

"Where on earth am I?" she began, in English, and looked bewilderedly first at Schreckermann and then at the Professor.

"You are quite safe, my dear Miss Harvel," said the Professor, in perfect English, "quite safe, and there is no cause for alarm. Please look at me for a moment."

He took up a position at the foot of the couch, gazing down at her quietly, but with a penetrating and persistent stare. I would have given worlds to have been able to warn her on no account to meet those persuasive eyes. But I could not move even a muscle in her defence, and after a moment she raised her eyes and fixed them on his face.

There was complete silence in the room for the space of a minute, and all I could hear was the thudding of the blood in my ears. Then Beatrice gave a little sigh, her head fell back on the pillow, and her eyes closed, her small hands clenching and unclenching once or twice.

The Professor moved swiftly to her side, and, bending over, made a few passes up and down her face. Then he stepped back and began to speak.

"Who are you?" he said, still in English.

Beatrice at once answered him in an impersonal and perfectly expressionless tone, as though she were involuntarily repeating a message.

"I am Beatrice Harvel."

"Where do you live?"

"At Les Pervenches, Boulevard des Tranchées, Geneva," she replied.

"What is your work?" continued the Professor.

"I am secretary to Monsieur Lavelle of the League of Nations," went on Beatrice, still in the same monotonous voice.

"Did Mr. Thomas Preston call to see Monsieur Lavelle yesterday?"

"Yes."

"At what time?"

"Shortly after six o'clock."

"Were you present when they met?"

"Yes."

"Did Mr. Preston mention a certain document to Monsieur Lavelle?"

"They talked of it."

"Who had given it to Monsieur Lavelle?"

"I gave it to him myself."

"How did you obtain it?"

"Mr. Preston gave it to me."

"What did Monsieur Lavelle do with the document?"

"He deciphered it."

The Professor paused, and I noted the strained attention with which the others were listening.

"Did he decipher it completely?" went on the Professor.

"Yes."

"Where did he put it?"

"In a Registry *dossier*."

"What is that?"

"It is a file in which papers are kept."

"Are there many such in the Secretariat?"

"Thousands."

"What did he do with the *dossier*?"

"He gave it to me to take to the Registry."

"And you did so?"

"Yes."

"What is the Registry?"

"A place where the *dossiers* are kept when not in use."

The Professor passed his tongue once across his lips.

"Are the *dossiers* numbered?"

"Yes."

"What was the number of the *dossier*?" he continued.

Fritz bent forward, drawing in his breath sharply; the Professor made a gesture for silence.

"4/90347/81756," replied Beatrice, in the same toneless voice.

"Repeat that number, please," said the Professor, and as she did so he wrote it down on a piece of paper.

"Did Monsieur Lavelle show you his solution of the cipher?"

"Yes."

"Can you remember it?"

"Yes."

"Will you repeat it, please?"

Here Beatrice, who had hitherto been speaking in English, to my astonishment, broke into German, though I knew she was almost entirely unacquainted with the language.

"*Wir, die Siebenschläfer, überzeug——*"

"Stop!" said the Professor. "That will do. You will remember nothing of what I have asked you when you wake, do you understand?"

"Yes."

"You have already forgotten what was in the document?"

"Yes."

"Try to repeat its contents."

"I cannot; I have forgotten them."

"It is now seventeen minutes to eleven. At noon precisely you will wake up, do you understand?"

"Yes."

106

The Professor ceased his interrogatory, and the others in the room relaxed their attitudes of strained attention.

I do not like to write any further my impressions of that hateful scene. But I would ask any who may read these lines to realise that I loved Beatrice, and to imagine what it was for me to see her will subdued to the purposes of a man who carried with him so positive and penetrating a suggestion of evil that since meeting him I have ceased to believe that wickedness is not merely the absence of good, as the modern sentimentalists have persuaded themselves, but a firm reality as objective, concrete and tangible as the devil who gnaws his bone upon the eaves of Notre Dame. The Professor seemed himself to know what was passing in my mind, and to presume that the torture he inflicted upon me, which wrung invisible and unsuspected nerves about my heart, was greater than anything he could have achieved by merely physical means. He was, indeed, on the point of turning to me, when the experiment was concluded, in order to relish its effect, and I was steeling myself to endure the smooth periods in which he invariably expressed himself, when there was, to my joy, a merciful interruption.

It came from Josef, the manservant, who suddenly entered and informed him that Adolf Baumer had arrived, and was asking to be admitted.

"Bring him here immediately," said the Professor.

He arranged the quilt decorously about the sleeping Beatrice and prepared to give his attention to the new arrival.

I found it in my heart to be almost sorry for little Adolf. His performances had been the reverse of brilliant, and personally I pitied anyone who was obliged to report unfavourably of his activities to such a master.

Adolf, entering the room, looked white and exhausted, and had evidently been taking violent exercise. At the sight of the Professor, his face assumed an expression of mingled deference and terror.

"At last, Herr Professor!" he exclaimed. "I am thankful, indeed, to find you again."

His expression, however, belied his words.

"So," said the Professor. "And may I ask you what you have been doing with yourself? Sit down, my little friend, and take your time. We have been rather anxious on your behalf, and I propose to give you my undivided attention."

He indicated a chair. Adolf sat, or rather collapsed, upon it, and, taking out a large and dirty red handkerchief, wiped his brow. He was a deplorable spectacle—a two-days' growth of stubble on his chin, his face streaked with sweat and grime.

He began an account of his adventures, frequently interrupted by Fritz, from the time when he had been kidnapped by de Blanchegarde and Réhmy at the Moulin Rouge, to the moment of his escape. He was describing how Karl von Emmerich, also kidnapped by Réhmy and de Blanchegarde, had been thrust into the cellar with him at Versoix, when Karl himself protested.

"The fellow's mad," he said. "I've never set eyes on him before."

Adolf looked at him bewildered.

Then he caught sight of me, whom he had not previously noticed, and his jaw dropped for, despite the gag, I was still an obvious replica of my double.

"Good God!" he exclaimed. "There are two of them."

"As you see," said the Professor.

Adolf pointed to me.

"That's the man who was thrust into the cellar," he declared. "Which of them is Karl von Emmerich?"

"The real Karl von Emmerich is beside you," said the Professor. "The other gentleman, who is for the moment deprived of the use of his limbs, is Mr. Thomas Preston, with whom we are shortly to deal."

"Then I must have handed the document to the wrong man," stammered Adolf.

"Your inference is undoubtedly right," replied the Professor. "I congratulate you on your powers of deduction. Our Adolf," he continued, turning to the others, "is really quite a sagacious little person. I'm often sorry that he is not a little more robust."

The expression of fear on the little Jew's face deepened. He began to make excuses, but the Professor cut him short.

"Pray don't apologise," he begged. "You made a very natural, though somewhat unfortunate, mistake. Happily we are now in a position to repair it, and there will be no danger of its repetition, as we are taking steps to remove all possible chance of Von Emmerich's identity being mistaken in the future. Pray continue your most interesting narrative."

The Professor, presumably as a result of his experiment with Beatrice, or possibly in anticipation of his experiment with me, was, it seemed, in a genial mood. Adolf, slightly reassured, proceeded with his story, describing how he had escaped, with my assistance, and how he had been pursued by the two Frenchmen in the motor car. It appeared that, unfortunately for him, Réhmy had taken a corner too fast and had hit a telegraph pole, buckling a wheel. The last Adolf had seen of them was Gaston running down the road after him, while Réhmy, whose head, it seemed, had been cut by the broken glass from the wind-shield, was tying it up with a handkerchief. Adolf had easily out-distanced Gaston on the errand-boy's bicycle, which he had eventually abandoned, going down to the lake shore, where he had stolen a boat in which he had crossed the lake, and with some difficulty found his way to the villa.

"Quite a sagacious little person," repeated the Professor, at the conclusion of Adolf's tale, "but I think that in future I shall keep you under my personal supervision.

"As for those two Frenchmen," he said, turning to Fritz, "I have known of their operations for some time, but till now I was not disposed to regard them as dangerous.

"Meanwhile," he continued, "our first care must be to obtain the document which has been causing us so much trouble. That is a task which I propose should be undertaken by Major Adler and Herr Schreckermann. You will accordingly proceed at once to the Secretariat of the League of Nations. You already possess, my dear Major, some acquaintance with the building in which that pious company of doctrinaires pursue their useless though innocuous vocations, but I hope it will be unnecessary for you to illustrate, as on the last occasion, your deplorable disregard for the sanctity of human life."

So it had been Fritz who had struck down Lavelle. I there and then swore that, if ever I got free from the Professor, an eventuality which at that moment did not appear at all probable, I would avenge the brutal murder of my friend, even if I had to search Europe from end to end in order to do so.

It will be seen from this that I had not yet had time to appreciate to the full the hopelessness of my situation. I was still too completely under the dominion of the feelings aroused by the experiment with Beatrice to realise the fact that in all probability I should share the fate of my old friend within the next hour. I was not, however, left long in doubt as to the sequel.

"When we have obtained the document," went on the Professor, "our continued presence in Geneva will no longer be necessary. It will therefore be best to move at once to Basle, that is unless Herr Schreckermann's financial operations are not yet concluded."

"I am quite ready to leave, Herr Professor," said Schreckermann. "I signed the last necessary contract yesterday afternoon."

"Good," said the Professor. "In that case you will take the small car and proceed with Major Adler direct to Basle. If you are unsuccessful in obtaining the document——"

"You need have no fears on that score, Herr Professor," interposed Fritz. "I think I am equal to obtaining a document."

"I have every confidence that you will do so," replied the Professor. "Please report to me here by telephone within the next hour the result of your researches. You can then proceed, as I have said, direct to Basle. I will follow, myself, in the large car from here, with the rest of the party. Meanwhile, pending the arrival of your telephone message, I shall devote myself to winding up Section Q, and arranging for the disposal of Mr. Preston."

"What are you going to do with the girl?" enquired Fritz.

"I propose to leave her here," said the Professor, "where she will be at liberty to return to Geneva on recovering from her trance. Her part in this affair has not hitherto been large, and a few helpful suggestions from me will, I trust, remove any impression made on her mind by our activities. We do not want to be burdened with an unnecessary passenger."

I breathed a sigh of relief. Beatrice, unless Fritz failed to obtain the document—and I had little doubt that he would be able to do so—would soon be free.

Fritz, however, instead of taking his departure, walked up to the couch and looked earnestly at Beatrice as she lay asleep. I saw the pupils of his eyes enlarge and his breathing become more rapid. He put out a hand and fingered gently the tress of hair that lay across the head of the couch, and, turning to the Professor, said: "It would be a pity to leave her behind, Herr Professor."

A cold fear struck at my heart as I listened.

The Professor looked at Fritz with an odd smile.

"You think so?" he asked.

"She's a lovely creature," said Fritz, looking at Beatrice in a way that made my blood boil.

"My dear Major," said the Professor, "a thousand apologies! But I am afraid it never occurred to me. In one who has wooed that elusive mistress, Science, the more human impulses tend to be less importunate. She is, as you say, a remarkably perfect specimen of her kind, though I have no reason to believe that her mental attributes are in any degree remarkable. That side of her, however, is probably of less account so far as you are concerned."

He reflected a moment, directing as he did so a whimsical eye in my direction.

"I am sure," he said at last, "that our friend, Mr. Preston, would not like to think he was leaving this young lady without protection or support. Perhaps, my dear Major, it would be well to take her with us, as you suggest. Your industrious, if occasionally misdirected, efforts certainly merit some reward, and I am well aware that you have always regarded the cult of Venus as the most appropriate relaxation of the warrior. I need hardly say that, should the lady in question prove temporarily blind to your many admirable qualities, despite the removal from her life of Mr. Preston's doubtless predominating influence, my services as an expert in the arts of suggestion are entirely at your disposal."

So saying, the Professor bowed formally to Fritz and Schreckermann, who immediately left the room on their mission to the Secretariat.

Of all moments that was the bitterest of my life. The thought that Beatrice was shortly to be handed over, a willing victim, if the Professor's powers were really such as he claimed—and I had but just witnessed an exposition of their quality—to the brute who stood looking from her to me with an expression of malicious satisfaction, was beyond endurance. My passion became too much for me, and, losing all control, I tore at my bonds in a fury that was scarcely sane and altogether hopeless and futile.

The Professor looked at me with a mild reproach, as though it pained him to see a reasonable creature moved to so childish an outbreak. Then he again pressed the bell and, on the appearance of Josef, directed the removal of Beatrice, still in her trance, to another room. This was shortly accomplished, with the aid of another manservant, and I was left alone with three men of whose intentions towards me I could have little doubt.

As the curtains swung to behind Beatrice, the Professor, with his usual tranquil air, turned to Karl and Baumer.

"And now," he said, "it remains to deal with Mr. Thomas Preston."

CHAPTER XIII

I AM NOT THE MAN I WAS

There was a short silence, broken by Baumer, who asked permission of the Professor to retire, in order to make himself more presentable. Little Adolf was of a nature that instinctively shrank from witnessing deeds of violence, and, evidently deeming, with reason, that my hour had come, he had no wish to remain.

As he rose to go, the Professor stayed him with a gesture.

"By all means, my dear Baumer," he said, "make such changes in your toilet as undoubtedly appear to be necessary. But kindly attend to my instructions. You will have certain duties to perform before we leave."

He turned to Karl von Emmerich, who was lounging on the chair from which he had witnessed the experiment with Beatrice.

"It is essential, my good Karl," continued the Professor, "that you should not be incommoded in any way by the police of Geneva, who are at present looking for a noted murderer. We must accordingly convince them that you have ceased to exist. The opportune arrival of Mr. Thomas Preston will, I hope, enable us to achieve this small deception without any serious difficulty. The police shall be informed by our friend Adolf that the body of a Mr. Thomas Preston, alias Karl von Emmerich, wanted in connection with the murder of a French chauffeur at Zürich, has been found on the shores of the lake not far from this villa. Adolf himself will claim the merit of this happy discovery, which will be duly confirmed by the police themselves on their arrival.

"While Adolf is thus lending his valuable assistance to the police of Geneva, I will take steps to ensure that the body of Mr. Preston shall be duly forthcoming, and that it shall present the appearance of having been in the water for some little time, shall we say, as from yesterday evening. For this purpose, I will prepare a solution which will have the double effect of paralysing Mr. Preston at the moment of his immersion, and of hastening the subsequent process of decay."

"Certainly, Herr Professor," said Baumer, turning a little white. "I will go at once to the police, and you may look for my return within an hour."

112

The Professor nodded, and Baumer quitted the room.

"While I am preparing the injection for Mr. Preston," said the Professor to Karl, "you will perhaps make arrangements for our transport, with Miss Harvel, to Basle. We will make the journey in the large car, and the servants can follow by train."

Karl rose to his feet and, drawing himself to attention, clicked his heels.

"If I may venture, Herr Professor?" he said.

"Certainly, my dear Karl."

"I would remind you that Miss Harvel is hardly dressed for travelling in an open car."

"Fräulein Elsa is here?"

"Yes, Herr Professor."

"Kindly instruct her to make the necessary arrangements. She will doubtless be able to find something suitable."

Karl left the room, and I was now alone with the Professor.

He came close to me and stood gazing at me quietly in silence for some moments.

"I am sorry, Mr. Preston," he said at last, "that it should have come to this, but you leave me no choice in the matter. I warned you clearly of the consequences that were bound to result from any interference with our plans. You chose, however, to disregard my advice. Hence the unfortunate position in which we find ourselves at the present moment. In the circumstances we must reconcile ourselves to the inevitable and try to believe that the event in which you are about to figure is less deplorable than it seems. You are a young man, Mr. Preston, and the thought of so abruptly terminating what doubtless appeared to be a promising existence is perhaps distasteful. Personally, however, I have always endeavoured to view death in the light of an interesting scientific change, and, for your consolation, I can inform you, as a man of science, that I am by no means convinced that your existence as a sentient being will be wholly discontinued as a result of the step we are at present contemplating. I need hardly say that you have my very best wishes for a long and successful career in whatever state of being you may find yourself within the next half-hour."

At this point, the remarkable man once more summoned his servants and directed them to remove me to what he described as the garden chalet, saying as he did so that I was doubtless in need of a few moments of reflection in order to fit myself for the coming change and that the building in question was admirably suited for the purpose.

I was picked up and carried, helpless as a log, through the laboratory and out into the garden by the silent Josef and his equally impassive companion. They took me some fifty yards to a small wooden hut situated at the shore-end of a stone jetty jutting into the lake. Here they laid me, with all the respect that was due to one who was already dead, upon a pile of faggots, which appeared to be all that the chalet contained, and, leaving me to my own devices, took their departure, shutting the door behind them.

I will spare you my reflections. They were of the bitterest kind, and it would do no good to repeat them. Indeed, I doubt if I could find adequate words to express what I felt when I realised that it was partly my own rash impatience which had placed me in the power of these scoundrels and had involved Beatrice in a fate which even now I shudder to contemplate. I regarded my death as quite inevitable, and it was rendered doubly bitter by my impotence to save the girl I loved. I do not easily abandon hope, but I unhesitatingly confess that at that moment, helpless as I was and destined shortly to test the Professor's doctrine concerning a future life, I was within an ace of utter and complete despair.

Action alone could save me from utter panic, and it was mercifully allowed me at least to struggle with my bonds. I was lying half on my back and half on my side, in a condition of extreme physical discomfort, owing to the tightness of the cords round my wrists, when I discovered, on trying to move, that my feet were less strongly secured. I found that I could even move them slightly, and this discovery sufficed to divert my thoughts from the desperate speculations to which my condition had given rise. I rolled over on my back, and, raising my feet in the air, kicked and struggled for some moments, with the result that I succeeded in loosening appreciably the cords round my ankles.

My next action was to endeavour to get to my feet, which, after several attempts, I succeeded in doing, though at the cost of some difficulty and pain. Once upright, I took stock of my surroundings.

The building in which I stood apparently consisted of a single chamber, unfurnished and bare except for the bundles of faggots and a few old sacks. It had one window, looking out towards the lake and opposite the door. I shuffled towards the door and tried it with my shoulder, but it was fast, as I had expected, though closer examination revealed the fact that it possessed no apparent keyhole and was therefore presumably bolted on the outside. I stood for a moment thinking hard. I was not in much better a position than when I had first been deposited in the chalet. True, I had the partial use of my legs, but my arms were still securely bound and the silk handkerchief was fast over my mouth.

It was very silent in the chalet and in the garden outside, though from time to time I heard a piercing shriek from the direction of the villa. I was puzzled to account for these dreadful cries till I remembered Ahasuerus, the Professor's parrot. Apparently he was protesting against his enforced removal, and I hoped whoever had the task of inducting him into his travelling cage would be severely bitten during the process.

Presently I heard another sound, this time from the direction of the lake. There was borne to my ears the faint gurgle of water beneath the bow of a boat and the occasional creak of a rowlock. Some fisherman, I thought, forgetting the season of the year, and I became filled with the vague hope of being able to attract his attention. I shuffled and hopped across the floor until I got to the window, only to find that it was too high up in the wall to enable me to get a view. Returning to the pile of faggots, I succeeded, after several attempts, in rolling one towards the wall, on which I was able to perch precariously. This brought my head above the level of the sill, and I gazed out, craning it this way and that in an effort to locate the boat.

I soon caught sight of it. It was heading rapidly for the end of the jetty, which I have already mentioned. It contained two occupants, one at the sculls, with his back towards me, and the other at the tiller, in the stern sheets. The man at the tiller was leaning forward, as though engaged in conversation with the man who was rowing, and he appeared to be wearing a close-fitting white hat. Presently, however, he raised his head, and I saw that what I had mistaken for a hat was in reality a bandage beginning low on the forehead and covering most of the head.

Hope sprang alive and undefeated from the depths of despair, for I recognised beneath the bandage the face of my friend, Etienne Réhmy, whose companion could be no other than de Blanchegarde.

I could have shouted for joy till I remembered that, gagged as I was, I could not even whisper to them of my urgent need. I was obliged to watch them, in a silent agony of impatience, as they approached the jetty. They reached it at last and Gaston shipped his sculls, grasping a ring in the stone and steadying the boat while Réhmy jumped ashore. A moment later they were walking along the jetty in my direction. I noticed that Réhmy, despite the bandage round his head, did not appear to have been badly damaged by his encounter with the telegraph pole, for his stride was firm and steady and his face had its usual colour.

Should I be able to attract their attention? The chalet, though at the shore end of the jetty, was not directly opposite to it, but somewhat to the right, so that if they continued on their way to the villa they would inevitably pass me by and walk straight into the arms of the Professor.

I thrust my chin over the sill to hold myself erect and, throwing my weight upon my left leg, I kicked the wooden wall of the chalet as hard as I could with my right. Owing to the fact that the cords round my legs were only loose, and that I was thus not altogether free from them, I could not swing my foot very far and consequently could not make much noise.

They were almost abreast of me now, and I redoubled my efforts, with the result that, just as they were passing me by, I overbalanced and fell to the floor, knocking up against the wall, dislodging some of the faggots, and making a considerable noise. I was struggling to regain my feet when the door slipped open and an arm with a pistol gripped in the hand of it was thrust into the room. It was followed by Gaston, a tight look on his eager face, and his brown eyes blazing with excitement. I had by this time rolled to my knees and so remained facing him, gazing at him over the top of the handkerchief, with a look I strove to make as intelligent and speaking as possible.

He did not recognise me at first but covered me with his pistol. Then, seeing that I was bound and therefore helpless, he slipped it into his pocket, and, stooping down, removed the gag from my mouth.

"Quick, Gaston," I said, almost before the handkerchief was off my mouth, "there's not a moment to lose."

"*Mon Dieu!*" he cried. "What have they been doing to you?" And taking out a knife he began hacking at the cords round my wrists.

"Where's Réhmy?" I asked, as he worked.

"Watching the villa," replied Gaston.

"Fetch him at once," I said. "We must decide immediately what to do."

By this time he had freed my right hand and, while he went for Réhmy, I was soon able, with the help of his knife, to complete the task of liberating myself unaided, though my hands and wrists were so stiff from the pressure of the cords that I found it very difficult to use them.

Gaston returned with Réhmy, and I rapidly recounted what had happened since my arrival at Bellerive.

When I had finished my hurried tale, both Gaston and myself looked instinctively to Réhmy for our instructions. He was, as ever, cool and methodical, ticking off the points on his fingers, as though they were items in a schedule.

"You say that Fritz and Schreckermann have gone to the Secretariat of the League of Nations to get the document?"

"Yes."

"And they will telephone the result to the Professor?"

"They were instructed to do so."

"Meanwhile Adolf is informing the police that the body of the man they want for murder has been found here in the lake. Has he started yet for Geneva?"

"I believe he has."

"That leaves only Karl and the Professor."

"Elsa, the woman with the pheasant feather in her hat, is also here, and there are the servants," I pointed out.

"Where is Karl?"

"He was ordered to prepare for the journey to Basle."

"They are going by car?"

116

"The Professor, Karl, and presumably Elsa will go by car with Beatrice. The servants follow by train."

"Where is the Professor now?"

"At the villa, preparing what he calls an injection. He may be here at any moment."

Réhmy thought a moment and then said:

"It's too late now to get the document. We can't even warn the Secretary-General. It would take ages to get through to Geneva by telephone. Fritz will have arrived at the League of Nations by this time. Our immediate object must be to get safely away from here with Miss Harvel. After that, if Fritz has succeeded in getting the document, we must follow it to Basle."

At this point, Gaston, who had risen some little time previously, and was standing near the door, called to us to be silent.

"There's someone coming," he said.

We moved towards the door, and I looked out.

"It's Karl von Emmerich!" I exclaimed.

Karl was just leaving the villa as I spoke. He walked across the grass straight towards the chalet, whistling as he came.

Gaston touched me on the arm.

"We must be ready for him," he whispered.

It was evident that the chalet was Von Emmerich's destination. But when he had arrived within ten yards of it he stopped, and an expression of surprise came over his face. Réhmy and I simultaneously realised that what had caught his attention was the fact that the door was no longer bolted but that it stood ajar.

I felt a pressure on my left wrist and, stepping back from the door, I looked round, to find Gaston, his eyes shining, holding the largest of the sacks—which, as I have said, together with the faggots, were all that the chalet contained. He motioned to Réhmy and myself to get out of the way, and we slipped to one side.

A moment later the door was kicked open and Karl, still whistling, entered.

"So, you English dog——" he began in German.

At that moment, however, the sack came over his head, and I dived for his ankles, like a full-back collaring a three-quarter. He crashed with a thud, and Réhmy, jumping on top of him, seized him through the thick folds of the sack by the throat.

"Quick," whispered Gaston. "He mustn't make a sound."

While Réhmy gripped him, I pulled the sack aside, and, snatching the silk handkerchief, pushed it between his teeth and made it fast.

He struggled furiously, but the three of us were too much for him, and he was soon secured.

"What next?" I panted, rising to my feet and brushing my hands.

"You must change clothes," said Gaston briskly. "Then you can slip into the house and find Miss Harvel."

"But the Professor," I objected. "He may come at any moment."

"If the Professor comes," said Gaston grimly, "his victim will be ready for him."

"You don't mean——" I began.

"I mean," said Gaston, "that the Professor has decided to murder a man who is bound and helpless and unable to utter a cry, a man with the features of Thomas Preston and wearing Thomas Preston's clothes. I mean that the Professor shall carry out his intention and that as a result of it there will be one ruffian less in the world."

I looked at Réhmy. He nodded.

"It's the only way," he said. "There are only two of us. We can't hope to overpower the Professor and his armed servants. At any rate, we cannot afford to risk it. Besides, you may need our help with Miss Harvel."

The mention of Beatrice decided me. I suppressed my first impulse of pity for the wretch who would be left to suffer my doom vicariously and began to remove my clothes.

Meanwhile Réhmy stood by the door, watching the garden for the arrival of the Professor.

I tore off my coat, waistcoat, and trousers.

"Quick," said Gaston. "Everything must be changed. We must leave nothing to chance."

I did as I was bid, while our victim heaved and struggled vainly beneath the sack. It went to my heart to abandon my British passport, but the body would be searched and everything had therefore to be transferred.

Divesting him of his clothes was a more difficult matter and required our united efforts before we had it satisfactorily accomplished. We tied his feet and removed the upper part of his clothes, and then tied his arms and repeated the operation lower down. During the process I noticed a large scar just above his left knee, the mark of an old wound.

All this time we were in a fever of impatience. If the Professor should come, our chances of putting up an effective resistance would not have been very great. Only two of us were armed, and he had at least two, if not more, capable and well-armed servants.

Réhmy was particularly anxious. As I afterwards discovered, he was less preoccupied with the chances of a struggle than with a plan which he had already begun to form in his mind for the recovery of the document. For the success of this plan it was essential that the Professor should not interrupt us in the work of substituting Karl for myself. It will perhaps convey some idea of the almost inhuman coolness and resource of this devoted servant of the French Republic that he should even at this perilous moment be thinking ahead of our immediate problem.

By this time, Karl was dressed from head to foot in the clothes of Thomas Preston. We bound him with the same cords as had been used on me and gagged him with the silk handkerchief, finally laying him on the faggots, where I had lately been deposited by Josef and his companion.

"What is the next move?" said Gaston, as he rose to his feet.

"I'll go to the villa," I said, "and see if I can find Beatrice. Meanwhile, you two might conceal yourselves near the main entrance. You can't help me in the house, and you cannot afford to be seen. As soon as I have located Beatrice, and if the coast is clear, I'll take her to the Professor's car, slip away and pick you up just outside the garden."

"Excellent," said Réhmy. "We will go and hide the boat. The Professor would think it odd if he saw it tied up to the jetty."

"We'll deal with that at once," said Gaston.

"Take this," he said to me, handing me a police whistle, "and blow it three times if you are in any difficulty. We shall be within earshot, and we'll get to you if we have to shoot our way through."

I nodded, and, looking out, saw that the coast was clear.

A moment later we all three slipped from the chalet, bolting the door behind us. Gaston and Réhmy made straight for the jetty, where I soon heard sounds of a boat being cautiously propelled across the water, while I went towards the villa. Halfway across I looked round and saw that my French friends were steering for a clump of willows about fifty yards down the bank, in which they would be able to conceal the boat.

I stepped on to the verandah, and my heart beat appreciably faster when I saw that I was about to meet the Professor himself, followed by his two menservants. He was carrying a small phial and a hypodermic needle, perhaps the same as that which he had used on Beatrice. We met on the verandah, and for a moment I feared that I should not be able to deceive him. His first words, however, dispelled my apprehensions.

"So you have been talking to our English friend, my dear Karl," he said. "I'm sorry to have kept him waiting for so long, but I found that I had no more of solution twenty-six made up, and it required a little time to prepare it."

He looked at me quizzically, and, though I put up a good front, I was inwardly weak as water.

"Doubtless," he continued, "you would like to be present at the little ceremony which is about to take place. You are obviously a man of simple pleasures. I'm afraid that is impossible, however. I am expecting a telephone call at any moment from Major Adler, and there must be a responsible officer in the house to answer it. I would accordingly ask you to remain in the villa."

I collected all my courage and suddenly heard myself say:

"And the English girl?"

The Professor smiled.

"You men of action are all alike," he complained, "always inordinately interested in any member of the opposite sex. Miss Harvel is by this time, I trust, comfortably awaiting us in the car. If she is not already there, please see that she is taken thither without loss of time."

I clicked my heels, as I had seen Karl do and replied, *"Zu Befeh, Herr Professor."*

He smiled at me and proceeded to the garden, followed by the two menservants, one of whom, I noticed, was bearing a length of rope, to which an iron hook was attached.

I entered the house, intending to slip out as soon as the Professor was out of sight and look for the car, which was presumably in the front drive. Immediately inside, however, I came face to face with Elsa. She was arrayed in the costume in which I had first seen her, complete to the hat with the pheasant feather in it. She smiled up at me coquettishly, while I almost groaned with vexation. She, of all persons, was the most likely to penetrate my disguise. Besides, time was precious.

"Karl," she said, "you have been teasing the Englishman."

"It's too bad," I muttered, assuming an expression of sulky ferocity. "The Professor won't let me see the end of him."

"What a shame!" she exclaimed, as though I were a small boy deprived of a half-holiday. "I'll go myself, Karl, and tell you about it afterwards. I have nothing left to do. The English girl is already in the car. She will be waking up soon, as it's nearly twelve o'clock."

And with that she ran from me into the garden and was lost to view.

"That's a devoted little creature," I thought. "And certainly she has the sweetest notion of amusing herself."

I glanced at my watch, or rather Karl's, and saw that it was five minutes to twelve.

I strode on into the hall, intending to cross it and open the front door into the main drive, where I hoped to find the car.

At this moment, however, there was a sharp ring at the telephone, and I was reminded of the message the Professor was expecting. It would be well to find out whether Fritz had succeeded in obtaining the document.

I took off the receiver, which was in the hall. Fritz was speaking, and he enquired for the Professor. I said that the Professor was engaged with the Englishman, but that I would take him a message.

120

"Karl von Emmerich speaking," I concluded.

"Tell the Professor," said Fritz, at the other end of the wire, "that we have the document and are proceeding at once to Basle."

"Very good," I replied. "The Professor will be delighted."

"I should hope so," grumbled Fritz.

It occurred to me that this was a priceless opportunity to ascertain the quarters of the gang in Basle.

"One moment, sir," I said. "I am sorry to trouble you, but I've forgotten the address in Basle, and I don't want to increase the unfortunate impression I have already made on the Professor by my blunder in Zürich. Would you be so good as to repeat it?"

"33, Martinsgrasse," replied Fritz. "Do they tell you nothing at Hanover?"

"I had my instructions, Major," I coldly rejoined, "but no details."

"Very well," he grumbled. "We shall expect you sometime late this evening," and he rang off.

I hung up the receiver and hurried away.

There was no time to lose. At any moment the Professor might be back, before I had succeeded in getting away with Beatrice.

I opened the front door, and my eyes were gladdened by the sight of the powerful green car, which had nearly run over me in the courtyard of the Secretariat, drawn up at the steps. It was empty except for the slight form of Beatrice, propped up in the back seat and covered with a rug. She was wearing clothes which doubtless belonged to Elsa, and were of a rather vivid blue.

As I approached the car, twelve struck from a clock situated over the garage attached to the house. As the last stroke died away, Beatrice opened her eyes. She looked at me in bewilderment for a moment.

"Where am I, Tom?" she asked. "What's been happening? And what on earth am I wearing?" she exclaimed, as she caught sight of her arm in its vivid blue cloth.

"It's all right, dear," I assured her, as I jumped into the driving seat. "I will explain everything later. You are quite safe—at last."

I am pretty good with cars, and I noted with satisfaction that this was a big Ballot, a French car which had won many races and a make which I had frequently driven. I put my foot on the self-starter, the engine sprang into life, and a moment later we were through the gates of the villa and safe in the road beyond.

CHAPTER XIV

I GO IN SEARCH OF MY UNCLE

I ran the car slowly down the road leading to the villa and pulled up where it entered the main road to Geneva. There was no sign of my French friends, and I waited anxiously for some seconds. At any moment, someone from the villa, or even the Professor himself, might appear. In that case, I could not decide what I should do. I was armed, for I had found a pistol in the pocket of the coat that had belonged to Karl von Emmerich, but with Beatrice to look after, I felt it would be too great a risk to stay and put up a fight. I had therefore almost decided to drive on should any of the gang put in an appearance, when Gaston's face, flushed with exercise, appeared over the hedge.

"Good!" he exclaimed, as he caught sight of me. "Here he is, Etienne, safe with the lady," and they both scrambled through and arrived breathless in the roadway.

I was standing beside the car, the engine quietly ticking over. Gaston, with a quick smile, pushed past me, and, entering the car, took the wheel, motioning Réhmy to get up beside him. Réhmy, as he got in, said to me in a low voice:

"Be very careful with Miss Harvel, Preston. Remember that she will know nothing of what she said in her trance. Talk to her quietly. We will introduce ourselves later on."

I nodded and took my seat next to Beatrice, grateful for the tact which had prompted them to leave us together.

As we started, I leaned forward and tapped Réhmy on the shoulder.

"Fritz and Schreckermann have got the document," I said. "Adler telephoned a few minutes ago and I spoke to him myself. They are starting for Basle immediately."

"We must follow at once," he replied, and began to tell Gaston my news.

I turned to Beatrice, who met me with a smile.

"Now tell me all about it, Tom," she said. "Who are the gentlemen in front?"

122

"Beatrice darling," I said softly, "thank God you are safe."

"Safe," she echoed, and I noticed that she did not resent the endearment. "Have I been in any danger?"

"You're feeling quite all right?" I asked, looking at her anxiously.

"Perfectly well," she answered. "I'm just a little tired, that's all. But why this mystery? What's it all about? And you haven't told me whose clothes I'm wearing. I think they're perfectly awful," she added, glancing down distastefully at her coat.

"Beatrice," I said, "you've just escaped from my grandmother."

She looked at me in astonishment for a moment, and then I could see she was making an effort to remember.

"I was speaking to you on the telephone," she said, "when I think I must have fainted, for I don't recollect anything more until I saw you by the car just now, except that I fancy I woke up once and found that someone was looking at me."

I shuddered.

"Dearest," I said, "you've had a very narrow escape."

And I told her how she had been carried off by the Professor, who had visited her *pension* in the guise of a doctor, alleging that she was ill. I recounted how he had evidently drugged her and removed her to the house from which we had just escaped.

"But what did the Professor want with me?" she interrupted. "And how did you find out where I was?"

I was rather at a loss to answer the first question, so I told her in a few words about my providential meeting with Réhmy and de Blanchegarde outside the League of Nations, of the little Jew whom they had held captive, and of the means we had taken to get him to disclose the whereabouts of the Professor and his followers.

"My friends in front were splendid," I said. "We owe them a great debt, for without their help we should never have got away."

"I'll thank them myself in a moment," she said.

She was silent a while and then added:

"Thank goodness, the document is safe with M. Lavelle. I must go to the Secretariat at once. He will be wondering what on earth can have happened. But I must get rid of these horrid things first," and she looked disapprovingly upon the garments of the fair Elsa. "I'll ring him up from my *pension*."

I looked at her for a moment, and then decided that, despite the shock, it was best for her to know the truth about Lavelle at once. I found her hand beneath the rug and pressed it tightly.

"You won't be able to ring up poor Lavelle," I said gravely. "Beatrice darling, he is dead. Those ruffians killed him last night."

She turned white and her lips tightened.

"Oh, Tom!" she said, and, releasing my fingers, she covered her face with her hands.

I put an arm about her shoulders. I could feel her slim body shaking with sobs; but after a moment she sat up and took her hands from her face. I saw the tears in her eyes, but her expression was firm and controlled.

"Tom," she said, "you can never go back now. You must not rest till you have avenged him."

I nodded my head, proud of her spirit in that moment of sorrow.

"I have already promised to do so," I replied. "And if God wills I shall keep my word."

We sat silent after this for some minutes, while the car ran slowly through Geneva. My own thoughts, strange though it may seem, were exultant. Beatrice had allowed me to make love to her, to call her sweet names; and for a girl of her temperament, whose scorn of anything in the nature of a flirtation had been the undoing of more than one of my sex, this could only mean the real thing.

Besides, I had work in front of me, and all my lingering doubts and scruples had vanished. I would see this thing through to the end, cost what it might. Beatrice herself had told me that there was now no turning back. I had at last the satisfaction of a straight path in front of me and a job that was as cordial in my veins. My enemies were fighting with the gloves off; so would I. They asked and gave no quarter; neither would I.

Beatrice, in her next words, confirmed the impression that she too approved of my devotion to the task, that she was, in fact, preoccupied with its details. She broke the silence that had fallen between us to ask about the document.

"I suppose," she said, "that they took it from poor Lavelle," and her voice trembled for an instant, "when they murdered him?"

I nodded, thinking it best that she should remain under this impression until it was time for her to know the whole truth.

"Yes," I said.

"They have gone off to Basle," I added, "and we are going after them immediately, as soon as we have put you in a place of safety."

She smiled suddenly.

"I shall be all right," she said. "Though even now I can't conceive why they wanted to make off with me."

I hesitated a moment before answering. Then I replied:

"They were afraid that I knew too much about their plans. They were holding you, I fancy, as a kind of hostage for my good behaviour."

The car was now approaching the outskirts of Versoix, and Beatrice asked where we were going. I told her that we were probably bound for the chalet rented by Réhmy, and a few minutes later I was seen to be right, for we drew up at the door, which was opened by my friend Jules.

We alighted, and, once inside, I affected the necessary introductions without further loss of time. Beatrice was soon thanking Gaston and Réhmy for the part they had played in her rescue. This she did very prettily, making a great impression, especially on the susceptible Gaston.

I was burning to hear how Réhmy and Gaston had traced me to the villa and whether the Professor had successfully disposed of Karl, but it was obviously better first to discuss our plans and recount the past events at leisure during the journey to Basle.

Gaston was already busy arranging a hasty meal, so I took Réhmy aside and informed him of what I had said to Beatrice.

"I have only one question to ask her," he said.

"Mademoiselle," he went on, "there is only one thing I want to know. M. Lavelle showed you the document after he had deciphered it?"

Beatrice nodded.

"Can you tell us what it contained?"

It went to my heart to see how earnestly she tried to remember the secret which the Professor, by his devilish suggestion, had obliterated from her mind.

"I wish I could," she said at last. "I remember it was in German, of course, but that is about all. It's dreadfully stupid of me, I know, and yesterday I believe I could have told you something about it. Now, however, it has completely gone from my mind. I'm terribly sorry."

"Do not distress yourself in the least, my dear Miss Harvel," said Réhmy, with a gentle courtesy that became him very well.

I had told him in the chalet of the scene with the Professor an hour or two previously; how he had suggested to Beatrice in her trance that she should lose all recollection of the purport of the document. He realised that here was a notable proof of the Professor's uncanny power. We were recalled by Gaston who announced that lunch was ready.

"An omelette and some passable red wine. I am sure you must be hungry, Mademoiselle," he said.

Réhmy glanced at his watch.

"We have no time to lose," he objected. "We really ought to be starting at once."

Here, however, he was overruled by Gaston, who, with the wisdom of his genial type, insisted that, without a meal, a man was only half his own master. I heartily agreed with him, for the strain of the past few hours had given me a ravenous appetite, and I fell on the food like a starving man.

We discussed our immediate plans while eating and, on my suggestion, we decided that Beatrice should go immediately to England and stay with

125

her people until the whole affair was over. She could easily do this, as a letter to the authorities in the Secretariat stating that she was suffering from shock at the news of the murder of her chief would prove an excellent excuse. She demurred, but I would hear of no alternative. I felt that, as long as she remained in Geneva, she was bound to be exposed to unknown and perhaps immediate danger. We were still ignorant of the full resources of the gang, but we had already had sufficient experience of their activity and ingenuity to take no unnecessary risks.

As a further precaution, I telephoned to Jerry Cunningham, asking him to come immediately in a taxi to the chalet. He would, I knew, keep an eye on Beatrice until she left that night for London, and would even accompany her to Paris, if he thought it necessary. Until her departure for the train, she was to remain at the chalet, ordered Réhmy, since it would be dangerous for her to return to her *pension*. Jerry and the manservant, Jules, could look after her and she could telephone to one of her friends to pack her trunks.

Once this arrangement was concluded, I felt a great load lifted from my mind. Beatrice would now be safe, and I was free to pursue the murderers of Lavelle, untrammelled by any further anxiety on her behalf.

As soon as we had finished our meal, Réhmy and Gaston left the sitting-room to make a few necessary preparations for the journey, and to give Jules his instructions.

I was at last alone with Beatrice, and I found that the constraint which came between us at our last meeting had now entirely vanished, as far as I was concerned.

She was standing on the hearthrug, her head in clear relief against the light pinewood walls of the room.

"Beatrice," I whispered, and, stepping forward, held out my arms.

"What is it, Tom?" she said.

I could only repeat her name, and at this she stretched out her hand, and a moment later she was in my arms. The sweetness of those moments I cannot describe. Documents, plots, the whole fantastic scene of adventure in which I had been called to play, without rehearsal, so prominent a part— all were forgotten, as I held her close and kissed her for the first time.

Presently she stirred and freed herself.

"You mustn't stay any longer, Tom," she whispered. "They will be waiting for you, dear, and you've no time to lose. But come back soon and safe."

"Till our next meeting," I replied, and, drawing her to me, I kissed her once again.

As she moved from my embrace I heard the footsteps of Gaston and Réhmy descending from above. Gaston put in his head to say that all was ready. I looked at Beatrice.

"Good-bye, Tom my dearest," she said simply, "and God keep you."

I turned and went out. In the hall I met Jerry, who had just arrived in a taxi from Geneva. I took him by the arm.

"I've scarcely a moment to explain," I said hurriedly. "But, look here, old man, I want you to keep an eye on Beatrice. She must leave Geneva at once, and I want you to see her to the Paris train. For heaven's sake, don't let her out of your sight. They have captured her once already."

"What, your grandmother?" he said, bewildered by my urgency.

"Yes," I replied, already struggling into my coat, "and my uncles and my fellow nephews and nieces. They're a pleasant crew. Beatrice will tell you as much as she knows. I must start at once for Basle—after my Uncle Fritz."

"Are they the lot who murdered that Frenchman at the League?"

"They are," I replied grimly.

He whistled.

"The Genevese papers this morning are full of it."

"They're devils, Jerry," I said, "cunning as weasels and absolutely ruthless. Thank goodness you are here to look after Beatrice."

"Don't you worry your head about Beatrice," he said, as we went towards the door. "She'll be quite safe here, and I'll see her to the train. If it's necessary, I'll travel with her."

"What about your young pupils?" I asked.

Jerry made a small grimace.

"They'll be thankful for a day's holiday from their kind tutor."

"Well, I'm awfully grateful, old man," I said. "Good-bye," and I opened the front door.

At the last moment, I turned and said, "Jerry."

"Yes?"

"There's another job for you when this business is over."

"What's that?" he asked.

"Being my best man at the wedding," I replied, and shut the door before he could answer.

Outside I found Réhmy and de Blanchegarde already in the car. Gaston was at the wheel.

"Quick, *mon ami*," he said. "With any luck we shall be in Basle before eight o'clock."

I jumped in beside Réhmy, and a moment later we swung into the road. I noticed at my feet a small suit case, which Réhmy told me Jules had fetched from my hotel, and in which he had packed some spare clothing. Réhmy forgot nothing.

"I also instructed Jules to pay your bill," he added.

I asked him what I owed him, but he would take no money, saying that I was unofficially working for his government and as such entitled, if not to a salary, at least to my expenses. Further than that, he thrust fifty pounds upon me in Swiss notes and American dollars, saying that it was essential I should be well supplied with money. This was true enough, and I stowed them away in Karl's pocket, which on examination proved to contain some two hundred francs in Swiss money and a large wad of the new German "*Rentenmark*" notes.

We sat silent a few minutes while Gaston drove the car down the long dull road to Lausanne, along the borders of the leaden lake towards Morges, where we should turn to the left and go through La Sarraz and Orbe to Yverdon.

"You haven't told me yet," I said presently, "how you reached the villa, and I have never properly thanked you for your opportune arrival."

There was not much, he said, to tell. He had pursued Adolf in the Peugeot, picking up Gaston on the way. The little Jew had had only a few hundred yards' start. They had soon come up with him; but just as they had arrived within some ten yards of him, he had swerved sharply to the right down a steep lane running towards the lake, and at right angles to the main road. In trying to follow him, Réhmy had turned too sharply for the speed of the car, which had skidded badly, and struck a telegraph pole at the corner, where the lane crossed the road. The shock had been a violent one, but fortunately the brunt of it had been borne by the near front wheel and its mudguard, both of which had been badly buckled. The shock had also shivered the wind-shield, and Réhmy's forehead had been laid open by the flying splinters of glass. Gaston had very fortunately escaped injury, but, by the time he had ascertained that Réhmy was not seriously hurt, Adolf was observed in a small boat rowing rapidly across the lake to freedom.

The two Frenchmen had therefore been compelled to retrace the short distance to Versoix on foot, where Réhmy's injury had been attended to by a local doctor, and a man despatched to salvage the car. At Versoix, of course, they had received the message which I had left for them, giving the address of the gang at Bellerive, and after some difficulty and delay had obtained a boat and started for the Villa Mortmain, where, as has already been related, they had found themselves only just in time.

"I know the rest," I said, "except what happened after I went into the villa in search of Beatrice."

"That's soon told," replied Réhmy. "We hid our boat under a clump of willows at one end of the garden, and had just got under cover when we saw the Professor come down the steps of the verandah towards the chalet. He had two men with him, and presently a girl came out of the villa and joined them."

128

"That was Elsa," I interposed, "Karl's lady-love, the girl who took me to the house in the rue Etienne Dumont."

"*Mon Dieu!*" said Réhmy with a low whistle. "Then she helped to kill her lover."

"Go on," I said.

"We lay crouching behind the willows and watched. The Professor entered the chalet first, followed by the two servants and the girl. A few minutes later the four of them reappeared in the reverse order, the two servants carrying Von Emmerich between them. They went to the edge of the lake and the two menservants lowered Karl into the water.

"We had seen quite enough, and at once made our way back to the road, where you picked us up. The last we saw of the people by the lake was the two menservants apparently engaged in dragging the body towards the shore by means of a rope."

"If you hadn't turned up," I said, "I should be at the end of that rope myself."

We sat silent awhile. I was very tired, and I think I must have dozed, for I was not conscious of the swift landscape on either side until we were nearing the end of the lake of Neuchatel, and the lights of that town were close upon us. We called a halt there for ten minutes while we drank coffee, for it was cold in the open car, and I afterwards relieved Gaston at the wheel.

We climbed the valley De Ruz to a little place called Dombresson. From thence the road wound sharply up the Mont Chasserel and down again to St. Imier.

I was filled with an extraordinary exhilaration as the car sped through the gathering darkness. She was a good car and I drove her fast and well, though I say it myself. We had long since left the mist and fogs of Geneva behind and were in the clear upland air, cold, with a tang in it liked iced wine. Switzerland, once you get away from the lakes and the valleys, from the petty, avaricious towns, to the great hills and spaces reaching up to the snow line, with their wooden villages and their simple-minded peasants, is grand enough; beautiful it is not—it is too harsh and built on too great a scale for beauty. But it is impressive and inspiring. All this I felt as we rushed along, past Tavannes now and Moutier to Delémont, where we halted for Réhmy to take my place. As we changed seats, he said:

"Gaston and I have been talking things over in the back, and he'll tell you what we think it best to do."

As we were going through Soyhières, where we swung right-handed, Gaston explained that it would obviously be best for me to drive alone to Number 33, Martinsgasse, where Fritz and Schreckermann would be awaiting me, and to leave Réhmy and himself at an hotel on the way. In my character as Karl von Emmerich, I could report to Fritz, explain the absence of the Professor by a convenient excuse, and endeavour to obtain possession of the document, on the ground that I had been ordered by the Professor to take it immediately to Hanover. Whether successful or not, I was to join Gaston and Réhmy at their hotel, and we would then concert further measures. To all this I agreed.

"You are running a great risk," said Gaston, "and we both of us feel that we have very little right to ask it of you."

"Nonsense," I said. "We're all in this business now from henceforth to the end."

We were by this time almost at Basle. The car had behaved magnificently throughout, though she had been driven at a maximum speed.

At Reinach, some few kilometres from the city, I again took the wheel, and a few moments later we drew up in the outskirts of Basle. My French friends descended here, leaving me to finish the journey alone, for we did not care to run any risk of being seen together now that our destination was reached. They settled to put up at "Die Drei Königen," to which they bent their steps, whilst I drove on and presently crossed a high bridge over the Rhine, entering narrow streets which eventually brought me into the middle of the town.

I enquired the direction of the Martinsgasse from a gendarme, and he indicated a small ill-lighted street lying behind the painted Rathaus.

Two minutes later I had stopped opposite Number 33. As I climbed from the car, stiff with the long drive, I looked at my watch. It was a quarter to eight.

130

CHAPTER XV

I PLUNGE INTO DEEPER WATERS

Before approaching the door, I took stock of the house. It was tall and thin, dating, so far as I could judge, from the eighteenth century. The windows were dark and shuttered and no light was to be perceived anywhere. Finding that I could gain little information outside, I walked up to the door, a massive oak affair with a brass knocker shining dully from the centre. I remembered the signals given by Elsa in the rue Etienne Dumont, and thought it well to knock in the same manner. Accordingly I seized the knocker, gave one heavy rap, then a series of light ones, and finally two short, sharp knocks. A panel which I had not previously remarked slid sideways behind a small grille, and two eyes moved shiftily behind the bars.

"Ephesus," I said.

"They are not dead but sleep," replied the individual on the other side.

A moment later the door was opened, and I found myself at the foot of a narrow flight of stairs, at the top of which stood on oil lamp, reeking foully, its dull flame casting weird shadows on the walls and ceiling of the landing.

"Major Adler is above, sir," said the man who had admitted me. "But we were expecting Professor Kreutzemark."

"He has been delayed," I answered shortly, and turned to the stairs.

I was halfway up when the man called after me.

"And the car, Herr Lieutenant?"

"I shall not need it again," I replied.

"Very good, sir," he said. "You will find Major Adler on the first floor, second door on the right."

I nodded and proceeded on my way, and the next moment was knocking on the door in question.

"*Herein*," said a voice which I recognised as that of my Uncle Fritz.

Entering the room, I found him lying on a settee drawn up close to a big stove—one of those porcelain affairs common to Germany and Switzerland, and ornamented with a profusion of figures and designs—a beautiful and valuable specimen of the old art of faïence making, brought to perfection by the Nüremburg craftsmen of the fifteenth century. The room was lighted by half a dozen candles and was consequently shadowy in the corners. It contained, so far as I could see, some old oak furniture and a large writing-desk in front of a window. It was very hot, all the windows being closed and shuttered.

At the other side of the room sat Schreckermann, sprawling in a huge chair, his waistcoat undone, smoking one of those pipes dear to the German bourgeois, with a stem about a foot long, and a bowl of china modelled to represent a skull.

A table stood between the two men, upon which were two large mugs of beer. Uncle Fritz and Uncle Ulric were evidently taking their ease after the labours of the day.

Adler looked up at me as I entered.

"So," he said gruffly, "you've arrived."

I clicked my heels and drew myself to attention.

"*Ja*, Herr Major," I answered.

I had decided, while driving through the streets of Basle, that with Fritz flattery was my best cue. He had seemed to me to be the type of Prussian who can most easily be managed by playing up to him, and I determined to conduct the interview as much as possible on orderly-room lines. I would be the eager but disciplined young officer, deferring respectfully to the crusty old major, to whom all the problems of life were as an open book.

"B-but wh-where's the Professor?" stammered Schreckermann.

I had expected this and was ready for it. Taking a pace forward, which brought me into the shadow, I drew myself up and repeated my next words in as toneless and official a voice as I could muster.

"The Professor, gentlemen, is coming later," I said. "He has charged me with the following message:

"He regrets that pressure of work has prevented him from leaving Geneva this evening. He hopes, however, to be in Basle by tomorrow at midday."

Fritz gave an exclamation of annoyance, and I hastened to soothe him.

"He bids me congratulate Major Adler and Herr Schreckermann on their excellent work," I added, in the manner of a subaltern entrusted with an official commendation.

"Humph!" snorted Fritz, taking it beautifully. "Not coming, isn't he? First time I've known the Professor late for anything. What's keeping him at Geneva?"

"I don't know, sir," I replied, "but I think it's something in connection with the disposal of the Englishman."

Fritz grunted again.

132

"He seems to be wasting too much time over that affair," he grumbled. "The Professor's much too fond of making his confounded speeches. Why couldn't he cut the fellow's throat and have done with it?"

"Well," he continued, now gruffly genial, "you needn't stand there any longer. You're not on parade. Take a chair."

I did as I was bid, pulling up an old oak armchair to the table, and keeping as far as I could in the shadow cast by the flickering candles. Although my resemblance to Karl was very remarkable, and although I was dressed in his clothes, I did not want to take any unnecessary risks.

Uncle Fritz was obviously pleased with my demeanour. He lolled back on the settee, the mug of beer in his hand, enjoying the opportunity which I was trying to afford him of being affably insolent to a military subordinate.

"Now, I suppose," he continued, "you want that document we've heard so much about. The arrangement was that you should take it at once to Hanover and deliver it to Captain Z."

I bowed.

"Those were the Professor's instructions," I answered. "I was to hand it to him personally."

"Once you've obtained the signature of that mystery man, our part of the job is finished. And who'll get the credit for it, do you suppose? Will it be the man who did the work, who saved this organisation? Not a bit of it. You, my young friend, will go off to Hanover and get all the praise and all the pudding, while I sit here and wait for the Professor to come and talk my head off."

"Really, sir," I protested, "I'm sure that no one realises more than the Professor the excellence of the work you have done. He was only saying as I left, Herr Major, that in his next report to the Seven——"

Fritz raised his hand in a gesture of arrest.

"That's enough, young man," he said, glancing at Schreckermann. "There are certain persons whom we prefer to be nameless."

He rose heavily from the settee and lounged across to the desk, reaching for his keys. He unlocked the top, and I heard him fumble among the papers which the desk contained. Presently he returned, bearing a single sheet of paper, which I recognised to be the document in question. This he placed in an envelope and handed it to me, saying:

"Well, orders are orders, and you'd better take the document at once. And you'll perhaps be more careful with it than that little rat of a Jew."

I took the envelope, and, putting it away in my pocket, rose to go, when Schreckermann stopped me.

"Don't go yet," he said. "There's n-no v-v-violent hurry. You c-can't get a train before nine o'clock. Have you had anything to eat?"

"No, but I can get something later," I replied.

133

"Sit down, young fellow," said Fritz, in the best of humour. "You can't work properly without food."

He waved me back to my chair, at the same time crossing the room and opening the door. I had apparently played my part rather too well. I had put Fritz in the humour to be hospitable, and I saw that it would be inadvisable to slight his friendly advances.

"Anton!" he bawled to some unseen person below. "Bring up some food and some more beer, and don't be long about it."

I was in a fever to depart, but was afraid to show my eagerness. Waiting for the food to appear, I studied my hosts narrowly. Schreckermann was obviously tired out by the events of the day. He had yawned several times since I had come into the room, and he had the air of a man who had rather be in bed. Fritz, on the other hand, was of a wakeful disposition, obviously elated and prepared to talk. Without in the least degree being drunk, he had evidently been relaxing after his strenuous labours. I thought it might be useful to encourage him to talk, particularly of recent events in Geneva.

"Perhaps, Major, you would tell me how you managed to obtain the document?" I said, as an elderly individual, wearing an apron of brown sacking, entered bearing a large jug of beer and some cold ham, sausages, and bread on a plate.

My suggestion was evidently most acceptable. Fritz seized the jug, re-filled the tankards, and poured me out a welcome drink. Then he raised his mug on high and, looking towards us, said:

"*Prosit!*"

We raised our tankards in response and drank.

Fritz stretched himself on the settee and began. He and Schreckermann, on leaving the Professor, had apparently dressed themselves in the uniform of the Genevese police. Thus attired, they had gone to the Secretariat, where they had asked for the Establishment Officer. This individual was the official in charge of the internal administration of the Secretariat, and as such would naturally be the person to be approached by the police. He was a Swiss, it appeared, and Fritz had experienced but little difficulty in persuading him that he was a member of the Genevese police, who had called with the object of obtaining clues in connection with the murder of M. Lavelle. He desired, he said, to examine the office of the murdered man. The Establishment Officer had accordingly conducted him to that room, where he had made a superficial examination. Before starting for the Secretariat, Adler had scrawled on a piece of plain quarto paper the following words: "From my examination of the letters contained in file Number 4/90347/81756, I——" He succeeded in slipping this sheet, unobserved by the Establishment Officer beneath some of the litter on Lavelle's desk, and then turned over the papers until he came to it. He had discovered it with an exclamation of surprise and interest, seized it, read it and immediately demanded to see the *dossier* in question, pointing out that the uncompleted note seemed to indicate that Lavelle had been working on this *dossier* just before his death and that it might provide a clue. The Establishment Officer had at once sent for the file, and on its arrival Fritz had succeeded in finding and extracting the document without being detected. He and Schreckermann had left the building a few minutes later and taken the road for Basle, removing their disguise at the first opportunity. It had all been perfectly simple.

I was forced to admire the cunning and audacity of a man who had committed a murder but the day before, arraying himself as a member of the police force and going to search through the effects of his victim.

Throughout the narrative I had been busily engaged on the cold ham and sausages. I loathe Leberwurst, but I felt that Karl probably had a keen appetite for it, so I worked away until I had finished the plate, endeavouring to look as though I relished the vile stuff.

Now that I had secured the document I was filled with a sense of quiet exhilaration. The journey was nearing its end. Neither Schreckermann nor Fritz had questioned my impersonation for a moment. I had only to get out of the house, find Gaston and Réhmy, and we should soon all three of us be on our way to Paris.

I suitably congratulated Fritz on his success and glanced at my watch. It was half-past eight.

"If the Herr Major will permit me," I said, "I should like to make a few arrangements for my departure," and I rose to go.

"Have you f-finished your s-supper?" asked Schreckermann.

I replied in the affirmative.

"Be off with you then," said Fritz, "and please don't murder the chauffeur on the way to the railway station."

He chuckled at his friendly little jest at my expense.

"I hope it won't be necessary," I replied, in the manner of a schoolboy squirming under the chaff of his betters.

"One moment," he added, as I turned to leave the room.

I paused, and he went again to the desk and fumbled among the papers. He returned bearing a sealed envelope.

"Here are your instructions," he said, "to be opened when you get to Hanover. Don't fail to fulfil them. You may have friends in high quarters, but you will kindly conform to your official orders."

"They will be obeyed to the letter," I said formally, and clicking my heels I turned and left the room.

I found on reaching the street that the car had disappeared, but there was a servant waiting with my suitcase. I went up to him and took it from his hands.

"I will look after that myself," I said. "You need not accompany me."

"But the Herr Major——" the man began.

"I have said I do not require your services," I interrupted angrily. "I prefer to go to the station alone," and, taking the bag from him, I hurried down the street.

Arrived at the Rathaus, I found a taxi and ordered the man to drive to the German railway station. There are two stations at Basle, one on the German railway system and the other on the Swiss, distant at opposite ends of the city and separated by the Rhine. I thought it inadvisable to go straight to the hotel, where I had arranged to meet Gaston and Réhmy. The Major, I knew, left nothing to chance, and not improbably he was having me followed, more particularly as I had refused the services of his accredited servant.

Arrived at the railway station, I dismissed the taxi and made my way to the barrier of the platform for Hanover. Then, assuming that I had given sufficient evidence of my good faith, I doubled on my tracks and came again into the street.

Outside there was not a vehicle to be had.

I decided to walk, knowing that the hotel, which, it will be remembered, was "Die Drei Königen," was not very far away.

I set off at a good pace and, crossing the bridge over the Rhine, had soon arrived at my destination.

I entered the hotel and, to my great satisfaction, saw Gaston himself, sitting within view of the reception office, busy with the evening papers. He saw me arrive and at once came eagerly to meet me.

"I've got it," I whispered.

"Splendid," he returned. "Come with me upstairs at once. We have taken a private sitting-room."

We ascended to the first floor and in another moment I was shaking hands with Réhmy. I told them rapidly of my interview with Fritz, and finally produced the document. Réhmy, who had listened with grave attention, took it from my hand, saying as he did so:

"You managed them beautifully, Preston, but I'm afraid your subsequent behaviour was a little rash. One doesn't throw an expert off the trail by just walking into a railway station and out again. Such manœuvre would be far more likely to attract suspicion than to remove it."

Then, seeing me crestfallen, he added:

"Never mind; these are merely the tricks of the trade, and I don't for a moment suppose you were being shadowed."

He turned his attention to the document, which he examined very carefully for an appreciable time, Gaston meanwhile comforting me for my lapse of discretion.

"Our friend Réhmy," he said, "would have got on to the train for Hanover and out the other side, and left the station by a secret exit. He leads me an awful life."

At this point, Réhmy, who had come to the bottom of the document, made an exclamation.

"What is it?" said Gaston.

"Do you know who these men are?" said Réhmy turning to me.

"I know something about Von Bühlen, Kaufmann, and Von Stahl," I replied, "and Lavelle informed me that the Seven Sleepers were the seven richest men in Germany, as I told you yesterday afternoon at the chalet."

"Yes," assented Réhmy, "Lavelle was right. Von Armin, Mulhausen, Herzler, Crefeldt, and Steinhart are each of them richer than even Stinnes. I wonder what it all means."

"The document appears to be some sort of undertaking between them," I suggested. "I remember Beatrice in her trance gave us the first four words."

"Which were?"

" 'We, the Seven Sleepers, convinced——,' " I repeated. "It sounds like the beginning of a legal document."

Réhmy nodded and looked again at the paper in his hand.

"The document now awaits the signature of Captain Z," I put in, "whoever he may be. Without that extra signature it is apparently quite useless and incomplete."

"Just so," said Réhmy, folding up the document and giving it back to me. "Without that signature, it is, as you say, incomplete."

He looked me straight in the eyes, and for a moment there was silence in the room. It was broken by Réhmy himself.

"I am going to tell you," he said, in the manner of one weighing his every word, "what I believe to be the real significance of this document, and what I should conceive it my duty to do if I had the opportunity. We have here a paper signed by the seven richest men in Germany. These men apparently require the signature of an eighth person (whose identity is concealed even from some of the conspirators themselves) before they will take whatever action is contemplated. This seems clear from the fact that the activities of the gang are at present wholly concentrated upon obtaining this necessary signature and that we have found no trace of any other immediate object or intention.

"I could, of course, send this document at once to Paris as evidence that, in spite of the capitulation of the German Government, conspiracy is still active among the German secret societies and that certain prominent persons are probably implicated in these movements. But this is already common knowledge at the Quai d'Orsay. What we require at this stage is *proof* —proof that will convince the world, proof that cannot be explained away or confuted. I believe that we have at last the chance to bring the matter home, and that this time the stakes are so tremendous that the whole world must hear of it and be convinced. I believe, in fact, that these men are preparing for nothing less than war."

"War!" I exclaimed.

"War," repeated Réhmy firmly. "What else can be implied by those enormous purchases of Schreckermann? I also believe, from my knowledge of the present position of parties and interests in Germany, that no further step will be taken until two essential conditions are fulfilled. Two things, in fact, are necessary."

"Which are?" I interjected.

"Money," Réhmy replied, "and a leader. The money, if my suspicions are correct, is here"—he tapped the document, which I still held in my hand, as he spoke. "The leader, I believe, is in Hanover. He is none other than Captain Z. I am convinced that we are on the trace of a gigantic conspiracy, but it is a conspiracy which does not even exist till the man in Hanover has put his name to the document we have here. That is the reason why we have hitherto failed to discover anything vital or conclusive. The whole enterprise is in suspension; and while it remains in suspension we may conjecture and suspect, but we cannot *prove*."

He paused and looked at me with the same directness as when he had started his exposition.

"It is my duty, as a servant of the French Republic, to obtain that proof," he continued. "It should be my object, if practicable, to go to Hanover, discover Captain Z, and obtain his signature. Then the document would be complete. The final proof of it would be in my possession, and I should have succeeded in unmasking the whole conspiracy. It would be a clean sweep, a great task magnificently accomplished."

He paused again, and I could see that he was much moved. His eyes were shining, and there was a look in his face as of a man dedicated to a splendid mission, but wistfully aware that it was possibly beyond his reach.

And now he was not looking at me at all. He had dropped his eyes to the table, as though fearing to let me see in them the appeal which he could not entirely suppress.

"Captain Preston," he said, "you are the only man who can deliver that paper to Captain Z and obtain his signature. I am not urging you to attempt it. The risks are too great. But, my God," he ended suddenly, "what a magnificent opportunity!"

There was another short silence in the room. Réhmy, breathing a little fast, sat motionless, his eyes on the table. I stole a look at Gaston, whose eyes were brilliant with excitement, his hands clenched, and his whole aspect tense with emotion.

"Very well," I said. "I will start for Hanover immediately."

Gaston was beside me in a moment, gripping my hand.

"You mustn't do it," he cried. "The chances are fifty to one against you. Surely, Etienne, there is some other way."

But Réhmy did not move.

"Captain Preston is right," he said.

Gaston took him by the arm and began to speak to him in a low voice and in rapid French. Perceiving that he was desirous of talking privately to Réhmy, I moved away. I had scarcely grasped as yet what my decision implied.

I went to the window and, pulling aside the curtains, looked down into the street. Two thoughts were uppermost in my mind, first Beatrice, who in an hour's time, I hoped, would be in the train on the way to Paris, and the mission which I had voluntarily undertaken and from which I could not now in honour withdraw.

I was turning away from the window, prepared to assist Réhmy to override the objections of Gaston, when I saw something in the street below that took me in three strides to Réhmy.

"You were right in blaming me just now," I cried. "I've spoiled everything by my carelessness. Fritz and Schreckermann are in the street below."

"What!" they exclaimed simultaneously.

"I saw them just now from the window. There are two or three men with them."

I went back to the window and saw that Fritz and Schreckermann were crossing the street.

"Quick," said Réhmy, "we mustn't on any account be found together. They would know at once that you were Thomas Preston. We must separate immediately."

"Wait," said Gaston to Réhmy. "They will be suspicious in any case if they find we have been using the same hotel, and once their suspicions are aroused they will soon discover the real identity of our English friend. We must throw them off the scent."

"They have entered the hotel," I announced from the window. "We must do something at once."

"There is only one way out of it," said Gaston. "You are Karl von Emmerich, you came to this hotel on your arrival in Basle. On reaching the station to depart you suddenly remembered that you had left some of your things behind. You called to pick them up, and, on your arrival, you were assaulted by us, bound hand and foot, and robbed of the document. You will tell this story to Fritz when he finds you, and Fritz will at once set his organisation in pursuit of Réhmy and myself, leaving you to go straight to Hanover unmolested."

"Then you leave the document with me," I interpolated.

"Of course," said Gaston. "We leave it with you and you can take it direct to Hanover, obtain the signature of Captain Z, and meet us there. We will lead Fritz away on a false trail, shake him off as soon as we conveniently can, and join you at Hanover."

"We must have a rendezvous at Hanover," said Réhmy. "I suggest the Kröpcke in the Theaterplatz. It's the best café in Hanover. Always meet in a busy place to avoid suspicion. Today's Wednesday. Friday any time after two in the afternoon."

Gaston had already left the room. He returned as Réhmy finished speaking, carrying a bottle and a bundle of handkerchiefs and scarves.

"Quick," he said. "We must pretend to chloroform you."

Réhmy took a scarf and tied my wrists and ankles, while Gaston poured a portion of the contents of the bottle on to a handkerchief.

"We kept little Adolf quiet with this," he chuckled.

At that moment there was a furious knocking on the door.

"That will be Fritz," whispered Gaston. "We must be quick."

I lay down on the carpet. Réhmy thrust the document into my inner coat pocket, and Gaston laid the handkerchief over my nose. A sweet sickly smell mounted to my nostrils, causing my head to swim.

"It's all right," whispered Gaston. "I've mixed it with water."

Diluted as it was, however, the chloroform was powerful enough, and I was already beginning to lose consciousness. In a mist, I saw Réhmy and Gaston rush for the door. Réhmy tore it open, and I dimly perceived Fritz and Schreckermann on the other side. Without the slightest hesitation, Gaston struck Fritz a violent blow, and in a flash he and Réhmy were in the corridor outside and running down the stairs.

The next instant Schreckermann was bending over me.

He tore the handkerchief from my face.

"W-What the devil's happened?" he cried.

I could not answer immediately. The chloroform had been almost too much for me and I lay gasping. By this time, Fritz had risen and charged into the room like an infuriated bull, blood dripping from his nose.

"Water," he barked to Schreckermann, who disappeared on the word, returning a moment later with a jug. Fritz deluged my head with its icy contents, and the treatment had the desired effect. My brain cleared, and I gasped in German.

"Quick, Major! After those two. They've taken the document."

With an oath, Fritz sprang to his feet.

"You blundering jackass," he roared. "What in heaven's name have you done now?"

"I couldn't help it," I replied in a weak voice, raising myself on my elbow. "I went straight to the station this evening after I left you, but remembered at the last moment that I had left some luggage here."

"Luggage!" roared Fritz. "What on earth were you doing with luggage in this hotel?"

"I took a room here on my arrival in Basle. I came along to pick it up and was suddenly assaulted by those two men. They doped me just before you arrived. You'll catch them if you're quick. I can't come with you, I'm finished for the moment," and I sank back with a groan.

"H-He's right," said Schreckermann, who had been untying my bonds. "Quick, Major, let's follow them. We must leave Von Emmerich."

Fritz glared at me fiercely, and then turned and followed Schreckermann, who was already halfway out of the room.

"You'll hear of this from the Professor," he flung back at me over his shoulder, and on that he disappeared through the door.

CHAPTER XVI

I JOIN A DISTINGUISHED REGIMENT

It was some time before I recovered from the effects of the chloroform, despite the cold-water treatment applied by Fritz.

Presently I rose and searched the apartment for towels, in order to dry my dripping head. This was soon accomplished, but I found my collar and tie thoroughly soaked with water, and the mirror showed me that I presented a very disreputable appearance. As I had my suitcase with me, however, these defects were soon remedied, and I next gathered up the various belongings of my two friends and packed them into their respective suitcases.

I descended, ordered the bill, and asked for a railway time-table, intending to get to Hanover without delay. From the time-table, it appeared that the next train did not leave till 11.35 p.m., and it was an express to Frankfurt. Looking at my watch, I discovered that it was twenty-five past nine. I had accordingly some two hours to wait.

My first step was to settle with the proprietor. I explained to him that the two gentlemen whose account I was paying had already left to catch the Paris train, and had asked me to settle everything for them. I then found the hotel porter, ordered him to take my bag to the station, to purchase me a first-class ticket to Hanover, with sleeping accommodation if available, and to meet me at the train. I also told him to register the baggage of Réhmy and de Blanchegarde to Hanover to await arrival.

These details settled, I left the hotel on foot, thinking it unwise to remain there any longer than was necessary. I crossed the new Rhein-Brücke and took refuge in a small Bierhalle, in the Clara Platz, opposite the Church of St. Clara, and sat where I could command a view of the street, without myself being easily visible.

Ordering a glass of brandy, I filled my pipe and started to think things out. I had two things to fear, first that Gaston and Réhmy had been unable to lure Fritz and Schreckermann in pursuit of them and that my disgruntled relatives would shortly return, in which case my interview with them would be of a most unpleasant nature, and secondly that the formidable

Professor had discovered the trick which we had played upon him in the Villa Mortmain and might arrive at any moment.

I had noticed, on consulting the time-table, that there was a train leaving the Swiss railway station on the other side of the town at 9.16 p.m. for Boulogne and Paris, and it struck me that it was just possible that my French friends might have taken that, in order to lead Fritz and Schreckermann well away from my vicinity.

As for the Professor, I could only await events. I did not see that there were any possible precautions I could take, and I fervently hoped that it would prove impossible for him, even if he discovered his blunder, to reach Basle before the following morning at the earliest, by which time I should be well on my way to Hanover. Of course the whole business was desperately risky. If the Professor discovered that he had killed Von Emmerich instead of myself, and further that I had started for Hanover, there was nothing to prevent him warning whatever organisation existed in that city to be ready for me as an impostor. In that case I should be walking straight into a trap.

The sudden decision to go to Hanover had naturally upset our previous plans, and the fact that we had had no time before the unexpected arrival of Fritz to make any fresh arrangements, added to my difficulties.

In one sense, however, my task was simple. There could be no going back; the only thing for me to do was to go forward and trust to events. So far, indeed, despite several serious relapses, fortune had favoured me. I could only hope that my luck would hold.

Half an hour was consumed in these reflections, at the end of which time I thought I had best be leaving for the station. Before moving I examined the street attentively. For some five minutes I saw nothing to cause me any anxiety. A number of pedestrians passed of whom I took no particular note. I could see those on the other side of the road more clearly than those nearest me, owing to a lamp-post which stood opposite the window, shedding a circle of light on the pavement, into which each passer-by stepped in his passage.

I watched this light for some moments, and presently noticed that a man whom I had just seen go past the lamp from right to left was now going past it from left to right. As I watched him, he turned again, and once more began to walk down the street. I caught sight of his face as he entered the circle of the lamplight. It was vaguely familiar, but for the moment I could not place it. Then I remembered. I had seen him earlier in the evening. He was the man who had handed me my suitcase when I had left Number 33, Martinsgasse. I watched him for some moments, and saw that he was indeed, as I had thought, patrolling the opposite side of the pavement, keeping an eye on the Bierhalle. He had presumably kept me under observation the whole time and had followed me thither from the hotel.

Satisfied with my observations, I left the window, and debated what I should do.

Finally, I summoned a waiter and asked for a map of Basle. When this was brought to me I studied it closely. I then requested the same waiter to order me a cab, after which I walked to the door of the Bierhalle and stood awhile on the threshold, in full view of anyone watching from the street, while I waited for the cab to arrive.

When it drove up, I told the man to drive me to the Matthaus Kirche, which I had seen on the plan to be not far from the Badischer Bahnhof, the station for Hanover. The cab was a ramshackle affair with a great hood covering the passengers' seats, and shaped somewhat like the hood of a perambulator. It was quite possible to speak to the driver while the vehicle was in motion. When we had gone some distance, therefore, I leaned forward and tapped him between the shoulder blades, at the same time bidding him to continue to drive on while he listened to what I said.

I offered him twenty-five francs to go to the Matthaus Kirche, where he was to slow down, or even stop for a moment, after which he was to drive back by a roundabout way, over the Johanniter Brücke, to the Bierhalle. This he promised to do, and I passed him up the money.

I then watched my opportunity to leave the cab. It was not long in coming. We passed through a dark and narrow thoroughfare, and, in turning a corner, the cab slowed down. I instantly opened the door and jumped from the cab, bolting between two dark houses into a little alley, which fortunately opened in front of me. There I waited and looked out.

A moment later I saw the fellow who had been watching the Bierhalle go past. He was on a bicycle and was following the cab at a leisurely pace. I wished him joy of his evening ride, which promised to be long and tedious, and, slipping out of the alley, made off in the opposite direction.

After one or two enquiries, I found my way to the Badischer Bahnhof, where I went to ground in the restaurant. There I ordered a light meal, for, despite the rude plenty of my Uncle Fritz's table, I was still hungry. The station restaurant was an admirable place. It had many doors, some leading to the outside world, some to the platforms, and others again to shaving saloons and bathrooms.

I finished my meal at ten minutes past eleven, and, after paying for it, slipped unostentatiously through one of the many doors, arriving eventually, via the bathrooms, on the platform for Hanover. There I found the porter from the hotel with my luggage and my ticket. He had secured me sleeping accommodation, and a moment later I was installed in a first-class sleeping compartment, with the door locked.

Ten minutes afterwards the train was under way. I was due at Frankfurt at 6.40 the following morning, and I turned in almost immediately and slept fairly soundly.

At Frankfurt next morning, having a few minutes to wait, I went to the buffet and ordered some coffee. It was the first time I had entered Germany since the War, and I gazed about me with interest. I saw little, however, which called for remark. There were the same square-headed men and ill-dressed women, but I noticed that an air of general shabbiness pervaded everything. There was a noticeable difference between the first-class passengers and the second- and third-class, the first category being well, if somewhat vulgarly, turned out, whilst the others bore obvious marks of poverty, and, indeed, when I reflected that the collapse of the mark had inevitably entailed the ruin of almost all the middle classes, which, perhaps more than in any other country, form the backbone of Germany, the condition of the persons whom I saw was easily explained.

I must own that when I reached Frankfurt, I had no little apprehension that I might be detained. It was almost certain that by this time the Professor was in possession of the facts, unless by some happy chance things had gone better than we had dared to hope, and once his suspicions were aroused, I was in a far worse case than when I had been in Switzerland. I was now in Germany, where the Professor could presumably call in the assistance of the authorities if he needed their collaboration. He would in any case be in a much stronger position to deal with me on German soil. As an Englishman with stolen papers and masquerading as a German subject, my position was precarious enough quite apart from any support he might be able to command on behalf of the Seven Sleepers.

I accordingly avoided the general waiting-room and took shelter behind a little newspaper kiosk on the platform, where I was screened from possible observation or remark. Nothing untoward occurred, however, and I boarded the train for Hanover without being in any way molested.

I was fortunate in having a compartment to myself, and now that I had been somewhat refreshed by some much-needed sleep I emptied the pockets of the suit I was wearing and examined the contents with interest.

In addition to the pocket-book which I had already investigated, there was the passport of Karl von Emmerich, by means of which I had entered Germany, and several letters. It occurred to me that if I were to impersonate Karl successfully, it was essential that I should find out as much as possible of his occupation and general habits. The servant at Number 33, Martinsgasse had addressed me as "Herr Lieutenant," I remembered, and Karl had therefore evidently been in the German Army. On closer examination of his papers, I discovered his regiment. He had, I found, been an officer in the third regiment of foot guards, a famous corps which had fought with great distinction throughout the War, though they had more than met their match in the Coldstream at Landrecies during the retreat. Apart from that, however, and the fact that he appeared to belong to an East Prussian family, having been born at Heiligenbeil, I could learn nothing.

I turned to the letters. The first one I opened was a bill, apparently from a tailor, for a new uniform, from which I judged that Von Emmerich was still on the active list, though, so far as I was aware, the Prussian guard had been disbanded or completely transformed shortly after the armistice.

The second was from his mother and contained various domestic news, most of which was unintelligible to me. The conclusion of it, however, was significant. It ran as follows.

"You will, I hope, my dearest Karl, be careful to bear yourself well in your new and difficult task. Almighty God has graciously preserved you throughout the terrible War. He will, I know, support and strengthen you in your present work. Remember, dearest boy, that you come of a family which has had the honour to serve the Kings of Prussia since the days of the Great Frederick, and though, alas, an Emperor no longer rules in Berlin, you must never be false to the great and honourable traditions of your house. Do your duty bravely, no matter down what paths it may lead you. In doing so, you will prove a valiant son of Germany and make proud the heart of your old and loving,

"Mother."

There was something very moving in this appeal. Karl was obviously a cherished son, and I found myself hoping that his mother would never learn the facts of his unhappy death.

The third letter was the inevitable billet-doux, from some lady of Karl's acquaintance in Berlin, imploring him not to lose a moment in coming to see his beloved Freda on his arrival in that city.

I spent some little time in assimilating these few facts. The part I had to play would obviously be much more difficult than hitherto. Up to the present I had only had to impersonate my double for a short period and with a well-defined object. Now, however, I had been suddenly called upon to work more or less in the dark. I was to deliver a letter to a Captain Z, whoever he might be, obviously a person of great importance, and one of whom even the redoubtable Fritz stood in awe. I was ignorant alike of his identity and of his precise whereabouts. I could therefore form no adequate idea of the length of time during which I should be compelled to continue my impersonation. Gaston and Réhmy, travelling roundabout as they were, could not be expected to arrive in Hanover until the following day at the earliest.

146

Finally, I opened the sealed envelope given to me by Fritz the previous evening, containing the instructions as to my movements on arrival at Hanover. These were somewhat elaborate.

My first action was to telephone immediately to Number 5061 Linden. On obtaining that number, I was to ask for Heir Hüber, and inform him that I had arrived safely with the parcel of flour. I was then to leave the station, and, taking the first turning to the right, proceed to a small Weinstube, "Das goldene Herz," which I was to enter. I was to seat myself at the fourth table from the door on the left-hand side, and call for half a litre of Rhine wine and two glasses, after which I was to wait there until a man wearing a mouse-headed tie-pin entered and sat down at the table. I was at once to offer him a glass of wine, saying as I did so, "Do you prefer wine or beer?" To this he would reply, "Wine that maketh glad the heart of man." All further necessary instructions would be given to me by him. "On no account," the letter ended, "are you to hand the document to anyone except personally to Captain Z." At the foot of the paper was written in red ink: "Destroy immediately after reading."

I read the instructions through two or three times, until I was sure of them. I then tore up the paper into small pieces and scattered them from my window.

The remainder of my journey was uneventful enough. The train sped out of Saxony into Hanover, through Cassel, near which, I remembered, Napoleon III. had been imprisoned, and Göttingen, with its university. For the most part we ran through rolling country, well cultivated and populous, with little brick villages and many farmsteads scattered over it. It was a day of drifting cloud, and a high wind was blowing.

I lunched in the Speisewagen. Food on railway journeys is never good, but that must have been quite the worst meal I have ever eaten.

Punctually at 2.02 p.m. I stepped on to the platform at Hanover station. I went at once to a telephone box, and after some time got through to Number 5061 Linden, where I enquired for Herr Hüber. Presently I was answered by a gruff male voice, asking what I wanted. The manner of the man was distinctly unamiable, and I suspected that my message had interrupted him in the digestion of his lunch.

"Is that Herr Hüber?" I enquired.

"Yes," came down the wire. "And who may you be?"

"I'm sorry to disturb you," I said, "but I have only just arrived. I am bringing you the parcel of flour."

At this, there was an appreciable change of tone.

"I beg your pardon, Herr Lieutenant," he said. "We were not expecting you so soon. We had received word from Major Adler that there were difficulties."

"They have been overcome," I said coldly.

"My congratulations," he replied. "We will lose no time in meeting you."

I rang off and left the station.

Hanover proved a larger and far pleasanter town than I had anticipated, though I could see but little of it in my brief walk from the station to "Das goldene Herz."

I had some little difficulty in finding the place, for it was hidden away in a small angle of the street. On the outside it was no more than a door from which a flight of steps led to an underground cellar. Down these I walked, and, pushing open a pair of green baize doors, found myself in a long, low stone room, much overheated. Little tables were arranged all round the walls, beside which were stools and barrels.

I seated myself at the fourth table on the left-hand side, and, summoning a waiter, asked him to bring me half a litre of the best Rhine wine, two glasses, and a newspaper.

He returned with the wine and "Das Berliner Tageblatt" which I read while awaiting the arrival of the man with the mouse-headed tie-pin.

The articles in the newspaper were in a vein that was now familiar. Germany must submit to her late enemies with a good grace, trust to their generosity, and resume her place the better for her chastening among the nations of Europe. I could not help reading these inspired declarations in the light of Réhmy's recent diagnosis of the general situation and of the adventure to which I was committed. They now seemed to me deliberately intended to mislead.

Some quarter of an hour passed, during which several persons entered the Weinstube. None of them corresponded to the description which had been given me in my letter of instructions, and I continued to sip my wine and read my paper with half an eye on the door.

Presently it opened to admit a short, dark man of about thirty-five, with a deep scar on his forehead, and an empty left sleeve. He was wearing the ribbon of the Iron Cross in his buttonhole. His clothes were neat but somewhat shabby. He glanced round the Weinstube, and his eye lighted on me. He moved straight to my table, his hand to his tie as he walked, and I noticed that the knot was transfixed by a pin bearing a mouse as its head.

As he came to my table, I rose and pointed to the chair.

"Sit down," I said. "Do you prefer wine or beer?"

"Wine," he answered immediately, "that maketh glad the heart of man."

I poured him out a glass of wine and sat waiting. He gave me a sharp penetrating glance and then raised his glass.

"Your health," he said, and, in a lower tone, "My congratulations to Section Q."

148

I bowed.

"Herr von Emmerich?" he continued, with an interrogatory glance.

"At your service," I replied. "And you?"

"Hauptmann von Salsnig.

"We did not expect you so soon," he continued. "Major Adler telegraphed to us that there were difficulties."

"There usually are," I said shortly. "But we have dealt with them."

"You arrive just at the right moment," he observed. "Everything here is ready. Hüber has made all the necessary arrangements, and we can arrange a meeting for you this evening. You know," he added, "it has been touch and go with us here. We had the greatest difficulty in persuading *him* to see anyone."

"Persuading whom?" I asked.

He looked at me in surprise, and I realised that I had blundered.

"Captain Z, of course," he replied. "It was only when we assured him that you were bringing him all the necessary guarantees that he consented to receive you. It's lucky your father was an old friend of the family."

This was news to me.

"Yes," I said.

"You are some sort of connection, aren't you?" he continued.

"Distant, distant," I replied, since he obviously expected me to say something.

"Well, Lieutenant von Emmerich, the great point is that we have induced him to see you. 'I will trust a von Emmerich,' he told Hüber. 'I know the family.'"

I endeavoured to seem suitably gratified.

"I am glad that we have inspired such confidence," I said.

"But you will have to go very carefully," he said. "I warn you it's far from plain sailing as yet. He has been very difficult to approach, very difficult. More than once Hüber has been almost driven to despair."

"You may rely on me, Herr Hauptmann," I replied gravely.

"I am sure of it," he said. "Remember that the document is our strongest card. It goes further than we ever dared to hope."

"It does indeed," I replied, draining my glass.

Von Salsnig rose to his feet. "I presume you will come at once with me to Hüber's? Should Captain Z be unable to see you tonight, you will be able to have your interview with him first thing tomorrow morning for a certainty."

"I am ready," I answered, and, picking up my bag, I followed him from the Weinstube.

Outside there was a car, into which we climbed, my companion taking the wheel. He chatted pleasantly during the drive, which occupied some twenty minutes. We passed through the more populous portions of the town, my companion indicating various objects of interest including the old Aegidien Kirche. A tablet on the outer wall records the end of seven men wretchedly done to death.

"*Absit omen*," said Von Salsnig, as we passed it by.

Reaching the suburb of Linden we drew up eventually in front of a large house standing in its own grounds.

We were shown into a room on the ground floor, half smoking-room, half study. There were a good many books in it and the furniture was massive and heavy, in the best German style, the walls being adorned with antlers and other trophies of the chase.

A fat man, arrayed in a purple silk dressing-gown and an enormous pair of fur slippers, was seated at a desk. He rose as we entered, and Von Salsnig presented me in the formal German fashion to Herr Hüber.

"Lieutenant von Emmerich, I am delighted to make your acquaintance," said Hüber. "Pray sit down. I trust you have had a pleasant journey."

"Perfectly," I answered.

We chatted for a few moments on unimportant subjects, Herr Hüber yawning frequently and excusing himself by saying that my arrival had disturbed him in his siesta.

"I am afraid I was a little short on the telephone," he continued apologetically. "But you took me entirely by surprise."

I murmured that it was of no consequence. I noted with interest the efforts made both by Hüber and Von Salsnig to be scrupulously polite to a humble lieutenant of the third regiment of foot guards. Quite obviously courtesy was not with either of them a gift of Nature. It merely meant that I was a necessary link in the chain they were forging. For some reason I was a man who would be agreeable to Captain Z and who would be trusted by that mysterious individual for the sake of his family and traditions. And yet I was Karl von Emmerich, a man whom I knew only as a bully and a murderer. It was a puzzle which I could not read, the only ray of light being that pathetic letter from his mother, which at least showed me that somewhere at the heart of this conspiracy there was a stern spirit of devotion, antique, perhaps misguided, but essentially fine in its limited way, and suggesting that the man I was to see might be of a different quality from the others whom I had so far encountered.

A telephone bell rang somewhere in the house.

"Excuse me," said Herr Hüber. "I expect it is the message for which we are waiting."

He got up from his chair and padded across the room.

Von Salsnig and I remained silent, seated opposite each other by the stove. Now that the moment was almost come, I felt a tightening round my

150

heart. I was about to enter the presence of an unknown individual, obviously a man of great importance and of an uncertain temper, an old friend who, for all I knew, had dandled the infant Von Emmerich on his knee. It was a position full of possibilities, and I wished my French friends were not so far away.

The door opened and Hüber returned.

"He desires you to dine with him this evening," he said.

I bowed slightly.

Hüber came up to me and put a podgy hand on my shoulder.

"We are on the threshold of great events," he said. "We have done our part. The rest now lies with you. Be open with him and all may yet be well."

CHAPTER XVII

I DINE WITH A GREAT MAN

We carried on a desultory conversation for some minutes, Hüber continuing to yawn repeatedly. At last he rose.

"If you will excuse me," he said, "I will go and finish my interrupted siesta. The advice of my doctor is both excellent and expensive, and I endeavour to follow it to the best of my ability."

He quitted the room, leaving me with Von Salsnig, who suggested that, as there was nothing for me to do until I was to fulfil my dinner engagement with Captain Z, he should first show me my room, and afterwards, as it was not yet three o'clock, take me to see something of the city of Hanover.

I acquiesced, for I did not wish to arouse any suspicions, though I should have much preferred to remain quietly by myself and collect my wits for the forthcoming dinner-party.

I was taken to a rather over-furnished bedroom on the next floor. I decided, as I unpacked, that the most significant element in the situation was the fact that my unknown host was apparently ignorant, to a degree which I could not determine, of the plans of the conspirators, and that they evidently considered that my influence with him largely depended on the circumstance that he knew my family. I was expected to create a good impression and to complete their schemes by obtaining his signature of the document, a result which was of vital importance to them, but which would not be easy to secure.

Lying on the bed was a uniform of some kind, which on further examination proved to be the mess kit of an officer in the third regiment of foot guards. In the buttonhole was the ribbon of the Iron Cross, second class. As I was looking at it, Von Salsnig entered, and enquired whether I was ready to accompany him. Glancing at the uniform, he said:

"You see, we have had some of your kit sent from Leipzig. We thought it best that you should wear uniform tonight. It will make a good impression."

"I am quite willing to do so," I replied doubtfully, "if you think it will do any good."

"It can do no harm," he rejoined.

We walked downstairs together and out into the street. On my companion's suggestion, we visited the Schloss Herrenhausen, the building from which George, Elector of Hanover, had set out to become King of England. It is a miniature Versailles, the gardens complete with statues, orangery, and an open-air theatre.

Now that our official business was concluded, Von Salsnig proved himself to be an interesting and companionable person. He talked first of the Great War in which he had served as an artillery officer, and I found myself engaged on a discussion of army gunnery which threatened to become technical. Fortunately, I remembered in time that I was supposed to have served in the foot guards, and would therefore not be expected to know much about the sister arm.

As we wandered through the gardens and examined the great tropical plants in the glass houses, I found it more and more difficult to play my part with ease. I was taken for granted, which, while it lessened the risk of discovery, made it far more difficult for me to obtain an adequate grasp of the approaching situation. I was naturally assumed to be familiar with the whole scheme, and I could not therefore make the slightest attempt to gain further information in the course of casual conversation. Indeed, I soon found that my companion maintained a marked reserve on the subject, and I did not dare to press him. I consequently returned from our walk about six with no very clear idea of what was in store for me.

At my suggestion, we stopped at a little Weinstube in the Georgstrasse, the main thoroughfare of the town, for a glass of lager beer, but we did not stay long, and about half-past six I was back in my room changing into the uniform of my late lamented twin.

At ten minutes to seven Von Salsnig knocked heavily on my door and announced that we should be going.

I picked up Von Emmerich's cap and heavy grey overcoat, lined with scarlet silk, which was, I noticed, similar to those worn by our own foot guards.

As I passed through the hall, the portly Hüber, who had by now discarded his purple dressing-gown for a check suit of Teutonic pattern and shade, came forward.

"My best wishes go with you, Herr Lieutenant," he said. "If all goes well, the future of the Fatherland is assured."

I suddenly realised that the man was deeply in earnest and that these were not merely conventional words to speed the parting guest.

His little eyes, set like currants in his fat face, blazed with enthusiasm, and it was brought home to me that the old German spirit, which had driven the grey-clad masses through Belgium to Verdun, still survived in some of the men who had fostered it.

Outside, a taxi was waiting, and a moment later I was seated beside Von Salsnig, bound for an unknown destination. We drove for about twenty minutes past the railway station to the Eilenriede, a kind of park. We pulled up in front of what appeared to be a moderate-sized villa of two stories, compact, plain, and grey-plastered, with a small flight of steps leading up to the front door.

"Good luck," said Von Salsnig, as I got out of the car and approached the steps. "You will report to us immediately the result of your interview."

I rang the front door bell. It was answered by a maidservant, who relieved me of my overcoat and cap.

She showed me into a small room opening from the hall, saying that she would inform a certain Herr Kenrich that I had arrived.

I looked eagerly about me. The room was evidently an office, for it contained the usual uncomfortable office furniture, including a safe in one corner, and two desks, one a massive roll-top affair, and the other, at some distance from it, of less elaborate construction. Obviously, I was now in the working quarters of Captain Z and his secretary. Over the larger desk hung a big, signed portrait of the ex-Kaiser, in field-grey uniform, his head surmounted by the silver eagle. I gazed with interest at the portrait of the unheroic madman who had brought his proud Empire lower than the dust, and had then deserted it, shamefully surviving the sole occasion where he might have perished with honour.

My reflections were interrupted by the entry of a neat blond-haired man in plain clothes, whom I supposed to be Herr Kenrich. I judged him to be in the neighbourhood of forty. His hair was greying a little at the sides, but his moustache, which was in the imperial style, was as yet untouched by time.

He greeted me with a quiet cordiality, addressing me by my Christian name, and congratulating me on my opportune arrival.

"We were unable to persuade the chief to wait for you in Switzerland," he said. "Your organisation has taken longer than it promised."

"There were unexpected difficulties," I began.

He held up his hand.

"Quite so. I understand, and I may tell you that personally I have every confidence in Professor Kreutzemark."

I hastened to agree.

"Make no reference to any difficulties," he continued. "He dislikes excuses, and is quick to ascribe them to inefficiency."

I bowed in silence.

"You will dine with him alone," said Kenrich. "He desires the interview to be quite private."

At that moment an electric bell rang sharply in the room. Herr Kenrich rose.

"Come," he said. "He is ready for you.

"Remember," he added, as we left the room, "he retires punctually at ten. At his age one has naturally to be careful, though he has an iron constitution."

We walked down the passage, and Kenrich threw open a door at the further end. He motioned me to advance, and as I passed through he announced my name in formal tones. I took two or three steps into the room and halted abruptly.

Standing on the hearthrug, regarding me closely, was one whose face was known from one end of Europe to the other.

It was Field-Marshal von Ludenburg!

I had the sense to come stiffly to attention, and click my heels. But my brain was in a whirl. The development was so totally unexpected. I had realised, of course, that I was to meet a person of some importance, but it had never occurred to me that he would be no other than the man who had succeeded Von Falkenhayn in the direction of the German armies, and to whose tenacity and strength the stubborn defence put up by Germany in the latter half of the War was mainly due; the man who had been the subject of an almost pagan idolatry, when the people of Berlin had driven great iron nails into his wooden statue.

I had recognised him immediately. He stood with his legs apart on the hearth-rug, a colossal figure (seventy-six years of age, as I was afterwards to learn). His huge square head, with its short grey hair cut *en brosse*, was directly facing me. Beneath a broad forehead, curiously unwrinkled by time, two fierce and fearless eyes peered out, puckered at the corners, and with deep pouches beneath them. From the nostrils of the firm nose, large but not too large in proportion to the rest of the face, two deep lines ran to the mouth, hidden by the great moustache, grizzled, turning up at each end and protruding appreciably beyond each cheek. His frame was in the same proportions as his face, rugged and immensely strong, and the great head was supported upon it by a short thick neck, bulging slightly where it was confined by a stiff linen collar. He was in everyday clothes, his left hand in the side pocket of his coat.

There was a moment's silence while I stood fronting him. Then he took a step forward and held out his right hand.

"I am glad to meet you, Von Emmerich," he said, in a curiously toneless voice. "You are extremely like your father."

I relaxed my attitude and bowed stiffly as I took his hand.

"I am deeply honoured," I began, but he cut me short.

"Compliments are unnecessary between old friends," he said. "Your father and I were comrades in arms as far back as '70. His death was a great sorrow to me. But he died as I once hoped to die, fighting for Germany."

A pair of sliding doors rolled back as he spoke and beyond them I saw a dark dining-room, and dinner laid for two on an oak table, illumined by four wax candles.

"Come," he said. "Dinner is ready."

As we moved to the dining-room, he shot a sharp glance at me.

"You are in uniform," he remarked. "Why is that?"

I paused for a moment before answering, and then replied boldly:

"I had hoped, sir, that this would not be the last time I should wear it."

He looked at me sharply again for a moment, and my reply seemed to satisfy him. Without further word, we entered the room and took our places.

The meal was a very simple one, some boiled fish, followed by veal and a plain pudding. For drink there was some light Rhine wine, and I noted that my host drank very sparingly.

As I picked up my napkin, he enquired after my mother.

I hastened to assure him that she was well, and began on the fish.

I was bewildered, but not frightened. Though I had only been in the room a few moments, I already felt the force of a great personality, partly as the result of its direct influence upon myself at that moment, and partly the result of all I had heard and read of his character and career. This was the man who had been the idol of the German people throughout the War, from the moment of his great victory at Tannenberg till the last bitter days when defeat and ruin had fallen upon his nation. I recalled too that, while all the other generals, and even the Supreme War Lord himself, had abandoned their posts in the hour of defeat, he alone had stood faithful to his country and had applied himself to the thankless task of demobilising the broken and despairing German armies.

"Now," he said, looking me straight in the face across the table, "tell me why you have come."

I passed my tongue once or twice across my lips, and, taking hold of all my courage, I began to speak. Although I had been quite unprepared for meeting this man, I had realised that whoever was to receive the document which I bore might quite possibly question me as to the undertaking. I had accordingly more or less made up my mind what to say.

I began with a few general statements on the deplorable condition of Germany after the War. Our country, I said, was on the verge of ruin. We were defenceless and broken. But there were still many thousands who hoped, apparently in vain, for better things, for the dawn of a brighter day, for the restoration of the German nation.

He listened to my platitudes in silence, and, so far as I could see, unmoved, but when I said that there was still youth in Germany in whom there yet lived the will and courage to serve their country to the death, his expression changed.

"You do well to speak of youth," he said. "By youth we may eventually be saved, if only it will be true to itself. But how have the young men of Germany spent their lives since 1918? They have wasted themselves in faction. They have been false to the dynasty and to the traditions of their fathers. We were defeated in war, but we might yet have remained loyal in peace and endeavoured to build again on the old foundations. Have the young men of Germany remained steadfast? On the contrary, they rejoiced in the overthrow of sound government, and now, when it is too late, they make cowardly and ineffectual protests by feeble rioting and the vile assassination of their leaders."

He paused, and there was a look of pain in his eyes. I saw his left hand clench on the tablecloth. In another man the somewhat formal periods in which he expressed himself might have seemed pompous, or at least exaggerated, but they fitted marvellously with his massive figure and the tremendous energy which informed his whole demeanour.

"What would you have had us do, sir?" I said, partly to break the silence that had fallen between us, which seemed unnatural to the part I was playing, and partly from an irresistible desire to see into the mind of this prodigious man.

"I would have had you keep the faith to which you were pledged," he replied. "There was but one way for our defeated country to recover her place among the nations. Had she remained true to her ancient ideals and been content to wait in confidence for the day of justice and redress, she might have been even at this moment a power in the councils of Europe. The virtues that made us great were loyalty, discipline, devotion to authority and, above all, courage. All these you have abandoned. You have been faithless to the government which you yourselves appointed; you have preferred licence to discipline; you have resisted authority; you have not even had the courage to stand by the men who were doing their utmost in your behalf. You have been false not only to your Emperor and to the sacred traditions of the Fatherland, you have been equally false to your republican masters, lacking the faith and courage to stand by them in their difficulties. There is no health in you."

"Mistakes," I pleaded, "are easily made in the bitterness of defeat."

There was no relenting at this, but, if anything, an added severity.

"You should have been prepared to face the bitterness of defeat. It is the supreme test. What do you think it cost me, who from early manhood to old age had seen our splendid armies formed and trained, to stand beside them when the Armistice was signed and to assist in their complete destruction under the control and direction of our enemies? I wonder if any man has ever been called upon to know the bitterness of defeat in such full measure? But I can tell you this, Von Emmerich, that, if your father had lived to see that day, he would have stood by my side when I signed the orders to demobilise, as, fifty years ago, he rode by my side into the conquered city of Paris."

He paused again, and I saw my opportunity.

"There is still a way, sir," I said, speaking swiftly. "And there are thousands of us who are ready to take it. But we can do nothing without a leader. A leader!" I cried. "Give us a leader, and the things of which you speak shall cease. We are organised and waiting."

"Organised," he broke in. "Murder clubs! Political caucuses! Chattering doctrinaires! It is an anarchy that you have organised. And there is not one among you who can remember his manhood."

"Sir," I said, deeply moved, so that I lost all sense of the part I was playing, and realised only the agony of a great man faced with the ruin of his country. "Sir, I think you do us an injustice. Find us a leader, and you will see that the old virtues can be restored. We are ready to fight and to spend ourselves in the cause of the Fatherland, but we cannot move hand or foot without a leader."

I looked him full in the eyes, and he stared back at me. His face was hard set, but I saw that I had moved him. I leant forward across the table.

"Sir," I said. "There is no need for further words. You are our leader, and you know it."

His face did not move, only his eyes, I thought, lit for a moment with some hidden fire. Then they dulled again, and he bent down towards his plate.

"Fine words," he said, "fine words, Von Emmerich. They do you credit, my lad, but how will you find again the power which you have destroyed? If I consented to be your leader and if, as you say, there are thousands of you who are ready to respond, to what should I be leading you? Can you fight without arms, without money, without food? And where are you to get these things? Had this country faced defeat with the same high courage with which it faced war, it might have been possible. As it is, we have nothing to build upon, nothing but good will, and you cannot drive the French from the Ruhr or the English from Cologne by singing 'Deutschland über alles'!"

158

"I have come to you tonight, sir," I rejoined, "to show you that we have at last secured the means to victory. I have here a document which I am charged to deliver to you and which, when you have read it, will, I feel sure, remove your doubts."

He stretched out his hand across the table.

I unbuttoned my jacket, pulled out the document from my pocket and handed it to him.

He looked at it closely for a moment.

"It is in cipher," he said at last.

"Yes," I replied, "but doubtless your secretary will decode it. Have you observed the signatures?"

He looked again, and there was a long silence. Then he raised his head.

"You give me your word as a gentleman of Prussia," he said, "that this paper has been signed by the actual men whose names appear at the foot of it?"

"Most assuredly I do," I answered.

He rose from the table and pressed a bell.

It was answered by Kenrich, who was evidently his confidential secretary.

"Kindly decipher this," said Ludenburg, "immediately, and bring it back to me here."

Kenrich bowed. As he was turning to leave, Ludenburg looked at me.

"Is there a code word?" he asked.

"Ephesus," I replied.

He glanced at Kenrich, who nodded, and left the room.

While Kenrich was busy deciphering the document, Ludenburg changed the subject of our conversation from my mission and it took a more general tone. He asked me where I had won my Iron Cross, and I was hard put to it to find a reply, but I eventually told him I had gained it in the attack on Villers-Brettoneux in 1918.

"Ah," said Ludenburg, "that was the end. Had we captured Villers-Brettoneux we should have won the War."

He asked what was the condition of the troops at that time, and I told him that we had been extremely exhausted, as by then we had advanced more than fifty kilometres, driving the enemy before us.

"Exhausted, yes," he mused. "We asked too much of you. Our hopes in those great days soared too high. A splendid goal was before us. We ought to have shouted in the ear of every single man, 'Push on to Amiens, put in your last ounce. Amiens means decisive victory.' But they could not do it. It was more than human endurance could bear.

"What were your losses?" he added, after a pause.

I had not the faintest idea, but I hazarded:

"Some forty per cent, sir, by the time we had passed Albert."

He nodded musingly.

"It was too great a task," he said. "You did all that men could do and even more."

There was silence after this, and I continued my dinner. A reckless daring had taken possession of me. I had forgotten my part entirely. My mind was filled with the spectacle of this man, a veritable reincarnation of the heroes of Valhalla. Implacable and deadly foe though he had been, the majesty of his nature, in the days of humiliation through which he was now passing, triumphed over and outshone his surroundings. His was a spirit strong enough to retain its courage to the end, and as I sat there watching the great figure, grey-haired, his last years embittered by the utter collapse of every standard which had guided his long life, with everything by which he had set store in ruins about him, I glowed with admiration to perceive that his indomitable will was still master.

Our conversation veered again presently to lighter subjects, and Ludenburg spoke of the old days with my father, duck shooting in East Prussia in the marshes of Posen.

I found he was a keen sportsman and had all his life taken every opportunity to shoot. He talked of old forgotten hunts and battues, in which he had hunted the wild boar and the fallow deer at Blankenburg in the Harz Mountains and at Mosukau. He was in the midst of a story about duck flighting on the Masurian Lakes, in which my father had apparently played a part, when Kenrich, his secretary, returned.

His face was very grave.

"The paper you require, sir," he said, placing the document, together with the transcription of its meaning, on the table beside Ludenburg.

Ludenburg picked up the deciphered message and read it slowly through.

I watched him narrowly, striving hard to keep all expression out of my countenance. I did not know whether I was expected to be aware of the contents of the document or not, and it was obviously my safest plan to adopt the purely official attitude of his secretary.

Presently he rose from the table and paced the room two or three times, the copy of the decoded message gripped in his right hand.

"Do you know what is in this message?" he said suddenly, turning and fixing me with a steady gaze.

I did not know what to answer, but I felt I must not show any hesitation.

"Not its exact terms, sir," I said, "only its general bearing. I was not present when it was drafted."

He leant across the table and handed the transcript to me.

"Read," he said.

And this is what I read. I reproduce it in German and English:

Wir die Siebenschläfer überzeugt, dass Deutschlands Feinde im Begriffe sind seine vollständige Zersplitterung vollzuführen verpflichten uns hierdurch, alle sich aus etwaigem gegen Frankreich, Grossbritannien, Italien oder irgendeine andere den Versailler Friedensvertrag unterzeichnende Macht eingetretenen Feldzug mit Zustimmung und Genehmigung der Reichsregierung ergebenden Auslagen für den Zeitlauf von mindestens sechs Monaten zu decken.

Diese Verpflichtung gilt jedoch nur mit der Massgabe, dass die Leitung des ganzen erwähnten Feldzuges dem Freiherrn General Feldmarschall Paul von Ludenburg ungeteilt überliefert sei, der zum Beweis, dass er diesen feierlichen Pflicht annimmt, neben den unseren auch seinen Namen auf diese Urkunde niedergeschrieben hat.

(*gezeichnet*)

Von Armin Steinhart
Mülhausen Von Buhlen
Herzler Von Stahl
Crefeldt

We, the seven sleepers, convinced that the enemies of Germany are on the point of accomplishing her complete destruction, hereby undertake to meet for a minimum period of six months all financial charges incurred with the sanction and approval of the Government of the Reich on account of military operations against France, England, Italy, or any other Power signatory of the Treaty of Versailles.

This undertaking is subject to the condition that the entire conduct of all the said military operations be entrusted to Field-Marshal Paul von Ludenburg, who, in token of his acceptance of this solemn duty, has set his name beside our own to this document.

(Signed)

Von Armin Steinhart
Mülhausen Von Buhlen
Herzler Von Stahl
Crefeldt

I had to read it through twice before I could thoroughly grasp its entire significance. Then, when its full force was brought home to me, I sat aghast at what I had in my hand. Certainly up to that moment, despite the forebodings of Réhmy, and the implacable manner in which the Professor and his subordinates had pursued us since the document had come into my possession, I had never fully realised the magnitude of the conspiracy. Here was the proof in my hand, naked and unashamed. I was frankly appalled at the enormous responsibility which had been thrust upon me, and which was now for the first time fully brought home.

I must have sat staring at the document for some time, when my reflections were broken into by the harsh voice of Ludenburg.

"Well," he said, "what have you to say?"

I made a great effort and summoned all my wits.

"It is even more liberal, sir, than I had dared to hope. It gives you an entirely free hand."

I handed the paper back to him, and he picked up the original document, and, folding the two together, gave them to his secretary.

"Place these in the safe immediately," he said.

Kenrich bowed and left the room.

Ludenburg resumed his pacing to and fro.

I sat in my chair, still numb with the shock of this discovery, waiting for him to speak. I could not find any words now to persuade him, no arguments such as had so glibly fallen from my tongue some hour previously came to my mind. I could think only of the ghastly shell-torn trenches of the Somme; of the uncut wire which I had seen round Fosse 8, with the bodies festooning it, of the sickening moment of fear when a great shell bursts close at hand. Were such horrors as that to be renewed?

I raised my head and looked at the old Field-Marshal, striving to divine his thoughts. His face, however, was set like granite, and I could read nothing there; one hand fiercely twisted his moustache, the other was clenched in the side pocket of his coat. Then he spoke, with an air of decision:

"You shall have your answer tomorrow," he said. "Call at noon."

I rose from the table and clicked my heels. Then I bowed and turned to go.

Ludenburg was apparently no longer conscious of my presence for, as I moved towards the door, that strange heroic figure fell on its knees, and, as I left the room, I heard his voice repeating just above his breath the opening words of the great Lutheran prayer, "Now help me, God of battles."

CHAPTER XVIII

I WITNESS A SIGNATURE

Outside in the hall I met Kenrich.

"Well?" he queried.

I informed him that I should have a final answer on the following day.

He nodded.

"We must leave him quite alone now," he said. "He knows all the facts, and he will make his decision unaided, as he always does."

He opened the front door for me himself, and I passed out into the quiet streets. I decided to walk back to the residence of Herr Hüber, for I felt the need of a breath of fresh air, and of time for reflection.

I need hardly say that I had found the part I was playing increasingly repugnant to me as my interview with Ludenburg had advanced. It was my mission to complete the evidence of a conspiracy by obtaining his signature to a document that involved him in the designs of a group of men whose character and methods, I was sure, would be utterly abhorrent to him. Had he been a person of the quality of Fritz or the Professor, my task would have been honest enough, but it went to my heart to be forced, by circumstances over which I had no control, to entrap so great-hearted a man into a position which would still further embitter his closing years and bring to a dark conclusion his long record of honourable service on behalf of his belovèd country and cherished ideals. I could see no way out, however; I was committed beyond question or doubt to the mission which I had voluntarily accepted from Réhmy and Gaston. I hated to deceive that heroic old man, but I felt obliged to adopt a course which, in ordinary circumstances, I should never have pursued. I had to think, not only of my obligations to Réhmy and Gaston but of the appalling possibilities revealed by that terrible document. The stake for which I was playing was nothing less than the peace of Europe, and the cause for which thousands of young men had fought and died during four long years of war. I could not risk losing the chance that was given me of unmasking this desperate plot, and of obtaining the crowning proof of its existence.

I soon saw that I had no choice. I must go on with the affair as Réhmy had planned it, and the name of Ludenburg, if he signed the document, must appear with the other parties to that fatal undertaking.

It took me some little time to find my way back to Hüber's, and it was almost eleven o'clock when I arrived at the house. Both Hüber and Von Salsnig were awaiting me, and no sooner had I entered the hall than they overwhelmed me with questions. I was in no mood, however, to satisfy their curiosity, and I maintained a purely formal attitude.

"You will know, gentlemen," I said, "shortly after noon tomorrow whether or not he will agree," and with this they were forced to be content, though I heard Hüber mutter something about "Prussian insolence" below his breath, as he lumbered off to bed.

I must have slept soundly, for I was dog-tired, and it was past nine on the following morning when I was awakened with coffee and hot water.

Much refreshed by my night's rest, I rose and dressed. For good or ill, today would be the crisis. My French friends were due to meet me that afternoon, and I should then be able to tell them whether or not success had crowned our efforts.

As I was descending the staircase, I heard Von Salsnig speaking on the telephone. I did not pay much heed to the conversation, but continued to walk downstairs. Suddenly, however, all my faculties sprang to attention.

"*Ja*, Herr Professor," he was saying.

I leaned over the banisters, and, to cover my eavesdropping, I took out a cigarette and lighted it.

"No, we have not had a definite answer yet," Von Salsnig was saying. "A decision has been promised by noon today.—What's that?—You think it best to let him go for the answer himself?—Certainly, if you have the matter in hand.—Yes, you may rely on me.—No, I will look after that myself. You need have no apprehensions."

He hung up the receiver, and I continued on my way downstairs. My anxiety in respect of the Professor, which had been partially driven from my mind by the events of the previous evening, returned in full force. It was considerably increased by the demeanour of Von Salsnig, whom I met at the bottom of the stairs. He was obviously embarrassed and gave me a very odd look as I said good morning. I made a few general remarks, to all of which he replied absently, watching me narrowly as he did so. The man had evidently been much disturbed by his telephone conversation, and he seemed to find it difficult to meet me at all naturally. I thought it best to take a bold course.

"I have had no instructions," I said, "as to the disposal of the document if it is signed. I imagine I am to take it immediately to the Seven."

Von Salsnig looked at me sharply.

"No," he said. "I have just received instructions that you are to bring it to us here. We shall ourselves arrange for its despatch."

"I do not quite see——" I began.

"Those are our instructions," he interposed, and then added, with an obvious effort, "You may be sure that if you are successful this morning you will not lose by it."

"Suppose I am asked," I said, "what is to be done with the document, what shall I reply?"

Von Salsnig reflected for a moment.

"Say," he replied, "that it will be forwarded to the Seven immediately, and that any further developments will be reported without loss of time."

I nodded, and went into the sitting-room, which was empty. Hüber had evidently not yet risen.

I was left alone in that room for over an hour, and during that time my forebodings were multiplied. I did not like the demeanour of Von Salsnig, coming, as it did, immediately after his conversation on the telephone. I had a sensation of being caught like a bird in a net. I could do nothing, however, but go forward. The only alternative was utter failure, since I no longer had the document in my possession. I must go to the villa of Ludenburg as arranged, and carry out the programme single-handed.

I suppose the strain was beginning to tell upon me, for I began to long consumedly for the moment when I should be able to communicate with Réhmy and Gaston. That blessed moment was not, thank heaven, far off. In a few hours they would be in Hanover and at the rendezvous.

Shortly after 11.30 Von Salsnig appeared.

"The car is waiting," he said.

It did not take us long to reach the villa of Ludenburg. Neither of us said a word during the drive, and I was by this time thoroughly alarmed by his attitude, but I could merely trust that the marvellous good fortune I had hitherto enjoyed would not desert me in the final hour. As we drew up in front of the villa, Von Salsnig said to me,

"I will wait for you here."

I nodded, and walked up to the front door. I did not see how I could elude Von Salsnig after the interview, but I was determined that somehow I would slip away to my French friends.

Herr Kenrich was awaiting me, and, as I entered the room, noon struck from a little clock on the mantelshelf.

"We will go into the office," he said, after a brief exchange of courtesies.

I followed him out of the room and across the passage. He threw open the door and stood aside for me to enter. An instant later I found myself once more in the presence of that tremendous figure. Ludenburg was standing by the safe as I entered the room. He looked at me a moment while I stood stiffly to attention, then, without a word, turned his back and grasped the handle of the safe. I heard a whirring click and the steel door swung back. He took the document from a shelf inside the safe and turned and walked across the room to his desk.

All this time I had not moved or spoken a word, though I was watching him with feverish interest. He sat down at the desk and unlocked it. He was in profile to me, but the strong face was unmoved, and I could infer nothing from his expression. Laying the document in front of him, he picked up a pen. Then he swung around in his chair, the pen between his fingers.

"What are your orders?" he said, in an official tone.

"I am to take the document to Herr Hüber, sir," I replied. "He will immediately forward it to the proper quarter."

"When do the Seven meet?" he enquired.

"As soon as possible," I replied. "I was instructed to inform you that you would receive the fullest details without loss of time."

He looked at me. Then he turned back towards the desk, and a moment later I heard the pen scratch on the paper as he signed his name in a firm hand beneath the signatures of the Seven.

I waited for him to speak, but he said nothing. He sat motionless, holding the document between his finger and thumb, as he waited for the ink to dry on his signature. A sudden sharp contortion twisted his features, to be gone again a moment later, leaving them calm and serene, and in his eyes I saw a look of high resolve.

He rose, and, placing the document in a plain white envelope, handed it to me.

"Sir," I began, "I have to thank you——"

But he held up his hand.

"You owe me no thanks," he said. "This is only the beginning. You are too young to know the cost. I have already, through the long night, weighed it and counted it to the last man and the last scruple. I have endeavoured to serve my country for sixty years. I will not fail her now. The youth of Germany has asked for a leader. Tell them I am ready."

He held out his hand as he finished speaking, and we exchanged a handclasp.

I turned and left the room, and, as I walked towards the door, I swear there was a mist before my eyes.

Outside I met Kenrich, who looked at me enquiringly.

"He has signed it," I said.

"God be praised!" he whispered. "Now there will be a man's work to do."

I merely nodded, for in that moment I could not trust myself to speak or to play my part. I felt like rushing back into the room and crying out that it was all a sham, that there would be no war, that he had been deceived. But it was forbidden me to do so.

I passed through the open front door, and, as in a dream, found myself on the pavement outside. As I stood there, I came back to realities, and I remembered Von Salsnig in the car. I looked up, but the car was nowhere to be seen. The long, well-kept, ugly German road was empty of all vehicles. This struck me as almost too good to be true.

I set off briskly to the left down the Seelhorststrasse, marvelling at my good fortune. Presently I saw a ramshackle cab with a still more ramshackle driver on top of it. I hailed him and was soon driving to the Café Kröpcke, which proved to be a large establishment in the middle of the town.

I descended from the cab, entered the café and sat down. It was not yet one o'clock, and Réhmy was not due to appear until two at earliest. I spent the time in keeping a sharp lookout for him, or for the friends of Hüber, and in eating a well-cooked steak with a poached egg on it, which I washed down with beer.

As I was finishing this meal and preparing to smoke a light, mild, German cigar, a shabbily dressed man with a pair of thick horn-rimmed spectacles on his nose, and a pronounced stoop, entered the café. He disregarded the efforts of the waiters to induce him to go elsewhere and obstinately insisted on seating himself at my table. I paid no particular attention to him beyond shifting slightly in my seat to obtain a better view of the door, which his position prevented me from seeing.

He, in his turn, appeared to be quite unconcerned with myself. He called for a glass of beer, and while it was being brought leant forward, and, picking up a newspaper at which I had been looking, asked me in gruff German if I had finished with it. I replied in the affirmative.

He looked idly through its contents and laid it down again when the waiter brought his beer.

"Not much news in the paper," he said, turning to me.

"Not much," I replied.

"Business very slack," he continued.

"Very," I re-echoed, wondering how long this old bore was going to sit there.

"I am a partner," he went on, "in a big firm, but we're not doing well. Times are hard."

"Really?" I said, stifling a yawn.

"Yes," he rejoined, apparently taking my interest for granted, "we manufacture saucepans, and other things, but principally saucepans—aluminium saucepans."

He paused an instant to relight the stump of a cigar in his mouth.

"I am a sleeping partner," he said, emitting a cloud of smoke. "There are seven of us."

I stared at him in amazement.

"Indeed," I said. "And where are your works?"

"I'll show you," he replied. "This is how you get to them."

He took a stump of pencil from his pocket and began drawing on the marble table-top between us. As he did so, he whispered in French:

"Have you got it, Captain Preston?"

It was Réhmy!

"Yes," I replied.

"Is it signed?"

"Yes."

"Who by?"

"Marshal von Ludenburg."

Réhmy's face showed for a moment his astonishment at my news.

"It's as bad as that," he muttered.

We carried on a short conversation interspersed with directions as to how to get to some impossible works on the outskirts of Hanover, while Réhmy told me what to do.

We were to wait, he said, for Gaston, who would arrive, he hoped, very shortly. He and Réhmy had led my Uncle Fritz and Schreckermann a magnificent chase, and Gaston had taken an alternative route to Hanover, still further to throw them off the scent, leaving him, Réhmy, to come on alone. He had adopted the disguise as an added protection. When Gaston arrived, we should all three at once proceed——

At that moment, a heavy hand was laid on my shoulder. I looked up and saw myself face to face with a sergeant of the green police (the constabulary of the German Republic).

"These are the men," he said. "I arrest you on charge of conspiracy against the German Reich, by undertaking separatist propaganda with the object of dismembering the German Republic and subverting the government of the country."

I gazed at him utterly bewildered, while one of his fellows clapped a pair of handcuffs on my wrists.

I turned round and saw that two policemen were performing a similar office for Réhmy.

"Quick," said the sergeant.

Before I could think what course to take, or could frame any protest, he had seized me by the elbow and was pushing me out of the café. Outside was a vehicle not unlike an English Black Maria, drawn by two horses. We were quickly thrust inside it, before the eyes of a curious little crowd which had assembled. One or two hoots were raised, and a red-faced, patriotic German lady struck Réhmy over the head with her umbrella, calling him a dirty traitor.

A moment later the doors slammed to and the vehicle started. We were on the way to an unknown destination.

CHAPTER XIX

I SEE RED

"What is the meaning of this outrage?" I began, as we started on our journey.

The police sergeant answered me with a scowl.

"You will see soon enough what it means," he growled. "It's men like you that are playing the enemy's game for him. You ought to be shot."

I must own that I heartily agreed with his point of view. No patriotic German could fail to execrate the separatist propaganda. But how on earth had I become liable to the charge?

I looked at Réhmy. He was sitting with his head bowed in his hands, and I felt bitterly sorry for him. A moment ago he had seemed on the threshold of success, but suddenly he was faced with the complete failure of all his plans.

I wondered for a moment whether I had been mistaken for Karl, and was suffering vicariously for any one of his numerous offences, but a moment's reflection showed me that if that had been the case the police would scarcely have arrested Réhmy in addition to myself.

I soon gave up trying to puzzle it out, and as I sat in that jolting windowless vehicle, between the impassive forms of two green-clad policemen, I fell into a kind of apathy. As we used to say in the army, I had, for the moment, lost the "offensive spirit." I suddenly felt very tired and leaned back wearily against the hard wooden seat, and I remember wondering whether they would let me smoke in prison, and what the food would be like.

After what appeared to be an interminable drive, though I do not think that in actual fact it lasted very long, we pulled up. The door was flung open and the sergeant ordered us to descend.

I followed Réhmy out into the open air and perceived that we were in a country road, opposite a garden gate, from which a path led up to a fair-sized house. A constable gripped each of us by the elbow and hustled us up the path. The door opened and we were conveyed across a wide hall, past the foot of a broad oak staircase, through another door, into a large and fantastically furnished room.

It was indeed a strange apartment in which we found ourselves. The prevailing colour was a dull, sombre red. The walls, the furniture, the carpet, even the boards were all alike of the same hue, and to complete the scheme there was a single picture in the room depicting a flaming scarlet sunset, over a tumbled mass of waters. I mention these details, though at the time I was not conscious of them. My whole attention was immediately riveted on a single figure, which rose from an armchair as we entered and stood facing us.

It was Professor Kreutzemark!

He stood at the further end of the room, his head touching a large curving mantelpiece of crimson teakwood. A glass of red wine was in his hand, and Ahasuerus perched on his shoulder. That evil bird chuckled malevolently at our entry, and twice emitted the sound of a cork being removed from a bottle of champagne. The Professor lifted a slim hand and gently ruffled its breast feathers.

"So," he said, "you have arrived at last, gentlemen. I am delighted to offer you such poor hospitality as my house affords," and he bowed suavely.

"I have no further need of you or your men, sergeant," he added, turning to the police officers, and pressing a bell as he spoke. "Josef will conduct you elsewhere, and I feel sure that a glass of Augustinerbraü will not come amiss."

The officers withdrew, leaving with the Professor the key of the handcuffs with which Réhmy and myself were secured.

"Pray be seated, gentlemen," the Professor continued, pointing to two chairs at opposite corners of the hearth.

"I have not yet had the honour of making your acquaintance, Captain Réhmy," he pursued, "though I have been so closely following your activities that I feel I know you quite well. As for Mr. Preston, he is by now quite an old friend, though hitherto he has cultivated a habit of sudden and unannounced departure, which in more formal society might be considered discourteous."

I looked at Réhmy. There was something like despair in his eyes, but his head was up, and his bearing controlled and courageous.

"I presume you are Professor Kreutzemark?" he said.

The Professor bowed.

"I am," he replied.

"The inventor of yellow cross gas?"

"The adapter, let us say."

"The murderer of Raoul Dupléssy," continued Réhmy, gazing at him steadily.

The Professor emitted a short sigh.

"I think we are wandering a little from the point," he said. "I have first of all to thank you both for having made such excellent use of your opportunities during the last twenty-four hours. You have done admirable service."

He paused and turned to me with a mocking smile.

"Did you really think, my dear Captain Preston, that your ingenious operations in this city of Hanover were unknown to me? You do me an injustice. I have been following your operations with the deepest interest, and in the confident expectation that you were an emissary far more likely to succeed with the distinguished person to whom you were accredited than the late lamented Von Emmerich, who I fear was considerably less prepossessing and less intelligent than yourself. I have now the honour to congratulate you on your remarkable success. You have obtained the signature we so greatly needed, and which I was somewhat doubtful of securing by our own unaided efforts."

So he had been playing with me. He had been watching me from first to last, and when I had done his work for him he had pounced. I had been congratulating myself on having displayed a certain amount of ingenuity and presence of mind, and all the time I had been working into his hands.

He evidently read my thoughts. He stepped forward, and, bending down, looked into my face. I tried to stare back at him, but even then I could not meet his eyes. He laughed sardonically.

"Is it bitter, my little Englishman?" he said. "Did you really think that you had outwitted us?"

"And you, Captain Réhmy," he continued turning to my friend, "did you really think that your academic methods could prevail against the resources of a scientific brain?"

He threw back his head and his pale face flushed. His triumph was complete, and he knew it so well that, for an instant, he dropped his mask and allowed me a glimpse of the real man beneath.

I could find no words with which to answer him, and indeed, when I had first entered the room and perceived him, I had decided to let Réhmy do all the talking that was necessary. I was so disgusted with myself, and so utterly cast down at the manner in which I had been duped, that I felt that if I took any further hand in the game myself I should probably make our position even worse than it was already.

Réhmy, however, even in that bitter moment, was equal to the Professor. He lifted his head and stared at him inflinchingly.

"My compliments, Herr Professor," he said, "you confirm our national impression of your countrymen as a race which leaped from the primeval forest straight into a well-appointed laboratory."

The Professor flushed, and his eyes narrowed to two slits.

"The worse for you, Captain Réhmy, if that impression be well-founded," he said softly.

I could see that Réhmy's shot had gone home and that the Professor's armour was pierced. He turned, however, with an admirable assumption of suavity and walked to a hanging wooden ring, upon which he deposited Ahasuerus.

As he turned back again, the door was flung open, and Fritz entered, evidently in a state of high excitement.

"Herr Professor——" he began, and then stopped short at the sight of us. "Donnerwetter!" he cried. "You've got them."

He came swiftly down the room and shook the Professor violently by the hand.

The Professor eyed him coldly.

"I have, as you see, my dear Major Adler, retrieved yet another of your unfortunate blunders," he said, after a noticeable pause.

Fritz stepped back from the Professor, his momentary satisfaction at finding us both by the heels effectively snubbed.

"It wasn't my fault," he said, employing his usual formula when things went wrong. "The initial blunder was your own, Herr Professor. You must have killed the wrong man."

"Quite so," said the Professor, who had now recovered his customary equanimity. "Quite so, Major Adler. I admit that for some two hours I was myself at fault."

"The document?" asked Fritz. "Have you also recovered that?"

"I have no doubt," replied the Professor, "that if you were to search in the pockets of Mr. Preston or of Captain Réhmy, you would find it without any serious difficulty."

Fritz needed no further prompting. He came up to me and tore feverishly at my coat. A moment later the envelope containing the document was in his hands. He could scarcely repress a shout of triumph.

"I thought so," murmured the Professor. "Now, Major Adler, if you will kindly look at the paper you have in your hand, I believe you will find that the eighth signature, which we so much desired to obtain, is at the foot of the document."

Fritz opened the envelope, took out the document and looked at it eagerly. An expression of unwilling admiration came into his face.

"Herr Professor," he said, "you are wonderful."

The Professor shook his head smilingly.

"Not at all, my dear Major. I have merely brought to bear a little common sense. Perhaps you would not take it amiss if I were to tell you what I have been doing during the last forty-eight hours. I am sure it would interest Captain Réhmy and Mr. Preston."

He settled himself against the mantelpiece and began. It seems that his suspicions had first been aroused by the disappearance of the car, which we had stolen for the drive to Basle. At first he had assumed that Von Emmerich had driven to a garage to fill up the tanks with petrol and that he would shortly return. An hour had elapsed, however, without any sign of the car or of Von Emmerich, and the Professor's suspicions had by this time been thoroughly awakened. It was not long before it occurred to him that a substitution of Von Emmerich for Preston might have been effected in the chalet; and, as the police of Geneva, led to the spot by Adolf, had already removed the body of his victim to the morgue, the Professor sent Adolf back to Geneva to identify the corpse. Adolf, on his return, reported that the body was that of Von Emmerich. He had identified it by the scar above the left knee, which I had noticed myself in the hut at Bellerive.

The Professor lost no time in vain regrets. He had gone at once with Adolf and his servants to the chalet at Versoix, hoping to pick up the trail of the Frenchmen. There they had caught sight of Miss Harvel (my heart sank when I heard her name), accompanied by a man who walked with a limp, dressed for motoring, and standing beside the big Peugeot which had evidently been quickly repaired. The Professor at once instructed the two servants to hide themselves close by the gate of the drive leading to the chalet, which, as you may remember, was situated at a short distance from the main road and screened by a belt of small firs. They had waited there until the Peugeot, containing Beatrice, Jerry, and the chauffeur, had come slowly down the drive. Josef and his companion had sprung on the footboard, overpowered Jerry and the chauffeur and gagged Beatrice. Jerry and the chauffeur they had deposited in the clump of fir trees, and Josef had then driven the whole party to Basle, where they had arrived very late the same night. The Professor had at once conjectured that I had gone to Basle with my French friends, and this conjecture was, of course, confirmed on his arrival in that city.

At Basle the Professor was at once informed of the events at "Die Drei Königen." Fritz and Schreckermann had by this time started in chase of Réhmy and Gaston, in the belief that they had run off with the document. The Professor was not for a moment deceived, and discreet enquiries at "Die Drei Königen" had elicited the fact that a gentleman corresponding to the description of Von Emmerich had taken the 11.35 train for Hanover. The Professor and his suite had accordingly taken the first available train for that city, and had arrived there early in the morning of the day on which Ludenburg had signed the document.

From the moment he knew that I had gone to Hanover, the Professor had decided to give me all the rope needed till the document was signed. Now that Von Emmerich was dead, I was, in fact, the only man who could have approached the Field-Marshal on that particular errand at once, and without embarrassing explanations.

The Professor had immediately informed Von Salsnig of the facts and instructed him to act accordingly. He had meanwhile arranged with the local police for my arrest, but had deferred it until Réhmy had also appeared on the scene, feeling sure that I should meet one or both of the Frenchmen after the conclusion of my interview with Ludenburg. This explained why Von Salsnig had not been waiting for me in his car when I had come out of Ludenburg's villa.

The cunning of the Professor took my breath away. He had relied on the certainty that we should not abandon our efforts until we had implicated Von Ludenburg, and he had allowed us to do his work for him. And now he proposed to reap the fruits of our labours.

I cannot adequately reproduce the smooth malice with which he revealed to us the extent of our folly and the faultlessness of his own deduction. Though we knew that worse might follow, we felt appreciably relieved when he drew his story to an end and glanced at his watch.

"Major Adler," he said, "thanks to our energetic and engaging envoy, Mr. Preston, we now have the document complete. It would be well to lose no further time in taking it to Leipzig, where the Seven are doubtless awaiting its arrival. They are to meet shortly and the document should go to them without delay. I propose, therefore, that you should start for Leipzig this evening."

Adler nodded.

"Very good, Herr Professor," he replied. "Meanwhile the English lady will, I trust, be safe with you."

The Professor smiled.

"She will be waiting for you on your return, my dear Major."

It needed but this to bring home the full bitterness of defeat, and Fritz was not the man to miss the occasion. He turned to me in triumph.

"You hear that?" he said in brutal satisfaction. "And this time we shall see that you don't play a vanishing trick."

I could make no reply. I was trying hopelessly to think of some way in which I could save Beatrice, when the door opened and a woman entered.

It was Elsa, in wild excitement, and she advanced straight to the Professor.

"You've captured them," she cried.

Turning round, she caught sight of me. Her face became suffused with a passion of rage, and she rushed at me, screaming:

"You killed him, you devil! You killed Karl. Leiber Gott, may you die in torment!"

She struck me twice across the face as she spoke. I did not flinch from the blows and her violence was suddenly exhausted. She drew back and covered her face with her hands.

"We had no hand in it at all," she cried desperately. "We were blind and helpless. I swear it was you that killed him."

She shuddered, and her slim figure was shaken with horror.

"I can see him still," she whispered. "In the water. His eyes were open. He could not even shut his eyes."

The Professor, who was watching this exhibition with contemptuous interest, turned to me calmly.

"I must apologise, Mr. Preston," he said. "Fräulein Elsa is not quite herself."

His callousness in the face of the distraught passion of this poor creature filled me with an increased abhorrence for the man.

"Pray try to calm yourself, Fräulein," he continued, looking towards Elsa. "Though I am not usually inclined to encourage the gratification of the cruder instincts, I will in this instance indulge your very natural desire that Captain Preston should suffer an adequate retribution. I am at present experimenting with a gas of a different, and, I believe, of an even more deadly, nature than those which I was able to place at the disposal of the German armies during the War. Hitherto I have been compelled to observe its effects on rabbits, dogs, and certain of the smaller mammals. Now, however, fate has been kind enough to put into my hands the means whereby I can observe its immediate effects on a human subject, and I propose that, when I have completed certain business upon which I am now engaged, Mr. Preston should enter the gas chamber. It may perhaps relieve the very natural distress of Fräulein Elsa if she is permitted to assist me in this experiment."

Elsa raised her face at these words, and a glow of satisfaction and appeasement gradually overspread her childish features.

"At least," she said in a low voice, looking me full in the eyes, "I shall know that Karl has been thoroughly avenged."

CHAPTER XX

I TAKE LEAVE OF MY GRANDMOTHER

It was Fritz that broke upon this interlude. He suddenly strode across the room towards the door, saying as he went:

"Well, Herr Professor. *I* had best get ready for the journey to Leipzig."

At the door he paused and turned.

"With your permission," he said, "I propose before I go to have a few words with the English lady."

"Certainly, my dear Major," replied the Professor. "The English lady is upstairs. Fräulein Elsa will show you the room."

Elsa, obviously delighted to perform this office for the Major, went quickly towards the door.

"This way, Herr Major," she said, and the door closed behind them.

The Professor turned and surveyed us once more.

"Now that your fate is settled, Mr. Preston," he said, "it only remains to make arrangements for Captain Réhmy.

"I do not propose, my dear Captain Réhmy," he continued, "that you should share Mr. Preston's fate, at any rate for the moment. You will accordingly do me the honour of remaining here as my guest. I feel sure that you must have a great deal of information which might in certain contingencies be of incalculable assistance to us in our work, and I am certain you would not wish to be unreasonably uncommunicative."

"You will obtain nothing from me," said Réhmy quietly.

"Well," said the Professor amiably, "we will leave that matter over for the present."

He rang a bell as he spoke, and a moment later the impassive forms of Josef and his nameless companion appeared in the doorway.

"Josef," he said, "you will remain on guard over these gentlemen until I release you. If they desire anything to eat, drink, or smoke, please see that they are immediately supplied. Should they, in spite of their handcuffs, attempt to escape, you are to shoot at once."

He walked across the room towards the door, but paused in the middle, and, turning to us, added courteously:

"Josef does not understand French. You need not, therefore, feel any embarrassment in talking to one another in front of him. I shall not keep you waiting very long, Mr. Preston, but you may count upon at least a quarter of an hour." So saying, he left the room.

We were now alone, except for Josef and his companion. Josef advanced and stood between us. His attitude was deferential in the extreme, but it accorded ill with the pistol in his right hand.

"Is there anything you would like, gentlemen?" he enquired.

I was about to protest against this final mockery of the Professor, but Réhmy rose superior to the occasion.

"Cigars, I think," he replied, "and a glass of wine."

Josef bowed and, turning to his companion who was standing by the door, passed him the order. The man left the room and returned a moment later with two glasses of wine and a box of cigars, which he handed to us on a silver salver.

I hesitated, but Réhmy said in French:

"Come, man, keep your heart up. Don't let them imagine that we're in the least affected by their insults. They have us at their mercy, but we can show them that our spirit is beyond their reach, that we can yet remain undefeated."

There was a quiet resolution in his face, which showed that this was no mere verbal flourish. I felt that Réhmy would suffer the last indignities with an unblemished contempt for his enemies.

I took the wine, but refused a cigar. Réhmy, however, took both, and the servant, placing the box of cigars beside him, withdrew from the room.

If ever I have had reason in my life to be grateful to any man, it was to Réhmy at that desperate moment. It was only his stout heart and unflinching courage which kept me from utterly breaking down. To a man of his profession, of course, the possibility of death, or worse than death, had continually to be faced. On his various missions as a secret agent he had constantly to take his life in his hand. He was consequently more ready to pay the forefeit of failure at any time than I was, and when that moment had come his demeanour was beyond all praise.

For me, the situation was different. Five days previously I had been an ordinary business man on my way home to a partnership and success. Now, suddenly, I was to die, and Beatrice was to suffer a fate which even today I cannot bear to think about.

We spoke but little, but sat there, sipping our wine, the glass awkwardly balanced in our manacled hands. I know that my own hands were trembling, but Réhmy was outwardly unmoved. His French pride would not permit him to sweeten in the least degree the triumph of our enemies. I strove to imitate him, but I fear I made but a poor job of it. The agony was too great, and I soon began to long for the end. I wanted to be done with it all quickly.

A quarter of an hour or twenty minutes must have elapsed before the Professor returned. He was accompanied by two men in aprons and shirt sleeves, staggering beneath the weight of a large cylinder, and a quantity of piping and other apparatus.

The Professor approached one of the walls and inserted a small key. A portion of the wall swung back revealing a small aperture into an adjoining room.

Under his instructions the men placed the cylinder on a stand, which they erected immediately in front of the aperture, and connected the piping to the cylinder. I should mention that the aperture was covered by thick curtains stretching to the floor and emitting a strong chemical smell.

I was reminded of the gas chambers through which I had passed in taking my gas course in England and at the Base during the War. We had been made to walk with our helmets on through a room filled with phosgene gas. The room, like this one, had been curtained in the same way.

The Professor directed the operations of his workmen, only pausing to inform me, with his invariably courteous smile, that he would not keep me waiting much longer.

On the completion of their task, the workmen, obeying an order from the Professor, put up the shutters in the room and drew down the blinds, after which they switched on the electric light (which was situated in a big red alabaster bowl, hung from the ceiling by three gilded chains), for, although it was only about four o'clock, the December dusk had already fallen.

The Professor, going to the door, called up the stairs to Elsa, who presently came into the room.

"We are quite ready," he informed her, "if you wish to be present."

He motioned to Josef, who produced a rope, with which the Professor's assistants tied Réhmy to his chair, to prevent him from intervening in any way on my behalf.

I fancied for a moment that Réhmy would lose control of himself and make a wild struggle with his manacled hands; but, with an effort, he preserved his impassive dignity and submitted to be bound.

Josef and the two men did the like for me, binding me, in fact, to my chair, so that I was quite unable to move, after which the Professor dismissed the two assistants, leaving us alone with himself and Josef.

"And now, Captain Preston," said the Professor, "if you are quite ready . . ."

I looked at him in silence, then at Réhmy, whose face was grim and hard set.

"Forgive me, dear friend," said Réhmy. "I am bitterly to blame for this. The task was too difficult. I should never have allowed you to undertake it."

"It was my own will and choice," I assured him. "You have nothing with which to reproach yourself."

Réhmy looked at me with eyes unutterably sad, but lit with a flaming anger.

"Farewell, Captain Preston," he said. "You have shown yourself a gallant gentleman; and I pray that this foul crime may be avenged."

I could not control myself to reply. The bitterness of death was upon me and at that supreme moment I could think of nothing but Beatrice and her sweet face, and my impotence to save her.

At a sign from the Professor, Josef bent to assist him in carrying me and the chair to which I was bound towards the aperture in the wall. At this moment, however, a sudden scream rang out somewhere above our heads. It came from an upper storey of the house and it was in a woman's voice.

Josef and the Professor stopped in the act of lifting me in the chair, and Elsa looked up from the cylinder, which she had been examining with curiosity.

"That must be the Englishwoman," she exclaimed. "I left her with Major Adler."

Again the cry rang out, and this time it was followed by the sound of a shot.

The Professor moved deliberately to the mantelpiece and pushed the button of the electric bell in the wall beside it. But there was no answering ring. He pressed it again, with the same absence of result. If he was disconcerted he did not show it.

"I am sorry, Captain Preston," he said, "but I must ask you to wait a moment while we ascertain what these unexpected noises may mean. Major Adler appears to be amusing himself rather oddly."

"Josef," he added, turning to the servant, who, impassive as ever, was still grasping the chair, "please see what is happening in the room upstairs."

Josef released the chair and, pulling his pistol from the pocket where he had thrust it as soon as I was safely secured, walked quickly towards the door.

Just as he reached it, however, it was flung violently open, and a figure appeared. It carried a smoking pistol in one hand, and with the other it suddenly, without hesitation or warning, dealt the astonished Josef a violent blow in the face, which laid him flat and made him drop his pistol on the floor.

It was Gaston de Blanchegarde.

I had been deposited facing the door and saw him at once, as his eyes ran swiftly round the room. Suddenly, he pointed his pistol at the alabaster bowl of light: there was a report; the bowl was shivered; and an instant later the room was plunged in darkness.

"Is that you, Gaston?" shouted Réhmy in French.

The Professor, startled entirely out of his usual equanimity, was heard in the darkness crying out upon Adolf and Adler, while Elsa, who had gone at once into hysterics, was uttering scream after scream.

The only light in the room was that given by the fire. At first I could see nothing, but in a few moments, my eyes being used to the darkness, I perceived, by the faint flickering light, Gaston and the Professor, fast grappled and rolling over and over on the floor beside the stand supporting the cylinder.

"Gaston," I cried, "we're handcuffed. The Professor has the key."

Suddenly another figure, which I could not distinguish, ran lightly across the room; bent for a moment over the struggling forms; snatched something from one of them; and an instant later was by my side.

It was Beatrice.

"Hold out your hands," she commanded, and, bending down, she inserted the key.

There was a click. I shook my handcuffs, and they fell to the floor with a crash.

"There's a knife in my pocket," I said urgently.

Beatrice found it and cut me free of the chair.

"Now look to Réhmy," I cried.

She hurried towards him, while I turned to assist Gaston. He was evidently on the point of overpowering the Professor, but, as I reached him, I saw that Josef, having recovered from the blow he had received, and evidently despairing of finding his pistol in the dark, was advancing with an uplifted chair, with the intention of bringing it down on Gaston's unprotected head. I dived for his knees and we crashed to the floor together.

As I struggled to my feet, I heard a slight hiss, and a sweet, sickly smell struck on my nostrils. "My God!" I shouted. "The gas!"

"Quick," I heard a voice say.

I turned blindly in the half-light and found that Beatrice was beside me. Seizing her by the wrist, I rushed to the door, tore it open and an instant later we were in the passage outside, with Gaston and Réhmy at our heels.

I shall never forget the picture which I saw through the open door. A log had fallen from the fire and a sudden burst of flame had scattered the darkness. The light was playing upon a thin stream of vapour issuing from the nozzle of the pipe which was connected with the cylinder. Elsa had apparently fainted, and she was lying not far from Josef, motionless upon the floor. The Professor was on his knees, apparently trying to rise. His movements reminded me of that form of nightmare in which the sufferer vainly endeavours to perform some urgent physical act, to run with leaden feet, or struggle with limbs that are nerveless and immovable.

Suddenly, to our surprise, Gaston darted back into the room and reappeared a moment later with Elsa in his arms. He deposited her in the passage, while Réhmy, with a face of iron, shut the door and turned the key which he found in the lock.

For a moment I hesitated, and Réhmy divined my thoughts.

"They must do as best as they can," he said. "We have no time to lose."

To give point to his words, we became aware of a furious hammering and a babel of voices some short distance away. Among the voices I thought I distinguished the tones of my little friend, Adolf Baumer.

"That's the servants," said Gaston. "I locked them into their own quarters, but they will be breaking out in another moment. Where's the front door?"

"This way," replied Réhmy.

We hastened down the passage to the front door. Réhmy opened it, and we tumbled down the steps into the garden. Here we left the path and took to the trees, which were mostly young firs and larches, and afforded us good cover from observation, either from the house or from the road.

It was well that we did so, for, as we made our way cautiously in Indian file towards the gate, a car drew up in the road outside. I at once recognised the occupants. It was driven by Von Salsnig, who was accompanied by Herr Hüber.

Crouching behind the friendly trees, we watched them descend from the car and go up the path towards the house.

Conveniently in the road, empty and unguarded, stood their well-appointed automobile. I looked at Gaston and Réhmy. It was a splendid chance and three of us realised it simultaneously.

"Wait till they go inside," I whispered, as Gaston moved impatiently.

We watched Hüber and Von Salsnig ascend the steps. They stopped for an instant opposite the open door leading into the house, and Hüber said something to Von Salsnig. They debated together a few moments and then they entered the house.

The four of us at once broke cover and bolted down the path, through the gate and into the road.

Gaston took the wheel, and I sprang to the handle, while Réhmy and Beatrice seated themselves in the back of the car. Fortunately, she started at the first turn of the crank.

As we sped down the road, there was a sudden outcry from the house. Our theft, it seemed, had been discovered.

CHAPTER XXI

I AM DELIVERED TO THE FRENCH AUTHORITIES

I had now time to feel the full force of the rapid events of the last half-hour. I was a man suddenly pulled back from the doors of death and the contemplation of worse than death for Beatrice. My brain was dizzy and for the first few moments in the car I must confess that I was scarcely conscious of what was happening. I just lay back on the seat, trembling slightly, aware of nothing definite except that Beatrice was present on the seat behind me, saved like myself for the moment and carried swiftly forward into the sweet-smelling countryside.

Then, suddenly, I found that Réhmy was leaning over to Gaston.

"The document!" he exclaimed.

I remember to this day my amazement that he should still be preoccupied with that fatal paper. I did not yet realise that I was still in the living world, and a dead man has no use for documents.

"Safe here," shouted Gaston, patting his breast pocket, "and, while I think of it, you might take a look at this," he added, pointing to a leather portfolio on the seat beside him.

"Thank God, he's got the document," I remember thinking. Personally, I remain convinced that, if Gaston had not had it in his possession, Réhmy would then and there have returned to the Professor's house in search of it.

I picked up the leather portfolio to which Gaston had pointed and handed it to Réhmy.

"Fritz was carrying that," explained Gaston. "I thought it might come in useful."

I was now almost alive again and my brain was beginning to work.

"How did you get the document?" I asked.

"Fritz had it," said Gaston briefly.

"What's happened to him?" I enquired, as we shot round a corner, apparently on two wheels.

"Dead," replied Gaston.

Before I could ask him for further details, Réhmy again leaned forward between us.

"We must decide at once what we are going to do," he said. "We can't continued to drive on at a venture. The police are probably after us already. They will be telegraphing all over the place the moment those men at the villa get on the end of a telephone. We must make for occupied territory. The nearest town is Dortmund."

While we thus took breathless counsel, Gaston continued to drive the car at a high speed into the open country. His eyes were still shining with excitement, and he glowed with the well-being of a man who had for once been allowed full liberty to indulge his natural impulses.

Réhmy produced a map from his pocket and he and Beatrice, spreading it between them, were soon engaged in a close study of it. Presently Réhmy raised his head.

"We shall be caught for a certainty if we keep to the car," he said. "But I think we might borrow it for another hour. Make for Hamelin, Gaston."

He handed over the map to me, with which to check our route. We had been heading in the opposite direction, that is to say, along the Lehrte road. Under my directions, Gaston made a wide sweep south in the outskirts of the town till we struck the main road. The signpost showed us to be forty-three kilometres from our immediate goal, and we set ourselves to get there if possible in as many minutes.

As we flew along, Gaston explained in snatches how he had come to our rescue. He had been on the point of entering the Café Kröpcke when Réhmy and I were arrested, and he had immediately followed the Black Maria at a suitable distance in a cab, in order to discover our destination. When he saw that we were conducted to a private house, and not to the town jail, he immediately divined that we had once more fallen into the hands of the Professor, or of his subordinates quartered in Hanover. He had spent a considerable length of time in reconnoitering the house, and had waited until dusk was falling before endeavouring to effect an entry.

His task had not been easy. All the ground-floor windows had proved to be bolted on the inside, and he had finally climbed up a drain pipe, aided by the roots of a thick creeper, and entered through a window on the first floor.

"By the luck of the devil, *mes amis*," said Gaston, "I chose the room in which Mademoiselle Harvel was imprisoned. I chose also the best possible moment for my arrival, for she was struggling violently in the arms of Fritz. In fact, the first thing that came to me as I jumped to the floor was her scream for assistance. I ran towards them at once, and Fritz was on me like a flash, but I put a bullet through him before he reached me. He dropped at my feet, dead as mutton."

"Gaston seldom misses," interposed Réhmy, who had been listening eagerly from the back of the car. "But how did you know that Fritz had the document?" he asked.

"He had been boasting of the fact to Mademoiselle Harvel a moment before," Gaston replied. "Mademoiselle Harvel, whose courage and presence of mind I shall never forget, told me at once that he had it. It was in his breast pocket, and I needn't say that it was very soon transferred to mine. Then I bolted into the passage, with Mademoiselle Harvel after me, and down the stairs. There was a green baize door in the hall below with a key in the lock, which I was careful to turn."

The servants had thus been for the moment imprisoned, and he had made at once for the only other door visible, which led to the room in which the Professor was engaged with Réhmy and myself. He had paused before entering to wreck the telephone, which was situated just outside the green baize door, in the hall, and he had also put the electric bell out of order, which, as you may remember, did not ring when the Professor pressed it. An instant later he had thrown open the door, seen what was happening and laid Josef flat upon the floor.

By the time Gaston had concluded his narrative, we were in the outskirts of Hamelin. We slowed down and ran the car into a field, where we abandoned it.

We then walked along the road towards the town, discussing our next move. Beatrice, I should mention, was without coat or hat, as indeed were Réhmy and myself, though Gaston was fairly respectable. We should have been completely frozen during the drive from Hanover, had not the car fortunately been full of rugs.

Presently the road along which we were walking became dotted with small houses, some just finished and others still in course of construction. We halted at one which was still partially unroofed.

Réhmy instructed Gaston to go forward into the town and purchase overcoats for ourselves and a hat and coat for Beatrice. He was then to look up a train going either west, to Herford, or south, to Paderborn, from both of which towns Dortmund was easily accessible.

While Gaston hurried to execute these instructions, we went to ground in the half-built house. Beatrice and I took cover in a room on the ground floor, evidently designed to be the dining-room or best parlour. Réhmy kept watch in the porch outside.

We sat down on the hard floor covered with shavings, side by side and looked at each other. Suddenly Beatrice burst out laughing. She shook with it uncontrollably, hysterical after the terrible strain of her abduction and imprisonment.

"Your clothes, Tom," she gasped. "What a w-wonderful sight!"

"Karl's clothes," I corrected her. "His taste was not infallible."

Then I remembered that Karl was dead. I had hardly realised it yet. Her face changed.

"Oh, Tom," she whispered, "thank God that your friend Gaston was in time."

I put an arm round her, and a moment later she was sobbing on my shoulder. I do not know how long we were in that little room. It might have been ten minutes or it might have been an hour. I was dazed by my sudden change in fortune and the exquisite joy of having Beatrice so near to me. We sat there, holding fast to each other, scarcely speaking at all, and forgetting everything except the fact that we were again together.

We were recalled to a sense of our danger by the appearance of Gaston in the frame of the door, coughing diplomatically, with several brown paper parcels under his arm and a cardboard box in his hand.

"Your hat, Mademoiselle," he said. "I have done my best, but I know it is quite unworthy of you."

Beatrice smiled at him and, opening the box, was soon engaged in putting on a small velvet toque of a vivid blue, and a brown travelling veil. Her costume was completed by a grey check cloak. I thought she looked perfectly charming, though she declared she looked like nothing on earth. Gaston had taken less trouble where I was concerned. He provided me with a mustard-coloured abomination, the overcoat largely affected by the travelling German, and a hideous chessboard cap. Réhmy was given a soft black felt hat and overcoat of inconspicuous hue. When we had put on these garments, Réhmy produced from an inner pocket quantities of false hair and spirit gum, without which, he explained, he never travelled when on duty. He was an expert in disguise, and transformed me rapidly as best he could by the addition of a short fierce moustache; he also clipped my eyebrows, thus skilfully altering the whole expression of my face. He himself adopted a short goatee beard.

As we completed these operations, Gaston, who had gone out of the house to keep watch, returned. During the interval he had removed his moustache, an operation which must have cost him considerable pain, for he had nothing but a pair of nail scissors, an execrably blunt razor, which he had purchased in Hamelin, and a puddle of rain water.

Thus disguised, we again set forth. It was now about six o'clock and quite dark. As we walked, we munched bread and cheese, while Gaston explained that there was a train for Paderborn which left at the half-hour.

Hamelin is quite a small town, and we soon arrived in the middle of it. We kept to the most crowded streets, speaking little, and then only in German. This necessitated almost complete silence on the part of Beatrice.

We walked down the Osterstrasse, past the old Rattenfangerhaus, sacred to the memory of the Pied Piper, and so into the Deisterstrasse and the

Bahnhofstrasse to the railway station.

Beatrice, Gaston, and myself entered the waiting-room, while Réhmy went off to purchase tickets. In Germany travellers are compelled to stay in the waiting-room and are only allowed on the platform on presentation of their tickets at the barrier.

We sat down in silence in a corner and took stock of our surroundings. There were, I suppose, about twenty persons waiting like ourselves, poorly dressed folk of the artisan class for the most part, with here and there a workman in soiled canvas overalls. Close to the platform, an undersized man, wearing a dark coat and felt hat, was standing. As I glanced at him, he turned in my direction, and I saw that it was Adolf. I looked away immediately, deciding on the instant to inform my companions, and suggest a quick retreat by the door from which we had entered. As I was about to do so, however, I glanced at the door in question, and beheld Réhmy entering with the tickets and immediately behind him Von Salsnig. I nudged Beatrice, and she moved along the seat to make room for Réhmy, who was coming through the crowd towards us.

As he sat down, I whispered to him:

"Look, Réhmy, when you can. Adolf and Von Salsnig. They're watching both the doors."

He looked up guardedly.

"You're right," he whispered back.

He sat still for a moment, while we both noted that the two men were undoubtedly on guard.

At last Réhmy said to me.

"There's no hope for it. We must try and slip through the barrier. The train goes in five minutes. We must pass Baumer and hope that he won't recognise us."

A queue of travellers was forming as he spoke. I whispered to Beatrice to stand immediately in front of me and keep her veil over her face. We joined the throng and moved slowly forward. My heart was beating fast. Réhmy was in front, with Gaston next to him, then came Beatrice, while I brought up the rear. Réhmy showed his ticket to the official at the barrier. He passed through to the platform without giving any sign that he had been noticed. A moment later Gaston and Beatrice were also through. As I was about to present my ticket, however, a fat German frau, with a large basket on her arm, pushed her way past, with the obvious intention of getting through before me. The official began to remonstrate, but I held my peace.

"Quick there," he shouted, "pass along."

The woman in front endeavoured to obey his instructions, but in doing so she let fall the basket, over which I stumbled just as I was going through the barrier. I put out a hand to save myself from falling and clutched an arm.

"Verzeihung!" I murmured.

Looking up, I saw that I was holding on to Adolf. He stared at me hard, and recognition was mutual.

"Herr Inspektor——" he began.

I gave him no time for more, but pushed past him and bolted for the train. Gaston's head was leaning out of a first-class compartment, and I jumped in just as the train was beginning to move.

I looked out of the window. Von Salsnig, Hüber, and Schreckermann were at the barrier in excited conversation with the railway official. Adolf was running along the platform, but the speed of the train was now too great for him to board it, and, as we swept out of the station, I saw them all standing in a knot on the platform, gesticulating freely.

I withdrew from the window into the carriage and communicated what had happened to me at the barrier and what I had seen to the others. We held a hurried counsel of war. The train, which was an express stopping nowhere on the way, was due to arrive at Paderborn in a little under the hour. From there we should normally have gone direct through Lippstadt and Soest to Dortmund, but it was obvious that such a course was now impossible. The police would be waiting in full force at the next stop to arrest us all. Besides, although Gaston and Réhmy were furnished with papers, I had nothing except the passport of Von Emmerich, of which the number and description had doubtless long since been telegraphed to every Zollhaus and frontier post. Beatrice had no papers of any description, the Professor having apparently got her into Germany in some mysterious way of his own. We were of course more or less disguised, but, despite Réhmy's clever handiwork, we were none of us inclined to put our trust in this method of deception, particularly as there were very few other passengers, and a group of three men and a girl would have been easily distinguishable. We were up against the whole official and unofficial forces of Germany, and the most desperate efforts would be made to detain us.

At last, on Gaston's suggestion, we decided that the best thing to do would be to pull the communication cord and bolt into the darkness as the train slowed down. Réhmy had a large scale map of the country, and we accordingly determined to trust to luck to make our way through the night to some little village off the beaten track, if possible somewhere between Begheim and Lippspringe, where we could either lie up for a couple of days, or else obtain some sort of transport to take us on our way, through Wiedenbrück and Bechum towards the frontier.

There was now no time to lose, and as soon as we had reached this decision, Gaston got up and put his hand on the ring which controlled the alarm signal. As he was about to pull it, however, the train began sensibly to slacken speed.

Réhmy stayed him with a gesture.

"Surely we don't stop before Paderborn?" I said, as the train slowed down still further.

Gaston went to the window and looked out.

"I don't see any signs of a station," he said, after a moment. "Perhaps the line is blocked in front."

We were running very slowly now, and were in fact almost stationary when Gaston gave an exclamation.

"There's some sort of goods train alongside," he said. "It's standing parallel with us. I can't see how far it stretches."

I looked out over Gaston's head. It was black as a coal mine outside, but I could see the goods train, a darker line of the dark, stretching back indefinitely. A fine rain was falling. Most of the blinds were drawn upon the carriages of our own train and none of the passengers, so far as I could tell, were stirring.

I suddenly had an idea.

"Suppose we slip out and climb into one of the trucks," I suggested. "We shall at least put Schreckermann and his company off the scent."

We acted at once on my proposal. We hurriedly pulled down the blinds of the compartment and turned off the light. Then Réhmy cautiously opened the outer door. Gaston slipped on to the footboard, then Beatrice, then myself, while Réhmy followed last. We shuffled along in the pitch darkness, clinging to the window-ledge of the carriage. Our own train was meanwhile creeping forward at a walking pace, and the manœuvre was therefore comparatively simple.

One by one we dropped off and stood on the track between the two trains. Then, with the utmost caution, we followed Gaston, who groped his way along the line of stationary trucks, which were on our left. Presently he stopped and whispered to me to come forward. I moved to his side, and he motioned me to bend down. He planted a foot on either shoulder and I slowly raised myself again until I stood erect, pressing myself against the side of the truck. He sprang off my back after a vigorous effort or two and disappeared into the blackness above our heads. A moment later I felt his outstretched hand as he leaned down towards us.

"Mademoiselle Harvel next," he whispered.

Réhmy and I picked up Beatrice and hoisted her heavenwards, till Gaston could get hold of her shoulders. Once she was safely in, Réhmy climbed up and then he and Gaston, leaning over, succeeded in pulling me after them.

We found ourselves in an open truck filled with baulks of timber. We felt our way along and discovered that they were not the same length as the truck, but some three feet shorter, and a space was thus left at one end between the baulks and the side of the truck sufficient to contain our party. The sides of the truck were higher than a man's head and we were thus entirely shielded from observation, except from directly above us. We settled down as comfortably as we could, and, after what seemed hours of waiting, we heard the train which we had just left gather speed and, with a grinding of wheels, move off again into the night.

We had no idea of the destination of the goods train or even whether it had an engine, but our doubts on that score were soon dispelled, for, with many groans and jerks, we started off in the direction in which we had previously been travelling.

I do not think I need attempt to describe the miseries of the journey. We rumbled on right through the night, stopping for long intervals. It was bitterly cold and damp, and we had no cover over our heads. Beatrice lay for all that time in my arms and I did my best to keep her warm. Dawn found us shivering and huddling together for comfort. We did not dare to smoke or talk, for we were mortally afraid that some official, during one of our frequent halts, might take it into his head to walk down the line and inspect the trucks.

At about nine o'clock it ceased raining and the clouds rolled away, revealing a watery sun. The first light of day saw Réhmy, whose devotion to duty no hardship could destroy, examining as well as he could the portfolio which Gaston had stolen from Fritz, and I noted that his face grew continually graver as he scanned the papers which it contained.

Nothing untoward occurred until about eleven o'clock in the morning, when the train came to what was evidently a final halt, and we heard a babble of voices and footsteps on the ground below us.

I remember wondering desperately whether I should be able to summon up the wits or make the effort to struggle with a further crisis. Gaston, however, had already risen stiffly from the floor of the truck, and Réhmy had the stern set look that I had come to recognise as his characteristic expression when going into action. He took command at once, motioning me to be still, and whispering to Gaston to mount cautiously on his shoulders in order to reconnoitre.

Gaston slowly drew himself to the top of the baulks of timber, where for a few moments he lay stretched, taking a cautious survey of the scene. Suddenly, while we waited below him in silent suspense, he sprang to his feet and, standing on the top of the timber, began shouting in French like a madman. We all three thought he had gone crazy until he called down to us excitedly.

"It's Dortmund, my friends. We are in the charge of the French armies."

Then, addressing someone below, we heard him say:

"Go and find your sergeant. There are two French officers on this train on an important mission to Paris."

He turned back to us with a shining face.

"It's all right," he said. "Our troubles are over. It's undoubtedly Dortmund."

After that my memory is a little confused. I was very weak and cold, and further hampered by Beatrice who, poor girl, was half-fainting from exhaustion. Somehow or other, we found ourselves lifted from the truck and handed to the ground, where we were surrounded by blue-clad, helmeted French soldiers, amid a babble of talk and gesticulation.

Réhmy turned to me.

"It's most amazing luck," he said. "We struck one of the goods trains carrying supplies of timber to the occupied areas. The best of it is that they are part of the reparation payments despatched by the German authorities to allay suspicion."

I recalled the paragraph I had read in the paper in the train from Genoa (was it days or weeks previously?) where it had been stated that large supplies of timber were being delivered by Germany as a guarantee of her good intentions. There was a splendid irony in the manner of our deliverance that struck me even at that moment of complete exhaustion and misery.

We were conducted to the bureau of the French engineer officer in charge of the sidings and were soon seated round a nearly red-hot stove, drinking steaming hot coffee. Questions were naturally asked, but Gaston and Réhmy did little to satisfy the curiosity of our interrogators, and Réhmy, as soon as he had recovered a little from the effects of the journey, went straight off to a telephone. He made such good use of it that within half an hour a large car, with a military chauffeur at the wheel, drew up outside, and we started at once for Essen.

At Essen we found a French general awaiting us, and apparently prepared to take my French friends for granted. He asked no questions, but welcomed us warmly and insisted that we should lunch with him. We accepted his invitation, but it was a brief meal and nothing of any importance was said. The meal, in fact, was scarcely over before an officer entered and announced that a special train, consisting of two coaches and an engine, which the administration of the railway of the occupied area had placed at our disposal, was waiting with steam up to take us on our way to Paris.

CHAPTER XXII

I INDITE AN EPILOGUE

I have not much more to write, for indeed the rest of the story is public property and has been made the theme of comment and report in every newspaper in the world. Of the full discovery and publication of the conspiracy of the Seven Sleepers and the immediate fall of the German Government, I need not speak, for this is not a chronicle of great events, but merely the personal record of one who became so strangely involved in them.

There is nothing to relate of the journey to Paris. It remains with me as a passage of deep content, amounting almost to a stupor, in which I was mainly conscious of an insuperable longing for rest, a profound thankfulness, and an exquisite sense of Beatrice, secure from further harm, and looking to me for an assurance that we were really safe at last. My French friends apparently suffered the same reaction. Even the spirits of the irrepressible Gaston were for the moment in abeyance. We huddled each of us in a corner of the carriage, dozing in uneasy snatches, till we were roused at last by the fortunate discovery that we were hungry and that dinner was being served in the wagon-restaurant.

Over dinner we recovered slightly, and Gaston insisted on champagne. We drank two toasts, I remember, one to France and her allies, the other to Raoul Dupléssy and Henri Lavelle, who had died in her service. Gaston also made a charming speech of congratulation when, in response to his romantic interest in Beatrice and myself, we told him of our approaching marriage.

When we got back to our compartment, Réhmy pulled down all the blinds and summoned the conductor, bidding him lock the door. He then produced Fritz's portfolio and showed us what it contained. At the request of Beatrice, he reconstructed, for our special benefit, the broad lines of the plot which had been so nearly successful. There was enough evidence amongst Fritz's papers to enable us to form a fairly clear idea of what had been intended.

There was in particular a detailed memorandum containing the entire scheme for the execution of what was described as the "Valentine" attack, so called (Réhmy explained) because it was planned to take place on the 14th of February, or in just under two months' time. The vital element of the attack was surprise. London and Paris were to be drenched from the air with the Professor's new poison gas. Large forces of aeroplanes, leaving from various bases on the western frontiers of Germany (the names of which were in cipher), were to loose this horror from the air over two sleeping and totally unsuspecting towns. The last sentence of the plan deserves quotation:

"It may be regarded as certain that the effects of the X3 gas, as discharged by the new projectors, will be to destroy all forms of vegetable or animal life within a radius of 400 square kilometres."

It was afterwards discovered from the papers of Von Stahl and Herzler, subsequently arrested at Leipzig, that, simultaneously with this attack, an army of two hundred thousand fully armed and equipped German infantry with a proper accompaniment of artillery, a new and swift type of armoured car, aeroplanes and all the other paraphernalia of modern warfare, was to advance through Alsace-Lorraine and the territory of the Saar Basin. The southern force was to move by way of Metz and Verdun, and the northern force was to occupy Lille and push forward to the Channel ports. The air fleet would meanwhile be ready to annihilate London and Paris, or any town in France or the United Kingdom to which the government of those countries might have succeeded in transferring itself in the most unlikely event of all or part of the allied ministries surviving the first surprise attack from the air.

It was clear from the papers that the Seven Sleepers, in financing these deadly operations, were not moved by any patriotic or honourable motives. They had come to the conclusion that unless something were done to restore the position of Germany, the Allied Governments would ultimately lay hands on the fortunes which they had amassed during the War, and during the subsequent financial chaos. They were convinced that in the final settlement of reparations their vast wealth would be confiscated in order to clear off their country's debt, and they had accordingly made up their minds to stake everything they possessed in a last desperate effort to retrieve the position in the belief that success would leave them masters of the situation.

"In fact," said Réhmy, in concluding his exposition, "the fate of Europe has for the last few days hung upon the fatal document which was so providentially thrust into the hands of Captain Preston on his arrival in Geneva."

Gaston put his hand into the pocket of his coat and laid the document before us. Its appearance had somewhat changed since I had first beheld it in my bedroom at the Pension de la Reine. It was crumpled in places and the marks of Fritz's broad thumb were apparent at the edges, but in the top right corner there was a more sinister change. The paper showed a neat round hole, and on the back there were two splashes of crimson.

We looked at it in silence.

"Your aim, my friend, was true," I said at last.

Gaston nodded with tight lips, and, folding up the document, put it back in his pocket.

On our arrival in Paris, we took Beatrice, who was still very tired and exhausted, to a little hotel in the Quartier Latin and drove at once to the Quai d'Orsay. It was that early drive through the streets of Paris that finally restored me to a sane and reasonable world. Paris is of all cities the one where life from hour to hour seems most to justify itself, where men have most skilfully come to secure terms with destiny, and where things violent and uncouth are rebuked or shruggingly dismissed. Paris came to me that morning like the clean dawn upon a nightmare. The figures which had followed me through the incidents of this tale, fading like ghosts at cockcrow, shrank to an indeterminate mopping and mowing in an obscure recess of memory, and I once more became a normal citizen of the modern world. I awoke to a sense of homely and permanent realities, my spirits rising to deny emphatically the grotesque illusions among which, during the last week, I had so authentically moved.

The clear city was waking to another day. As we passed through the narrow streets of the Quartier, descending towards the quais, life was on all sides fleetly renewed. From the iron balconies of the humble folk, gay with occasional flowers, shrilling with birds pendant in tiny cages, the women had hung their household bedding, or gay mats to sweeten in the nimble air and the clean December sunlight. Below them small cafés were being set for the morning with tables and wicker chairs, and a glimpse through open doors showed the *patron* or his men sprinkling the sawdust or putting a morning polish on brass and zinc. The tiny shops slid past, bright with the spoils of a market visited at dawn, or inviting a leisurely inspection of old prints and the miscellaneous hoards of the antiquary. Then, through the narrow end of the little street, the river gleamed, and in a moment we were running along the quais, the long line of the Louvre cutting the blue sky with a fine simplicity, packed with treasures whereby eager generations, ere the silence closed, had achieved a lovely immortality. Beside it passed the busy life of the riverside, barges moored and discharging their cargoes, or passing smoothly under the comely arches of a bridge, swift green trams gliding beneath the brown tracery of tree tops, and the reckless and gallant fuss of the Paris taxis. I was filled with a joyous conviction that life was continuous, triumphant, persistent, and not intended for defeat.

Then, suddenly, suspended above the fair bustle of the city, I saw, in my mind's eye, hovering silver specks, ten thousand feet up in the morning air, raining abruptly down invisible and remorseless death, making in a moment of that happy scene a desert and a shambles; and I felt incredulous wonder and a gratitude, impersonal and immense, that fate should have permitted me to assist in foiling the powers of malice and disorder which in every age must be encountered and freshly overcome if men are to keep and to increase their inheritance.

But we had now arrived at the Quai d'Orsay, where my exalted mood was, at the same time, chastened and fortified. Réhmy's chief, a grizzled general, wearing the Legion and Croix de Guerre, received us as though the salvation of the world was an occurrence of every day (as perhaps it is). Our interview was strangely official and our arrival seemed to be taken as a matter of course. Réhmy delivered the document which had cost so much, together with the portfolio Gaston had taken from Fritz. His chief received them, handed them to a secretary and gave instructions for their safe deposit. He finally shook hands with us and thanked me gracefully, but without emotion, for my collaboration.

Gaston and Réhmy then went off immediately to draft a formal report of our proceedings, and I returned to Beatrice.

She was still very tired and in no condition to continue the journey to London in the evening. We accordingly decided to stay for that day, at any rate, in Paris. I wired to Uncle James, announcing my imminent return, and to Jerry Cunningham, informing him of our safe arrival. The afternoon we spent in the rue de la Paix, choosing an engagement ring. The lure of the Paris shops was a potent factor in Beatrice's recovery.

* * * *

Beatrice and I were married on Christmas Eve in the old parish church at Steynhurst, beneath the rolling Sussex downs. Jerry was my best man, and both Gaston and Réhmy were present.

We walked down the aisle and into the cold December air to the tune of an ancient carol:

> *The holly and the ivy,*
> *When they are both fll grown,*
> *Of all the trees that are in the wood,*
> *The holly bears the crown.*
> *Oh, the rising of the sn,*
> *And the rn ning of the deer,*
> *And the playing of the merry organ,*
> *And sweet singing in the choir.*

I am again a man of commerce, and it is sometimes difficult for Beatrice and myself of a fireside evening to credit the part we played in the events which are here set down. When, however, I am inclined to doubt their reality, I have only to take from my bureau a small envelope which contains two incontestable relics of our strange adventure.

One is the ribbon of the Iron Cross won by Von Emmerich at Villers Brettoneaux. The other is a telegram which reached me on the morning of our wedding. It was brief, departing in this respect from the usual habit of its author:

"Heartiest congratulations and best wishes till we meet again.

"Anselm Kreutzemark."

I have never mentioned the telegram to Beatrice. She is superstitious about the Professor, and I think it best she should assume, with the world at large, that he came by his end in his own red room at Hanover. For myself, I sometimes wonder whether he meant anything in particular by his final phrase.

www.ingramcontent.com/pod-product-compliance
Lightning Source LLC
Chambersburg PA
CBHW011718240626
47153CB00009B/2903

* 9 7 8 1 6 6 7 6 6 3 0 2 9 *